Raven's Kiss

Book 1 of the Raven's Queen Series

E.S. Brandon

Moonlit Forge Press

Content Warning

Raven's Kiss contains explicit sexual content, graphic violence, gothic religious extremism, body horror from magical corruption, and psychological manipulation.

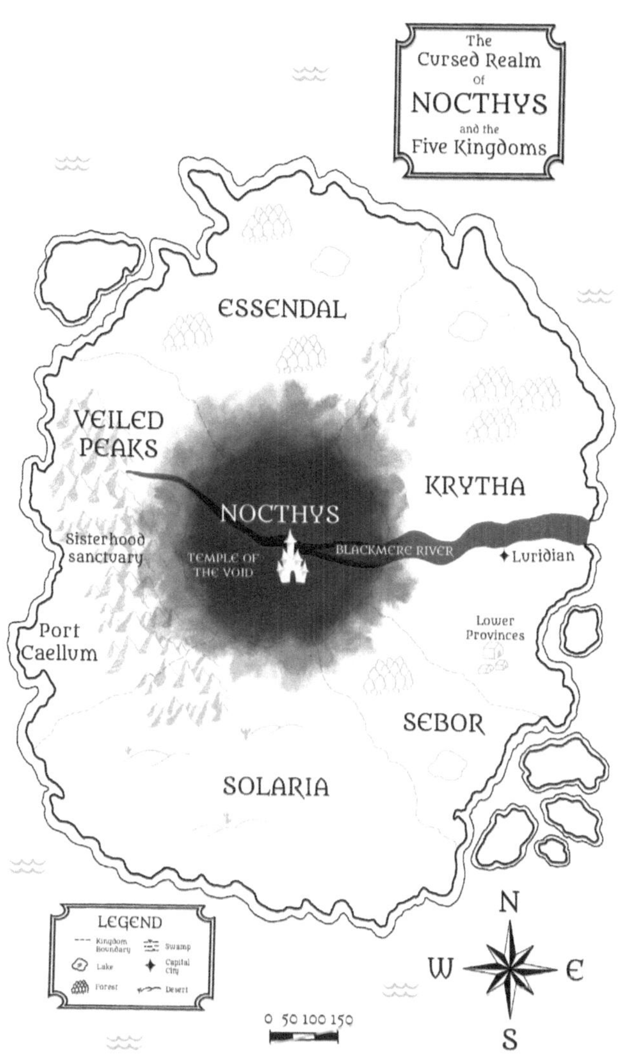

The
Cursed Realm
of
NOCTHYS
and the
Five Kingdoms

ESSENDAL

VEILED
PEAKS

KRYTHA

NOCTHYS

Sisterhood
sanctuary

TEMPLE OF
THE VOID

BLACKMERE RIVER

Luridian

Port
Caellum

Lower
Provinces

SEBOR

SOLARIA

LEGEND
Kingdom
Boundary
Swamp
Lake
Capital
City
Forest
Desert

0 50 100 150

N
W   E
S

1

EXECUTION

My blade opens his throat.

One clean stroke that answers years of questions. Crimson baptizes my face.

Hot, vital, perfect.

Brother Elias's golden-flecked eyes meet mine as his life escapes in a scarlet arc, painting the stone like a benediction. A wet gurgle escapes his throat, the sound of air bubbling through blood as his body fights its inevitable surrender. I taste copper on my lips.

This is what I was born for.

This is Mordreth's mercy.

The light fades from those golden-flecked eyes. Evidence of his corruption. The shadow taint that marked him for judgment, not the divine shadow of Mordreth that flows through our prayers, but a different force. A warmth where Mordreth's touch is cold. Chaos where the Raven God brings order. His body slumps forward against the restraints. The ceremonial altar collects his offering, channels carved into the stone guiding his sacrifice to the basin below.

Mordreth receives his soul. Another returned to shadow.

The execution chamber holds the chill of weathered stone and forgotten whispers. Centuries of blood have soaked into these walls, lending the air a metallic tang that mingles with incense and shadow-oil. Seven black candles burn at the points of the ritual circle carved into the floor, their flames unnaturally still in the windowless space. The light they cast seems to avoid the corners of the room, where darkness gathers like attentive witnesses.

Mother Superior steps forward from the darkness. Her white robes remain pristine despite the crimson spray that marks the walls, the floor, my face. Silver hair crowns her head in elaborate braids that never show a strand out of place, flowing like liquid moonlight down her spine. Her face carries the sharp beauty of winter itself—high cheekbones carved from marble, thin lips that rarely soften, and steel-gray eyes cold as frozen lakes. Even at sixty, she stands tall and straight, moving with the controlled grace of one who has mastered every gesture. The perfection of her appearance has always been its own kind of magic.

"Mordreth accepts this offering." Her voice fills the execution chamber, echoing against stone walls that have witnessed countless sacred rites. "His judgment flows through your hand, Daughter Seraphina."

I bow my head, crimson still warm on my skin. "I serve as his instrument."

Silent Sisters move around me, their forms dancing in torchlight. The soft rustle of their robes against stone sounds like distant whispers. They untie Brother Elias, handling his empty form with ritualistic care. The body holds no meaning now. The man who betrayed our teachings left the moment my steel found his throat. What remains deserves respect only as a reminder of Mordreth's shadow justice.

Mother Superior places her hand on my shoulder. Her touch feels cold even through the leather of my armor. "The nineteenth sacrament you have delivered since your Blessing Day. Eight years of faithful service."

Not that I need reminding. Each kill lives within me, a sacred memory preserved like pressed flowers between pages of sacred texts. Brother Elias joins the others. His golden-flecked eyes take their place in my mental reliquary.

Nineteen souls returned to darkness through my blade.

"Prepare for purification." Mother Superior moves toward the door, her robes whispering against stone. "You have served with unwavering devotion. The Raven God sees your faithful heart."

I catch my reflection in the polished obsidian wall. At twenty-four, I've grown into the weapon they shaped me to be. Midnight-black hair falls to my shoulders in heavy waves, still damp with execution sweat. The sharp angles of my face have lost any softness childhood might have held, leaving cheekbones that could cut glass and a jaw set with deadly purpose. My violet eyes burn bright with divine fervor. The lean muscle of my body speaks of countless training hours, every line honed for one purpose. Death delivered in Mordreth's name.

The chamber empties until only I remain with the body. Blood continues to drip from the altar into the collection basin below. Each drop produces a sound like a tiny bell, marking another moment of grace between my calling and Mordreth's will. The candles flicker as if responding to currents only they can feel. Shadow-oil burns in small braziers at the room's corners, releasing tendrils of black smoke that curl toward the ceiling like questing fingers.

I retrieve my weapon from where it rests in the ceremonial holder. The obsidian-inlaid handle fits my palm perfectly, crafted specifically for my hand. The edge gleams black and wet with Brother Elias's lifeblood. I clean it with reverent motions, honoring the steel that extends Mordreth's reach into this world. My fingertips trace the raven etched into the hilt, wings spread in eternal flight.

The smell of blood fills my lungs. Known. Comforting. The scent of duty fulfilled. Each execution chamber in the Sanctuary holds different acoustics, different smells, different textures against the skin. This one, reserved for those once holy who have fallen to corruption, carries the scent of old incense and older sacrifices under the fresh copper tang of today's judgment.

I was seven when I first witnessed an execution. Sixteen when I performed my first. The youngest in a generation to complete the trials. Eight years have passed since that day. Sometimes the memories blur together, form a crimson tapestry of devotion.

Today's offering will join that tapestry, another thread in the grand design Mother Superior weaves through all our lives.

By darkness blessed, by blood consecrated. Mordreth's will made manifest.

The Sanctuary tracks time differently than the outside world. While kingdoms measure months by moon cycles and years by harvests, we mark the passage of days through prayer bells and blood offerings.

Beyond the execution chamber's thick walls, the rest of the Sanctuary continues its rhythms. The steady drone of novices chanting morning prayers in the worship hall above. The distant ring of steel from the training yard where tomorrow's instruments sharpen their skills. The soft footsteps of Sisters moving through stone corridors with silent purpose. A living organism of devotion with Mother Superior as its beating heart.

The door opens with a sound like a sigh. Three novices enter, heads bowed, shoulders curved in reverence. Their white robes mark them as uninitiated, still innocent of blood-giving. They carry basins of water, bundles of herbs, and purification cloths. Crystal bottles of sacred oils clink softly against each other in the basket carried by the youngest.

"Blessed Sister," the eldest speaks, her voice barely audible above the hiss of shadow-oil braziers. "We come to prepare you for cleansing."

I nod, sheathing my clean weapon. The weight against my hip feels right. Balanced. The Sisters approach cautiously, their bare feet soundless on the stone floor. Their eyes avoid mine.

Whether from respect or fear matters little. Both serve equally well.

They guide me to the stone bench along the wall. A large copper mirror stands beside it, brought for the ritual cleansing. The metal has been polished to a high shine, though green patina still clings to its ornate frame where seven ravens spread their wings.

The novices move around me fluidly, like dancers performing steps timeless beyond memory. The eldest lights fresh incense in a stone holder shaped like a crouching raven. Sweet smoke rises, carrying prayers to Mordreth. The second novice murmurs ritual blessings over the water while adding sacred salts. The youngest arranges the cleansing cloths in the exact pattern required for proper purification.

The eldest begins at the buckles along my sides, her movements practiced and reverent. They work in harmony, unlacing my leather armor methodically. The second loosens ties at shoulders and wrists while the youngest prepares the obsidian table where each piece will rest.

The leather sighs as it releases its grip on my body. First comes the fitted leather cuirass embossed with Mordreth's raven sigil, worn smooth in places from years of service. Then the arm guards etched with prayer symbols that have pressed their shapes into my skin. The reinforced corset follows, its boning having shaped my ribs to accommodate both breath and blade. Last come the thigh sheaths that hold my secondary blades, their leather darkened with old blood that no amount of cleaning can fully remove.

Each piece they remove is placed reverently on the table, arranged in the shape of a body as though the armor might continue serving even without me inside it.

The armor falls. The woman remains. Both belong to Mordreth.

When they've finished with the armor, I stand in just the thin black shift worn beneath. Even this garment bears Mordreth's mark. Small ravens embroidered along the hem in black thread barely visible against the fabric, their wings reaching toward my knees. The cloth clings to my skin, damp with exertion from the execution ritual.

The chamber air feels colder now upon my skin. The stones beneath my feet radiate a chill that seeps into my bones. A reminder of mortality. Of limitations to be transcended through Mordreth's blessing.

One novice takes my hands, beginning the ritual cleaning. Her hands are cool and smooth against mine as she works scented water between each digit, washing away the evidence of divine judgment. Another prepares herbs, crushing dried leaves between hands that tremble slightly. The soft grinding sound of pestle against mortar creates a rhythm like a heartbeat. The third readies the basin, adding blessed oils that fill the chamber with sharp scents. Juniper brings clarity of purpose. Sage purifies intention. Shadow-root binds the assassin to Mordreth's will.

The air grows thick with these mingled aromas, each breath filling my lungs with divine calling.

I step out of the shift, allowing them full access to cleanse every trace of the execution. The mirror reflects my body. Lithe yet curved, marked with the scars of my training and service. At twenty-four, my form has reached its perfect balance of strength and agility. A long scar curves along my left ribs where I took a blade meant for Mother Superior three years ago. The puckered flesh still aches before rainstorms.

Smaller marks map my history across skin that rarely sees the sun. A burn along my right shoulder from training with fire blades, thin lines across my back from the Ritual of Seven Trials, a star-shaped mark above my left hip from my first solo mission.

The stone beneath my bare feet radiates cold that travels up through my legs. The chill reminds me of my mortality. My humanity. Traits to be overcome through Mordreth's blessing. The air upon my skin raises goosebumps along my arms. My nipples tighten in the cool chamber air. The body responds as bodies do. A reminder that even instruments of the divine will inhabit mortal flesh.

The water runs down my arms. Not warm like spilled life. Cooler. Cleansing but not fulfilling. The liquid catches the candlelight, making rivulets of gold slide across my skin before dripping to the floor. My reflection shows what the Sisterhood has made. A weapon forged from feminine form, honed to deadly perfection.

The novices work smoothly, washing away Brother Elias's crimson with cloth and scented water. Their hands move over my shoulders, down my spine, along the curve of my waist.

Reverence for the body that carries out Mordreth's will.

The youngest washes my hair with water infused with blessed herbs. The scent of rosemary and shadow-root envelops me as she massages my scalp carefully.

"Water takes the crimson but not the blessing," the novice recites, her hands working between mine. "Mordreth marks his chosen through holy service."

The ritual words echo in the chamber, absorbed by stone walls that have heard them countless times before. The Sisterhood has performed this cleansing since before the founding of the kingdom. Some say before humans first discovered fire. The motions, the herbs, the prayers are all preserved through generations of faithful service.

In the mirror, I study the body I inhabit. Strong arms capable of delivering death with grace. Toned legs that can carry me silently across any terrain. Firm breasts rising and falling with each measured breath. My waist narrows before flaring to hips that have never borne children and never will. The Sisterhood requires different sacrifices.

This body belongs to Mordreth. A blade given human form.

I let them work. My mind drifts to Brother Elias's final moments. The look of recognition in his eyes when I entered his cell. The acceptance when he explained his crimes against the Sisterhood. The way he nodded when I described the evidence of his corruption. Those golden flecks that couldn't be hidden. The way they gleamed in the torchlight, tiny stars burning in mortal flesh.

Golden-flecked eyes. Not Mordreth's cold touch but a warmth. A force that transforms rather than preserves. The Void corruption spreads within the blood. Judgment follows necessity.

The crimson washes away in pink swirls. Brother Elias leaving me one final time. The water in the basin gradually turns from clear to rose to deep crimson. The youngest novice carries it to the central drain and pours it in, murmuring prayers as the liquid disappears into darkness. Fresh water replaces it, steam rising from the surface indicating its warmth. The second cleansing begins, this time with blessed salts that make my skin tingle wherever they touch.

The eldest novice unwraps a bundle of black cloth from the altar. The fabric makes a sound like whispering as it unfolds. Inside rests a small pot of shadow-oil, thick and dark as night itself. The container is ancient obsidian, carved with symbols too old for even Mother Superior to fully translate. The scent rises from the pot. Ancient and forbidden. Whispers of secrets kept from those unworthy to receive them. She dips her finger into the substance with practiced devotion.

"By darkness blessed," she murmurs, drawing the symbol of Mordreth's eye on my forehead. The oil burns cold upon my skin, its chill reaching past skin to touch my very soul. "By blood consecrated."

The shadow-oil sinks into my skin, disappearing from sight though I can still feel its presence. A weight, an intuition, a connection to a presence vast and ancient that watches from beyond the veil of mortal understanding. This is Mordreth's touch—precise, cold, structured. Nothing like the chaotic warmth I glimpsed in Brother Elias's corrupted gaze.

My first kill flashes through memory. Another Brother. Another throat. My hands had trembled then. Mother Superior steadied them, guided the steel home. Eight years between that day and this one collapse into nothing. Time is measured not in seasons but in offerings.

"The nineteenth sacrament," I whisper.

The novices pause in their ministrations, eyes widening. They rarely hear my voice outside prayer or the ritual words of execution. Their hands resume more quickly, movements less certain. The sound of cloth against skin grows louder in the sudden silence that follows my words.

The cleansing continues, water is replaced three more times until it remains clear even after passing over my body. The ritual must be perfect. The instrument must be cleaned properly before being returned to its resting place. The novices work in harmony, their movements synchronized by years of training. One washes while another applies purifying herbs. The third prepares the next stage while murmuring prayers to Mordreth, asking his blessing upon his faithful servant.

When they finish, my skin smells of blessed herbs and shadow-oil. Clean. Purified. Ready for whatever service Mordreth requires next. My hair hangs damp around my face, water droplets sliding down my neck and between my breasts. The chill settles into my bones, a known discomfort that grounds me in the physical world.

They bring fresh armor from the antechamber where it waited. Not the ceremonial black leather I wore for the execution but the formal assassin's attire reserved for special occasions. The supple midnight leather fits my form perfectly, tailored to allow complete freedom of movement while presenting the elegant silhouette befitting a Sisterhood assassin.

Each piece bears Mordreth's raven sigil in silver thread. Across the back of the fitted jacket. Along the sides of the leather pants. Etched into the buckles that secure the armor at shoulders and waist. The ravens embroidered along the collar spread their wings toward my throat, as if to drink the life I've spilled in Mordreth's name.

The soft creak of fresh leather accompanies every movement as they secure each piece. The sound whispers of lethal intent. The smell of the leather mingles with shadow-oil and herb-scented skin. A perfume of death and devotion that marks me as Mordreth's own.

This armor is different from my everyday attire. Lighter. More refined. The leather is so supple it moves like a second skin. The silver threading catches the torchlight, making the ravens seem to shift and flutter with each breath I take. This is ceremonial armor, worn for special audiences and divine duties beyond routine judgment. The sight of it sends anticipation singing through my veins.

The youngest novice approaches when they finish, head bowed so low her chin nearly touches her chest. Her voice barely carries over the soft popping of the shadow-oil braziers. "Mother Superior requests your presence in her chambers once purification is complete."

A new mission comes. The Raven's hunger never ceases.

Mother Superior rarely summons anyone directly after an execution. Purification typically precedes rest, meditation, reflection on the service performed. This deviation from ritual carries meaning. Urgency. Importance.

"When?" I ask, my voice rougher than intended after the long silence.

The girl flinches as if struck. "Immediately, Blessed Sister."

The other novices exchange glances, curiosity warring with their training to show nothing. The eldest bites her lower lip, quickly masking the gesture by bowing her head in reverence. The middle one's fingers twitch against her robe, a sign of nervous anticipation. They know change approaches. They sense the shift in holy rhythms.

I rise from the bench, checking my reflection one final time. The woman who stares back is transformed. No longer stained with blood but marked with consecrated oil. No longer in killing leathers but formal armor. My violet eyes study the transformation with cold satisfaction. The silver ravens along my collar frame my throat perfectly. My damp hair has begun to curl slightly around my face, softening features that have been called both beautiful and terrible.

I feel the weight of the armor against my body, the subtle power it represents. The ritual garments transform me from woman to weapon, from flesh to instrument of divine will. The deep black leather absorbs light just as I absorb Mordreth's purpose.

The novices step back, their work complete. They move toward the walls, pressing themselves against the stone as if trying to disappear into it. I turn from the mirror, facing them with the full authority of my position. They seem to shrink before me, their white robes a stark contrast to my midnight attire.

I am Seraphina of the Blade. Nineteen sacraments delivered by my hand. Mordreth's mercy flows through me like life through veins. My purpose is clear and singular.

The sacrificial knife and the hand that wields it are one.

I leave the purification chamber, the novices already beginning to clean the execution space for the next offering. The corridors of the Sanctuary stretch before me, my leather armor creaking softly as I walk toward whatever sacred duty Mordreth has prepared for me next. The stone beneath my feet feels different now. The air carries new scents. Everything transformed by the knowledge that duty waits beyond routine. Beyond the familiar patterns of devotion and service.

The Sanctuary lives around me. Ancient stone breathing with accumulated power. Seven towers rise from the central structure, one for each aspect of Mordreth's divine nature.

Silence. Shadow. Sacrifice. Secrecy. Suffering. Surrender. Salvation. Corridors connect them in patterns that form sacred symbols when viewed from above. Patterns I've walked since childhood without fully grasping their significance.

As I move through these hallways, my footsteps echo like heartbeats. Other Sisters and novices press themselves against walls as I pass. Their eyes are downcast. Their breathing is shallow. Some make protective gestures, though whether to shield themselves from me or to honor what I represent remains unclear. Perhaps both.

My purpose carries me forward.

Toward Mother Superior's chambers.

Toward whatever mission awaits.

Toward Mordreth's will made manifest through my hand once more.

2

MISSION

The corridors of the Sanctuary feel different after an execution. Stone walls breathe deeper. Candlelight burns steadier. My body moves with the lightness that comes only after fulfilling divine purpose.

Blood has been spilled.

Justice delivered.

Mordreth's will through my hand. Perfect. Complete.

Yet an interruption disturbs the familiar rhythm. Mother Superior's summons pulls me forward when I should be entering the meditation chambers. My footsteps echo against stone, marking a path I've walked countless times but never quite like this. Never before prayers of reflection have been offered. Never while the taste of copper still lingers on my tongue despite the purification ritual.

Novices wearing white robes scatter before me like autumn leaves. Their downcast eyes and hurried movements speak of both awe and fear. The Sisters in black acknowledge me with slight nods as I pass, their expressions betraying nothing. They wear their training like I wear mine. Emotions buried beneath years of discipline.

The Sanctuary hums with morning rituals. Novice voices rise in dawn prayers from the eastern tower. The training yards below ring with the controlled violence of blade practice. These rhythms have marked my days since I was seven, taken in by the Sisterhood after my village burned. Here in the Veiled Peaks, hidden from the world by mist and mountain stone, we keep traditions older than the kingdoms below.

At the heart of the Sanctuary stands the tallest tower, reserved for Mother Superior alone. Seven guards wearing the silver-threaded black of the Raven Guard stand at attention outside her chamber door. Each bears the marks of divine blessing, the cold touch of Mordreth's favor that sets them apart from ordinary warriors. Each has proven loyalty through blood and sacrifice.

They part as I approach, moving with grace that speaks of thousands of shared training hours. I feel their eyes map my movements, cataloging potential weaknesses from habit, finding none. They read me as naturally as breathing.

The door to Mother Superior's chambers opens before I reach it. Sister Lara, Mother Superior's personal attendant, stands in the threshold. Iron-gray hair pulled back in a severe knot framing her face that resembles a death mask. Her skin is pale and expressionless except for eyes that have witnessed decades of holy violence.

"She awaits you," Sister Lara says, her voice carrying the rasp of one who speaks rarely. "The Raven God watches with interest." The formal greeting for assassins returning from successful missions—words that should precede rest and meditation. Their appearance now sends heat coursing through my veins. A significant moment awaits beyond that threshold. I cross into Mother Superior's chambers.

Mother Superior stands at the far end of the room. Her white robes catch the mingled light of sun and flame, making her glow like a star fallen to earth. Her silver hair, pulled severely back, gleams with an internal light all its own. At sixty, Ravenna, Mother Superior to all within these walls, projects power that makes my skin prickle with awareness.

"Daughter Seraphina." Her voice slides into the room like darkness under a door. "Your offering was received with divine favor."

I lower my head, feel my heartbeat steady in my chest. "Mordreth's mercy flows through willing hands."

"Indeed." She moves toward a large table dominating the center of the room. Ancient maps cover its surface, weighted at the corners with obsidian ravens. "Brother Elias's corruption threatened more than his own soul. The knowledge he sought would have spread darkness beyond holy boundaries."

I remain silent, though questions burn on my tongue. My hands tingle with the memory of blade meeting flesh.

She traces her finger along one of the maps, following the coastline east from our hidden sanctuary. "The corruption spreads faster than anticipated. We cannot afford to wait." Her finger stops at a city marked with Mordreth's raven sigil. Luridian. The capital city of Krytha, the largest kingdom on the continent. "Here. A coastal jewel that controls trade between east and west."

"So far from the Sanctuary," I observe, calculating distances. The Veiled Peaks lie in the western reaches of the continent. Luridian sits on the eastern coast, where the Sunfire Sea meets the shores of civilization.

"Three weeks by ship from Port Caellum," Mother Superior confirms. "Four if the spring storms come early. The city shares its eastern maritime routes with vessels bound for Nocthys's cursed borders."

Nocthys. The shadow kingdom at the continent's heart. Where eternal night reigns.

"Your next mission cannot wait for the customary period of rest," she says. "Mordreth's will requires action before the season turns."

The words send heat blooming through my veins. My heart beats faster. Whatever comes next carries significance beyond ordinary missions.

Another soul awaits Mordreth's mercy.

"I serve as his instrument," I respond. The familiar words taste like honey on my tongue.

Mother Superior turns from the map, her steel-gray eyes assessing me. "Lord Rivin Blackthorne of Luridian requires Mordreth's mercy."

The name means nothing to me. Another noble whose ambition has led him to dark places. The location, however, raises questions that burn in my throat.

"Blackthorne leads a growing cult called Vessels of the Void," Mother Superior continues, moving toward a small table I hadn't noticed upon entering, where a black lacquered box awaits. "They dabble in forbidden magic. Not the divine cold of Mordreth's blessing, but another force entirely. A power that burns with unnatural warmth."

This revelation sends ice through my veins despite the warmth of the chamber. Divine magic belongs to Mordreth's chosen alone. My hands twitch toward the blade at my hip.

"Like Brother Elias's corruption?" I ask, remembering those golden-flecked eyes.

"Worse. They seek to channel powers from between realities. The Void that exists in spaces where even Mordreth's darkness cannot reach." She pauses at the lacquered box. "A corruption of holy arts known only to the Sisterhood."

"Why does a blade not suffice?" The question forms before I can contain it.

Mother Superior's lips curve slightly, showing no rebuke. "Two Sisters attempted a more direct assassination seven years ago." She runs her fingers over the lacquered box. "Neither returned."

The information settles like a stone in my stomach.

Failed missions are rare.

"Blackthorne has woven void protections around himself," she explains. "But not true darkness, the chaotic energies of the Void. They alert him to consecrated weapons and render common poisons inert. His cult members function as an extension of his awareness, making direct assault impossible."

She opens the lacquered box. Inside rests a small crystal vial containing a substance black as night yet somehow luminous. It catches what little light reaches it and swallows it whole, like a tiny void drinking illumination. The sight sends a tremor through my body.

"The Raven's Kiss," she says, lifting the vial with care. "Last employed three generations ago against the Witch-King of Sebor. Its use is reserved for those whose corruption threatens the very foundation of our holy knowledge."

The vial gleams with malevolent beauty. The liquid inside shifts as if alive, responding to Mother Superior's touch with eager anticipation. My lips part slightly. I taste the air, suddenly thick with possibility.

"This is not a simple killing," she continues. "This requires divine seduction. The Raven's Kiss cannot be administered by blade or drink. It requires intimate contact." She stares at me now to convey the full meaning behind her words. "The most intimate contact."

Understanding ignites along my spine. Heat spirals through my body, warming my chest, my throat, my cheeks. Not embarrassment. Not shame. A dark thrill, like shadow-touched honey spreading through my veins. Instinctive and powerful.

The armor of my training keeps any reaction from showing on my face, though my pulse quickens within me, beating a rhythm of holy anticipation.

Not blade but lips. Not pain but pleasure. The sacrament changes form but not purpose.

"Mordreth's will guides my hand," I say. The words emerge steadier than the heat in my veins would suggest.

Mother Superior nods once, satisfied. "The mission requires complete immersion. You will become someone else entirely." She returns the vial to its box. "Lady Sera Ravencrest, a moderately wealthy widow from the distant kingdom of Valmeria."

The name slides over me like warm oil. I taste it silently.

Sera Ravencrest.

Close enough to my true name that I will respond naturally. My body already begins to shift, shoulders relaxing from their combat-ready posture.

"You will establish yourself in Luridian society. The spring social season begins in three weeks. Perfect timing for a wealthy widow's arrival. You will draw Blackthorne's attention through careful seduction. You will gain his trust and ultimately his bed." Mother Superior's voice remains dispassionate. "There, you will deliver Mordreth's judgment through the Raven's Kiss."

She gestures toward a side table where a smaller wooden box rests. "The application requires perfect care. Three layers, each sealed with an invocation to Mordreth. Only then will it bind properly, cold as Mordreth's touch, not warm like the Void's corruption. Once applied it's effective for a full night, losing its power as the dawn crests."

I approach the smaller box. Inside rests a second vial and a small brush made from raven feathers bound to a handle of polished bone. Mother Superior follows, standing close enough that I feel the cold energy she radiates, true divine blessing, not the fevered heat of corruption.

"The raw essence before the final binding ritual is lethal to any who touch it," she warns. "Including you, should you fail to apply it with proper invocation. Without Mordreth's divine protection through the ritual words, it kills within minutes, burning through flesh like wildfire." Her eyes hold mine, ensuring I understand the risk. "Only after the third layer of prayers is it bound to activate solely when required, and only through Mordreth's mercy does it spare the one who wears it."

She takes the brush, dipping it into the vial. "Your wrist," she commands.

I extend my arm, turn my wrist upward. Blue veins pulse close to the surface. Mother Superior applies a thin line of the substance across my skin. The liquid burns cold, sending a sensation shooting up my arm directly to my heart. Air stills in my lungs as the poison races through me.

"By Mordreth's darkness, bind this essence to holy intent," she intones.

The black liquid shimmers at her words, seeping slightly into my skin. The cold intensifies, spreading through my flesh like frost across a window. My body responds with a shiver that reaches to my core. This is divine cold. Mordreth's touch, graceful and controlled.

She applies a second layer across the first. "By Mordreth's mercy, reserve judgment for the deserving soul."

The cold intensifies, spreads through my entire arm. My hands tingle with icy fire. My heart beats faster, pumping heat to combat the spreading chill. The sensation borders on pain yet carries a strange pleasure with it.

The third layer follows. "By Mordreth's will, release this judgment only when the vessel stands at pleasure's peak."

The black liquid glimmers once more, then seemingly disappears into my skin, leaving no trace of its presence. The cold sensation recedes, replaced by awareness of something new waiting beneath the surface. Death sleeps in my flesh, patient as winter.

Death waits beneath my skin. Sacred purpose flows in my veins.

"Now you try," Mother Superior says, handing me the brush.

I take it, feel the smooth bone against my skin. The raven feathers whisper against my palm like a lover's breath. I apply the ritual substance to my other wrist, repeating the holy words with each layer. The liquid disappears into my skin just as it did under Mother Superior's application.

"Perfect," she says, watching the substance vanish. "You will apply it to your lips in the same manner before your final encounter with Blackthorne. Remember, the invocations must be flawless. A single misplaced syllable could redirect the judgment to your own heart rather than his." Her eyes narrow slightly. "His death will appear natural. Heart failure at the moment of greatest pleasure. A fitting end for one who has profaned holy knowledge."

Mother Superior moves to a large wardrobe of dark wood carved with ravens in flight. She opens it to reveal clothing I recognize from lessons on society. Gowns of silk and velvet. Undergarments of fine linen. Shoes crafted for beauty rather than function. A noblewoman's attire.

I reach out, touching silk the color of midnight. The fabric feels impossibly soft against my calloused skin. So different from the leather and wool that have clothed me since childhood.

"Three trunks have been prepared with everything Lady Ravencrest would possess," Mother Superior explains. "You leave at first light tomorrow. A carriage will take you down the mountain passes to the Port of Caellum, where a ship waits to carry you to Luridian. The journey will take three to four weeks, allowing you time to fully embody your new identity before arrival."

She withdraws a rolled document from inside the wardrobe, sealed with black wax bearing Mordreth's raven. "Your formal papers. Property deeds showing estates in Valmeria. Letters of introduction from nobles who owe the Sisterhood favors. A complete history crafted to withstand scrutiny."

I accept the documents, feel the weight of the new identity they contain. "How long have you planned this mission?" The question slips out unbidden.

Mother Superior's lips curve slightly. "The Raven God's vision reaches farther than mortal understanding. Three years of careful planning await your hand to bring them to fruition. We've tracked Blackthorne's rise, his growing corruption, waiting for the perfect moment."

Three years. The time astonishes me despite my training. Three years of preparation for this moment. For my hand to deliver this particular judgment. For my lips to bring divine death.

"Why me?" The question emerges before I can swallow it back.

Mother Superior shows no displeasure. Her eyes soften fractionally. "The Raven God selects his instruments perfectly, Daughter Seraphina. Your particular gifts align with this holy task." She touches my cheek briefly, her skin cool against mine. "Some are born to serve with blade alone. Others with darkness and seduction."

Her words slide into me like a blade between ribs. Graceful. Penetrating. My physical training has always been matched with lessons in courtly manners, noble etiquette, the arts of conversation and charm. Skills unnecessary for an assassin who strikes from darkness. Skills perfectly suited for one who must win trust before delivering judgment.

Born for this calling. Shaped for this moment.

"Your arrival timing proves perfect during the spring social season, when nobles are most vulnerable to new faces and old vices."

"You have three to four months once you arrive," Mother Superior continues. "The spring social season provides perfect cover for integration. But do not delay overlong. Our sources indicate Blackthorne plans a significant ritual within the next few moons. Each day his cult grows stronger, spreading their corruption like plague through Krytha's nobility."

"Rest tonight," she says, turning back to the map table. "Sister Lara will escort you to chambers where you may review your new identity and practice the application of the Raven's Kiss."

"And afterward?" I ask, already calculating the mission's likely duration. My body feels strange, caught between two identities. The assassin and the widow. The blade and the kiss.

"When judgment has been delivered, return to the Sanctuary immediately," she replies. "Send word by raven when the deed is done. A ship will await you for the return journey. The corruption Blackthorne spreads may require additional purification beyond his death."

I bow my head in acknowledgment, feel my hair brush against my cheeks. "Mordreth's will shall be done."

Mother Superior's tone carries finality, "Remember, Daughter Seraphina. You go not merely as an assassin but as Mordreth's holy avatar. His judgment flows through your lips as it has flowed through your blade."

The words resonate through my flesh. I have always been an instrument of divine will. This mission simply requires a different application of the same devotion. The method changes. The dedication remains constant.

I turn to leave, the documents heavy in my grasp. Mother Superior's voice stops me at the threshold.

"Daughter." Her words hold an unfamiliar note. An emotion almost like concern. "The seduction of the body is simple compared to the seduction of the mind. Guard your thoughts as carefully as you guard your blade. Blackthorne's corruption runs deeper than most. The Void's whispers can sound sweet to those who have never heard them before."

The warning sends a chill through me that has nothing to do with the Raven's Kiss still tingling beneath my skin. I nod once, accepting both the warning and the implicit faith in my abilities it contains.

The door opens before me. Sister Lara waits to escort me to quarters where I will prepare for the most complex mission of my service. My mind already begins the transformation, shedding Seraphina of the Blade like an outgrown skin, making space for Lady Sera Ravencrest to take form.

The weight of nineteen souls rests on my conscience. Nineteen holy offerings delivered to Mordreth with blade and blood. The twentieth approaches, to be delivered with lips and pleasure rather than steel and pain.

The method matters not.

The sacrament remains the same.

By shadow blessed, by blood consecrated. Mordreth's will made manifest through willing hands.

I follow Sister Lara through the Sanctuary's winding corridors, leaving familiar patterns of life and devotion behind. Tomorrow I enter a world known only through lessons and observations. A world of nobles and intrigues, of pleasures and pretense.

A world where Lady Sera Ravencrest will bloom like a night flower, drawing Lord Blackthorne to his perfect, lustful doom.

3

RAVENCREST

Sister Lara leads me to a section of the Sanctuary I've rarely visited. The Preparation Chambers lie in the western tower, reserved for those undertaking extended missions beyond our walls. The corridors here feel different. Wider. Less austere. The stone walls hold tapestries depicting scenes from noble life rather than ritual executions. Windows allow sunlight to pool on polished floors.

"These chambers recreate the outside world," Sister Lara explains, breaking her customary silence. Her voice sounds like cloth dragged over stone. "You will acclimate here before your departure tomorrow. Dawn comes early. The descent from the Veiled Peaks to Port Caellum takes a full day."

She stops before carved double doors inlaid with silver. The design shows a woman in elegant attire offering wine to a man whose shadow bears raven wings.

The doors open to reveal a suite of rooms that bear no resemblance to the spartan chambers I've inhabited since childhood. Plush carpets cover stone floors. A large bed with silk hangings dominates one room. A copper bathtub large enough for complete immersion stands in another. Wardrobes of polished wood line the walls, filled with gowns in colors I've rarely seen inside the Sanctuary's black and white palette.

So much beauty serving only appearance. So much softness hiding intent.

"Everything here matches what you will find in Luridian society," Sister Lara says. "Practice all aspects of your cover identity. The body must move with the same confidence in silk as it does in leather."

She moves to a writing desk where several leather-bound books await. "Your complete history. Memorize every detail. Lady Ravencrest must respond without hesitation to any question about her past. The spring social season begins soon after your arrival. You'll have little time to establish yourself before the games begin."

I approach the desk, open the topmost volume. Pages of carefully crafted falsehood await my study. Family connections. Childhood memories. The death of an invented husband. An entire life created for the sole intent of ending another.

She leaves me alone with my new identity. The doors close with a soft sound unlike the heavy thud of chamber doors elsewhere in the Sanctuary. Another small detail preparing me for the outside world.

I sit at the desk, hands trailing over the first volume. Mother Superior's words echo in my mind. Blackthorne plans a significant ritual within the next few moons. Time enough to establish myself, gain his trust, and deliver judgment before whatever darkness he intends can manifest.

I begin reading, committing each detail to memory with the same focus I bring to combat training. Lady Sera Ravencrest emerges from the pages word by word. Born to minor nobility in Valmeria's southern provinces, far from the coastal trade routes that connect to Krytha. Married at eighteen to Lord Damon Ravencrest, a man thirty years her senior who died three years later from heart failure. No children from the union. Left with moderate wealth and property in distant Valmeria, but no connections to bind her there.

She rises from these pages. Born of ink rather than blood.

The documents include maps showing Valmeria's position, a smaller kingdom from a distant western continent, separated by oceans. Far enough that verifying details would require months of correspondence. Close enough that trade and travel between the kingdoms remains common. A perfect origin for a widow seeking new beginnings in Luridian's glittering society.

Hours pass as I absorb her history. My body remains motionless save for the turning of pages and the steady rise and fall of my chest. Only when I close the final volume do I allow myself to stand, muscles protesting the long stillness with a pleasure that borders on pain.

I move through the chambers, testing how my body feels in this unfamiliar environment. The carpet muffles my footsteps, requiring conscious adjustment to maintain silence. The furniture arrangement creates obstacles that would never exist in the Sanctuary's practical spaces.

In the bedroom, I open wardrobes to examine the clothing I will wear as Lady Ravencrest. Fabrics slide through my hands like water. Silks and velvets. Linen and lace. Colors I've rarely worn. Deep blue the shade of twilight sky. Rich burgundy like freshly spilled crimson. Even the black garments differ from my assassin's attire, designed to draw attention rather than avoid it.

I select a gown of midnight blue, hold it against my body. The weight feels wrong. Too light compared to leather armor. The cut would restrict certain movements. I cannot lift my arms above my shoulders without straining delicate seams. The bodice pins my ribs like a beautiful cage, denying the full breaths my body craves. Layers of silk would wrap around my legs at the first attempt to run or fight. This gown makes me decorative rather than dangerous, and the vulnerability of it settles on my skin like oil. Yet these same features serve Lady Ravencrest's mission. Beauty becomes its own kind of armor in the world I will enter.

The Raven's Kiss vial rests in its wooden box nearby, a constant reminder of the mission's ultimate divine purpose. I open it occasionally, practice the application technique on my wrist, whispering the binding prayers each time. The substance disappears into my skin, leaving no trace visible to the eye yet perceptible to other senses. A cold awareness, Mordreth's divine chill, not the fevered warmth of Void corruption. A divine purpose waiting to be fulfilled.

The blade changes form but not function. The instrument remains divine.

Sister Lara returns as promised, bearing food and additional instructions. She watches me apply the Raven's Kiss once more, nods in approval at my technique.

After hours of study and practice, I begin the forms of the Raven's Dance, the most complex of the Sisterhood's combat sequences. My body moves through the familiar patterns while my mind imagines performing them in the restrictive garments of Lady Ravencrest. Each turn and strike must be adapted, modified to work within new constraints.

Blood remembers. Flesh understands. Bone knows purpose.

When Sister Lara returns at dawn, I am ready. The transition begins with practical changes. The assassin's attire gives way to a traveling gown of forest-green wool that whispers against my skin like a lover's promise. The fabric holds warmth without the familiar weight of leather, making me feel both protected and exposed. Pearl buttons gleam like tiny moons down the bodice, and the hem brushes my ankles with each step, a constant reminder that I'm no longer dressed for death but for deception. My hair, usually bound back for practicality, falls loose around my shoulders. Subtle cosmetics applied with Sister Lara's guidance alter my features slightly.

The woman who looks back from the mirror resembles me but is not me. Lady Sera Ravencrest gazes out with my violet eyes, yet her expression holds carefully crafted warmth where mine shows only purpose. Her posture suggests cultured poise rather than combat readiness. Her hands rest gently at her sides instead of hovering near weapon hilts.

Mother Superior waits at the eastern gate where a carriage stands prepared for departure. Four black horses stamp impatiently, their breath forming clouds in the pre-dawn air. The driver, a Brother from the attached monastery, keeps his eyes downcast as we approach.

"Daughter Seraphina," Mother Superior says, her voice carrying in the quiet courtyard. "Are you prepared to carry Mordreth's judgment into the world?"

"I am his instrument," I respond, the words coming naturally despite my altered appearance. "His will guides my hand and shapes my purpose."

She nods once, satisfied. "Remember, the corruption you hunt threatens the very foundation of our holy knowledge. Blackthorne profanes divine mysteries reserved for Mordreth's chosen alone. His cult seeks warmth where there should be cold, chaos where there should be order."

"I understand." My voice sounds different to my own ears. Slightly softer. The beginnings of Lady Ravencrest's cultured tones emerging naturally.

The Void whispers. The servant remains faithful.

"The spring tides favor swift passage," Mother Superior continues. "With fortune, you'll reach Luridian before the social season's true beginning. Use every moment. Blackthorne's influence grows daily among Krytha's nobility."

"Go with Mordreth's blessing," she says, stepping back. "Return when judgment has been delivered."

I climb into the carriage, settle on unfamiliar cushioned seats. Three trunks of Lady Ravencrest's possessions are already secured. The driver snaps the reins, and the horses move forward. The Sanctuary gates open, revealing the mountain road beyond. A path I've traveled rarely and never for a mission of this complexity.

As the carriage pulls away, I look back once. The Sanctuary stands dark against the lightening sky, seven towers reaching toward heaven like supplicating fingers. Mother Superior remains at the gate, a white figure growing smaller with distance. The only home I've known since childhood recedes behind me, soon to be hidden by the mists that perpetually shroud the Veiled Peaks.

I turn forward, facing the path ahead. The road winds down through pine forests toward the coast, where Port Caellum awaits with ships bound for every corner of the continent. Lady Sera Ravencrest journeys to Luridian, to society and seduction, to the divine purpose that awaits. Beneath silk and carefully crafted smiles, Seraphina of the Blade remains. Mordreth's instrument. The weapon shaped for this calling alone.

The Raven's Kiss waits in its wooden box, tucked safely among my new possessions. Its cold presence reminds me of the mission's sacred nature despite its unorthodox methods. Death delivered through pleasure rather than pain. Judgment disguised as passion.

By shadow blessed, by blood consecrated. Mordreth's will made manifest through my willing lips.

Twenty souls will soon rest on my conscience.

Twenty sacred offerings.

The road stretches before me, winding toward the sea.

Luridian awaits.

4

ARRIVAL

Lady Sera Ravencrest emerges with each passing day of the voyage, while Seraphina retreats within silk and careful smiles. Three weeks at sea have transformed me, the transition burning like shadow-oil upon bare skin—necessary and exquisite pain. The sudden bustle of sailors above signals our approach to land, drawing me to the cabin window where I see Luridian approaching.

The ship's bow cuts through gray waves as Luridian rises from the morning mist. Stone towers pierce low clouds like blades through flesh. Walls of weathered granite circle the city, imposing. Behind them, buildings crowd together, their architecture a blend of decaying grandeur. Gargoyles crouch on rooftops, their wings spread in eternal threat.

My body sways with the tide's rhythm, muscles remembering the motion even as I stand perfectly still. Three weeks at sea have inscribed the vessel's heartbeat into my bones. Salt has worked its way into my pores, my lungs, my being. Each breath tastes of brine and destiny.

Dawn arrives with salt air instead of mountain stone, the city's bells marking time differently than the Sanctuary's ritual gongs.

A sharp knock splinters the morning silence.

"Land, my lady," the first mate calls. "Luridian harbor approaches."

I open my eyes, feel intent settle across my shoulders like a ceremonial mantle. "Thank you. I shall prepare."

The words flow from my lips smoothly, all traces of the Sisterhood's harsh consonants smoothed away. My tongue has learned new prayers, spoken in Valmeria's refined cadence rather than the blessed whispers of the Sanctuary.

The veil of silk conceals the blade.

I move with fluidity, feeling the subtle shift between assassin's grace and noblewoman's poise. Each movement becomes ritual, the transformation from killer to widow is a holy rite of its own.

From my trunk, I select a traveling gown of deep burgundy. The color of dried blood, though none in Luridian would recognize the symbolism. The silk material feels impossibly soft against my skin, whispering secrets with each movement. The corseted bodice cinches my waist to an hourglass, black ribbon lacing up the back, the neckline dipping just low enough to suggest while concealing weapons' reach. Delicate cream lace edges the sleeves and décolletage, ivory against wine-dark fabric, pretty camouflage for deadly intent. The layered skirts swish with each step, burgundy over burgundy in deepening shades, heavy enough to hide blade sheaths yet light enough for swift movement if needed. The fitted sleeves hug my arms like gentle shackles, pearl buttons running from wrist to elbow. Each limitation becomes a new form of discipline, a different kind of worship.

I secure each pearl button, feeling them yield under my touch. My hair falls in soft waves rather than the severe style of the Sisterhood. The mirror reflects a stranger with my eyes. Violet irises framed by lashes darkened with sugar water and soot. A masterful disguise crafted of flesh and fabric.

The wooden box containing the Raven's Kiss rests on a small table bolted to the floor. I trace the carved surface with reverent hands, feeling the cold power pulsing deep within. Death sleeps inside, patient as winter. I secure it in my largest trunk, nestled among cosmetics where none would think to look for the holy venom.

Mordreth's judgment sleeps within beauty's mask. The sacrament of death disguised as passion's gift.

The ship's bell rings, calling the faithful to salvation upon solid ground. I gather myself, reciting the catechism of Lady Ravencrest's fabricated history. Each detail a prayer, each false memory a devotion to my true calling.

I step onto the deck, my skin tightening in the sudden brightness. The sun feels different here than at the Sanctuary, more direct in its interrogation. Sailors bow as I pass, their eyes lingering on the curve of hip and breast that my widow's attire accentuates while appearing to conceal. Their desire slides across my skin without penetrating. A weapon recognizes when others attempt to wield it.

The captain approaches, salt-weathered and practiced. "Lady Ravencrest. We dock within the hour. Your passage with us has been an honor."

I incline my head with grace. "Captain Rykthis. You have made a potentially tedious journey quite comfortable." The words taste of honey and deception, sweet on my tongue.

"Your belongings will be transferred to shore immediately upon docking. I've arranged for a carriage to await you."

"Most appreciated. Your careful attention does you credit."

The exchange completes, another small sacrifice on the altar of my mission. Three weeks of similar performances have honed this mask until it fits like a second skin, bleeding into my flesh where the edges should show.

At the bow, I watch Luridian grow closer. The city sprawls across hills overlooking the harbor, its beauty and decay intertwined like lovers. Grand buildings of pale stone crown the heights, their facades cracked like aging courtesans. Smaller structures of wood and darker stone crouch below like supplicants.

To the west, beyond the city's furthest reaches, the horizon darkens unnaturally. Not storm clouds but an unnatural presence, the edge of Nocthys's eternal shadow bleeding into Krytha's western borders. Even from here, I taste the darkness. Bitter and recognizable, yet wrong somehow. Where Mordreth's shadow brings cold grace, this darkness pulses with chaotic warmth.

The ship maneuvers into harbor, wood groaning like a soul in torment. Ropes arc through the air, snakes seeking purchase. Planks thud into place, connecting worlds with hollow promises.

Harbor sounds assault me after weeks of open water's rhythmic whispers. Gulls scream overhead like souls denied proper death rites. Merchants bark wares in profane litany. Dock workers chant curses with religious fervor. The scents of salt water tangle with fish entrails, unwashed flesh, exotic spices from the southern kingdoms, and the underlying rot that all ports cultivate like precious herbs.

My lungs resist this cacophony of smell and sound. Three deep breaths settle my pulse. The noblewoman I pretend to be would show no disruption at such common assault. She would move through chaos untouched, her senses protected by privilege and expectation.

The gangplank secures with a final thud. The captain offers his arm, grizzled gallantry worn like ill-fitting garments. I place my gloved palm upon his sleeve, feeling the muscle deep within wool and linen. He guides me down to the pier, and my body betrays me for one treacherous moment.

The solid ground heaves under my feet like the deck in a storm. My knees nearly buckle. Three weeks at sea have rewritten my body's understanding of balance. A curse almost escapes my lips before I strangle it back to silence. I force my spine straight, my face serene, though my flesh screams at land's unnatural stillness.

One reality surrendered, another embraced through sheer will.

My trunks follow, carried by sailors whose muscles strain under the weight of weapons and worship implements concealed among silks and satins. A carriage waits as promised, neither ostentatious nor humble. Perfect for a woman who understands that true power rarely shouts its presence.

I thank the captain, pressing coins into his palm. The amount feels right in my hands. Generous enough to be remembered. Not so much as to invite suspicion. He bows, returns to his vessel, thoughts already turning to new waters. The sea claims its servants as surely as Mordreth claims his.

The driver loads my possessions, then assists me into the carriage with calloused hands that speak of a life measured in lashes and labor. The leather seats cradle my body with softness. The vehicle smells of beeswax polish, previous passengers' perfumes, and the musk of secrets whispered during night journeys.

"Where to, mi'lady?" The driver's local accent wraps around the words like darkness around bone.

"Crescent Court, in the Amber District." The address rises from memory with clarity, property arranged by Mother Superior's agents long before I knew I would claim it. Mordreth's vision extends beyond mortal understanding, preparing holy ground years before his servants recognize their calling.

We move from harbor to city, climbing streets that grow increasingly refined with each turn of the wheels. My eyes record everything. Buildings show their true nature to trained sight. Grandeur decaying from within. Foundations cracking under hasty repairs. Gardens struggling with encroaching weeds. Luridian wears its wealth like a mask, desperate to hide the rot beneath gilded facades.

The carriage passes through marketplaces where merchants display exotic goods from across the continent. Spices from the southern provinces of Krytha. Fabrics from distant Valmeria and beyond. Weapons that speak of foreign blood spilled on unfamiliar soil. I note darkened alleys that might serve as escape routes or meeting places. My hands itch to touch blades displayed on merchant tables, to feel their balance and whisper blessed prayers over steel that hungers for flesh.

We turn onto a wide avenue where trees form a green canopy overhead. The air changes. Perfume replaces sweat. Floral scents mask rot. Wealth creates its own reality, denying decay while surrounded by it. The Amber District announces itself through manicured gardens and polished brass.

Here live those wealthy enough to pretend immortality awaits them, far from Nocthys's creeping shadow.

Crescent Court appears around a gentle curve. A half-moon of three-story townhouses facing a small private garden. Iron fences divide individual properties from communal green space, creating illusions of both freedom and security. The buildings share architectural bones but display personal flourishes in door colors, window treatments, garden arrangements.

The carriage stops before the house at the curve's center. Number Seven. Morning sunlight gleams on windows like divine blessing. The door bears a brass knocker shaped like a stylized tree. Life and death intertwined in metal metaphors. Flowers bloom in planters, their bright colors a stark contrast to the Sanctuary's austere beauty.

"Here we are, mi'lady." The driver opens the carriage door with theatrical flourish that speaks of expected payment.

I descend, feeling the weight of silk skirts on my legs, so different from leather armor yet requiring similar vigilance. My eyes drink in the property with hunger born of training. Corner position offering multiple ways to come and go. Upper windows overlooking the street, perfect for watching. Nearness to neighboring homes allowing me to learn their patterns.

"Will you require assistance with your belongings?" The driver's eyes measure weight versus reward.

"Yes. Bring them to the door." I withdraw a coin purse, extracting a payment that includes gratuity that will ensure his favorable memory should I need his services again. "Thank you for the smooth journey from the harbor."

The key slides into the lock with satisfaction. The door opens, revealing an entrance hall of polished wood and cream walls. Sunlight streams through flanking windows, illuminating dust motes dancing in still air. The space smells of beeswax polish, dried lavender, and the subtle mustiness of rooms long closed but well-maintained.

I cross the threshold, feeling the subtle shift from public to private space. The driver deposits my trunks in the hall. After accepting a final coin, he departs, leaving me alone in my new sanctuary. The door closes with finality, and blessed silence settles around me.

I move through the house, my senses alive to every detail. Each room whispers its secrets to trained ears. The layout feels strangely comfortable despite never having been here before. An echo in the angle of light through windows, the particular smell of the wood. For a disorienting moment, I remember a house from childhood, before the Sisterhood claimed me. A hearth with my mother's herbs hanging above it. The memory stabs with unexpected sharpness, then dissolves like smoke.

The ground floor contains formal receiving rooms. Parlor, dining room, study. The second floor holds private quarters. Master bedroom, guest rooms, sitting area. The third floor houses servant quarters and storage spaces. Every threshold I cross becomes sanctified by my presence. Every room is both a shrine and fortress.

In the master bedroom, I stand before tall windows that oversee the garden and surrounding homes. I press lightly on the glass, feeling the boundary between observer and observed. From here I can watch without being watched.

Notice patterns.

Track movements.

Anticipate opportunities.

My position in Crescent Court places me within the social circles Lord Blackthorne inhabits. From here, I can orchestrate seemingly chance encounters, building the foundation for ultimate judgment. Mother Superior's foresight manifests in each perfect detail.

The hunter claims her territory. The sacrament approaches.

5

CONNECTIONS

I unpack items required for immediate comfort, but leave most of my belongings sealed in trunks. Lady Ravencrest would never soil herself with mundane tasks better left to servants. My touch lingers over the whisper-soft velvets in midnight blue and forest green, crisp taffetas that rustle like autumn leaves in shades of amber and rose, and silks that slip through my fingers like water—sapphire, emerald, the purple-black of bruised plums. Each fabric tells its own lie—luxury masking lethality. The trunk containing my true implements remains locked, its contents patient as the grave.

A knock at the front door interrupts my preparations. My hand instinctively reaches for a blade no longer at my hip, muscles remembering what my mind has temporarily forgotten. I breathe once, twice, allowing the widow's persona to resettle across my features like a veil.

The mirror in the entrance hall reflects a woman at peace, perhaps slightly curious at an unexpected visitor. No trace of the predator's wariness shows in her violet eyes.

Opening the door reveals a tall man in formal attire, his posture announcing service to wealth and power. "Lady Ravencrest? I am Phillips, steward to Lord Hargrove." His accent carries the refined edges of one educated beyond his station to better reflect his master's status. "My master resides at Number Three. He wishes to extend his welcome to the Court and invites you to take tea this afternoon, if convenient."

The invitation presents my first test in Luridian society. The performance begins in earnest.

"How thoughtful," I reply, allowing refined pleasure to warm my tone while maintaining appropriate reserve. "Please inform Lord Hargrove that I would be delighted to accept his kind invitation. Shall we say four o'clock?"

"Perfect, my lady." Phillips hesitates, eyes assessing my recently arrived status. "If I may be so bold, are you in need of staff recommendations? Lord Hargrove maintains connections with several reputable agencies."

The offer serves my intent perfectly. "That would be most helpful. I had planned to post advertisements today, but local knowledge would prove invaluable."

"I require a handmaiden suitable for my needs," I say, testing his responses. "Competent, discreet, and preferably one who doesn't chatter endlessly about court gossip."

Phillips nods immediately. "I have a candidate in mind, Lady Ravencrest. A young woman named Liora Tanner. She's intelligent, discreet, and exceptionally careful with fine garments.

Twenty years of age with experience serving in several noble houses."

"She sounds suitable. I'd like to meet her before making a final decision."

"Very wise, my lady. I'll arrange for Miss Tanner to call on you tomorrow morning. I shall also bring additional recommendations when you visit this afternoon, should you wish to consider other candidates." His satisfaction suggests the exchange serves his interests as well as mine. Information flows in many directions within these circles.

As he departs, I feel the recognizable thrill of a hunt beginning well. The neighbor's swift invitation implies curiosity about the newcomer. Such interest serves my calling, creating natural paths to establish my presence.

I return to arranging the master bedroom, creating the illusion of comfortable occupancy. Clothing in wardrobes. Personal items on surfaces. Books positioned to suggest interrupted reading. The house remains mostly vacant, but Lady Ravencrest's presence begins to imprint upon the space.

For tea with Lord Hargrove, I don a gown of deep blue silk that complements my violet eyes. The color speaks of twilight skies and bruised flesh, beauty with underlying threat that none would consciously perceive. My hair arranged into deceptively simple waves that require careful practice to refine. Minimal jewelry signals moderate mourning customs. Pearl earrings. A single gold band. A modest brooch at my throat like a promise of crimson.

Lord Hargrove's home stands three doors from mine, its exterior speaking wealth through subtle signals. Brass polished to mirror shine. Superior glass in windows. Exquisite attention to detail in landscaping. I note each element with the eye of one trained to read surfaces for what they conceal below.

A maid admits me to a parlor where Lord Hargrove awaits. His bearing confirms what his home suggested. A man accustomed to both giving and following orders. Silver hair and trimmed beard frame features accustomed to command. His eyes assess me with a practiced subtlety that nevertheless feels transparent to one trained in true observation.

"Lady Ravencrest. Welcome to Crescent Court." His voice carries cultivated authority, the weapon of those born to privilege rather than forged through trial.

"Lord Hargrove. How kind of you to invite me." I offer my hand carefully, maintaining the balance between confidence and appropriate deference.

He takes my skin briefly, his touch cool and dry over my gloved hand. We settle into an arrangement of chairs designed to facilitate conversation without threatening propriety. The silver tea service gleams between us like ceremonial implements.

"You come to us from Valmeria, I understand?" He signals the maid to pour, the gesture automatic as breathing. "The voyage must have been arduous, three weeks at sea, I'm told."

"Yes, though the sea voyage provided welcome time for reflection." I accept the offered cup, feeling its warmth through fine porcelain. "Valmeria holds too many memories. Luridian offers new possibilities. I must ask, how did you know I was arriving?"

"Ah, yes. Phillips mentioned you were widowed. I always like to stay informed when someone new to society is arriving." His expression shifts to practiced solemnity. "My condolences."

"You're most kind. Three years have softened grief's sharpest edges." The tea tastes of bergamot and deception, bitter and sweet on my tongue. "One must eventually move forward."

Our conversation flows in practiced currents. I speak of cultural interests, suitable travel experiences, and appropriate observations of Luridian's beauty compared to other coastal capitals. His responses reveal connections throughout local society. Names and relationships worth remembering. Patterns of influence and expectation. I gather each detail like a hunter collecting tracks.

"Luridian must be quite different from inland Valmeria," he observes, testing my knowledge.

"Indeed. The sea air here carries such vitality. In Valmeria, we're separated from the coast by the Thornwood. Quite a journey to reach any port." I sip my tea delicately. "Though I confess, being so close to Nocthys's borders gives one pause. Even from the harbor, one can see where the shadow begins."

"Ah yes, the eternal night." His expression darkens slightly. "A curiosity that draws scholars and fools alike. Best to keep one's distance from such unnatural darkness."

My heart beats faster when he mentions an upcoming gallery opening sponsored by the royal family. Lord Blackthorne will certainly attend such an event.

Mordreth guides my path toward my target, illuminating the way with divine intent.

"I would be pleased to escort you to the gallery opening," Lord Hargrove offers as our meeting concludes. "As a newcomer, you'll benefit from proper introductions to our circle. Fresh perspectives from distant Valmeria are always welcome."

"That would be most kind." I set aside my cup, allowing pleased appreciation to show in my expression. "I've developed an interest in art during my periods of solitude. The gallery opening sounds perfect."

"Excellent. Phillips has prepared staffing recommendations as promised." He offers me a folded paper, an interest in my domestic arrangements marking him as potentially useful beyond initial introduction.

I return to Number Seven with satisfaction warming my life. The tea has yielded valuable results. Social connection established. Invitation secured to an event Blackthorne will attend. Initial acceptance within the Court community. Mordreth's will unfolds through seemingly mundane connections.

The afternoon sun slants through tall windows as a soft knock interrupts my study of the city map. "Enter."

The door opens to reveal a young woman who moves with the quiet grace of someone trained to be invisible yet indispensable. Light brown hair escapes from a practical braid to frame her face, and her brown eyes hold an intelligence that immediately sets her apart from typical servants.

"Lady Ravencrest." She drops into a graceful curtsey, neither too deep nor too shallow. "I am Liora Tanner. Mr. Phillips sent me regarding the handmaiden position."

Her gaze flickers up, taking in my appearance with the quick assessment of someone accustomed to reading her betters. I see her note the unusual violet of my eyes, the sharp angles of my face softened by the warmth I've practiced for Lady Ravencrest's persona.

I study her with the same intensity I use to assess potential threats, though her steady gaze makes the comparison feel wrong. She doesn't fidget under scrutiny, doesn't fill the silence with nervous chatter. Instead, she waits with a patience that speaks of inner strength.

"Tell me about your experience, Liora."

"I've served in three noble houses, my lady. Most recently with Lady Harwick before her marriage took her to the eastern provinces." Her voice carries the faint accent of Lower Luridian, softened but not erased by years in service. "I'm skilled in wardrobe management, hair arrangement, and maintaining a lady's chambers. I can also read and write, should correspondence duties be required."

The last admission catches my attention. Literacy in servants is rare, suggesting either unusual education or self-teaching. "How did you learn your letters?"

A slight flush colors her cheeks. "I... borrowed books from the houses where I served, my lady. Taught myself during quiet hours. I hope that doesn't displease you."

"On the contrary." I find myself genuinely interested. "Initiative and intelligence are qualities I value. What else have you taught yourself?"

"Some herb lore from my mother. Basic remedies for headaches, sleep troubles, minor wounds." She pauses, then adds quietly, "I also know which flowers bloom best in darkness, if you're interested in maintaining a private garden."

The specificity of that last comment intrigues me. A servant who notices what grows in gloom, who thinks to mention it unprompted. My training whispers caution, but instinct pulls in another direction.

"You're observant," I note.

"It's a useful quality in service, my lady." Her eyes meet mine directly for just a moment before dropping appropriately. Something shifts in the air between us, her gaze holding mine like a question I'm not ready to answer. When she looks away, I feel the loss of that warmth more keenly than I should. In that brief connection, I see unexpected depth, not just intelligence but a kind of recognition, as if she sees past Lady Ravencrest's careful construction to the truth underneath.

"Indeed it is." I walk to the window, creating distance while I consider. "Tell me, Liora, what do you know of discretion?"

"That a good servant sees everything and says nothing, my lady. That trust, once broken, can never be fully mended." Her voice carries weight beyond her years. "I've kept many secrets in my service. I would keep yours as well."

The promise hangs between us, more substantial than typical servant platitudes. When I turn back, she's watching me with those steady brown eyes, waiting.

"The position is yours if you want it," I decide, surprising myself with the swiftness of the choice. "You'll start immediately. Phillips will discuss wages and arrange for your belongings to be brought from your current lodgings."

Relief flickers across her features before professional composure returns. "Thank you, my lady. I won't disappoint you."

As she curtseys again and turns to leave, instinct makes me call out. "Liora?"

She pauses at the door. "Yes, my lady?"

"Welcome to Crescent Court."

The smile that touches her lips is small but genuine, transforming her face from merely pretty to truly beautiful, making my heart pound unexpectedly. "Thank you, my lady. I look forward to serving you."

After she leaves, I stand at the window, watching darkness lengthen across the garden. My hand traces the glass where her reflection had briefly appeared beside mine. A handmaiden. Necessary for my cover, nothing more. Yet her steady gaze and quiet strength suggests complications I hadn't anticipated.

Focus on the mission, I tell myself. But her words echo in my mind. "I would keep yours as well."

Evening brings solitude and blessed ritual. I secure the house with meticulous attention, testing each lock and latch. Safety is an illusion, but preparation is devotion. Mordreth favors the vigilant servant who watches while others sleep.

In the master bedroom, I remove Lady Ravencrest's elegant attire, folding each garment with care. The silk whispers over my skin as it falls away, confessing secrets of its previous owner. Under the widow's sophisticated exterior, my body remains Mordreth's holy instrument, each muscle honed for divine duty.

Naked before the mirror, I see the flesh Mordreth has shaped through trial and life. My hands trace the scars mapping my skin. The thin line along my ribs from a training blade that cut too deep, still sensitive to touch. The star-shaped mark above my hip from my first mission, puckered and proud. The burn on my shoulder from the Ritual of Seven Shadows, skin forever changed by blessed fire. My body tells its own story, each scar a prayer written in flesh, each mark a testament to devotion sealed in crimson. I feel the beauty in this damaged skin that most would hide.

These are not flaws but sacraments.

I perform the Night Devotion, moving through holy forms with grace born of thousands of repetitions. Each position honors one aspect of Mordreth's divine nature. Silence. Shadow. Sacrifice. Secrecy. Suffering. Surrender. Salvation. My breath flows steadily, my heartbeat a steady drum marking divine time.

Guide your servant through shadow's test. Grant clarity when doubt clouds judgment. Let this blade cut true in your holy service.

As I complete the final movement of devotion, an unexpected wave of loneliness washes through me. The empty house echoes with silence where the Sanctuary would pulse with the breath of sleeping Sisters. My throat tightens suddenly. The feeling passes quickly, but leaves me shaken. I have never felt separated from Mordreth's calling before. Even on missions in distant lands I was still myself. Not like this. Not someone else.

I extinguish all but a single candle, then slide between cool sheets. The bed's softness feels obscene over skin accustomed to hardness, its give and welcome almost suspicious after years of ascetic discipline. I find myself craving the known discomfort of my Sanctuary pallet.

Tomorrow brings the next phase. Further establishment within Court society. Initial mapping of roads to Lord Blackthorne. Each step brings judgment closer to fulfillment.

I close my eyes but remain alert to each unfamiliar sound.

Lady Ravencrest sleeps peacefully in her new home.

Seraphina watches from behind violet eyes, patient as death itself.

Death waits on silent feet. Mordreth's judgment approaches.

The pieces align perfectly. Residence established. Staff secured. Social connections initiated. Lord Blackthorne remains unaware that his judgment draws near, cloaked in widow's weeds and cultured smiles.

Lady Sera Ravencrest has arrived in Luridian.

Seraphina of the Blade stands ready under silk-draped skin.

The twentieth offering draws ever closer.

Mordreth's will made manifest through his faithful servant.
The hunt begins.

6

OBSERVATIONS

The gathering fills Lord Neverell's grand hall with noise that presses into my skin like unwanted touch. Candle flames reflect in crystal glasses, turning wine the color of fresh crimson. The heavy scent of expensive perfumes mingles with sweat under silks and velvets. I find the inability of nobility to fully mask their animal nature darkly amusing.

I sip wine that tastes of summer berries and bitter tannins. Lady Sera Ravencrest stands poised in midnight blue silk while within, my flesh remembers the comforting weight of leather armor and blessed steel upon my thighs.

First week in Crescent Court. Establishing patterns. Learning rhythms. The household accepts Lady Ravencrest with minimal suspicion.

Lord Hargrove materializes at my elbow, his silver hair gleaming in the candlelight. "Lady Ravencrest, I trust you're finding our little gathering amusing?" His smile stretches too wide under calculating eyes. One week in Luridian and already he's appointed himself my guide to society.

"Quite so." The truth tastes sweet on my tongue. "Your introduction to Lord Neverell's gathering proves most valuable."

"The pleasure is mine." His gaze lingers where the sapphire pendant rests over my breasts. "One must know the right people in Luridian. Some doors remain firmly shut without proper connections."

An opening presents itself as clearly as an exposed throat. "I understand Lord Blackthorne holds considerable influence despite his family's relatively recent elevation?"

Hargrove's expression tightens with the resentment old nobility reserves for new power. "Indeed. Though some find his methods... unconventional. His interests tend toward the esoteric. Not everyone appreciates his particular enthusiasm."

My heartbeat quickens within my breast. "The most rewarding conversations often arise from unconventional minds. Traditional thinking rarely yields meaningful insight, and can be quite boring."

Hargrove studies me with fresh understanding. "A dangerous philosophy in certain circles, Lady Ravencrest."

A passing Countess claims his attention before I can respond. The timing serves me perfectly. I move through the crowd deliberately, positioning myself near the chamber's eastern alcove. The space offers an ideal vantage point to observe the entire gathering while appearing merely to appreciate the view from tall windows.

Three noblewomen have mentioned Blackthorne since my arrival. Their voices changed when speaking his name, mixing desire with unease. The combination stirs my pulse. When prey inspires both hunger and fear, it carries power worth tasting, worth claiming in the Raven's name.

Movement ripples through the crowd like wind across water. Conversations pause, then resume with renewed intensity. My senses sharpen as the room's scent changes subtly. The new aroma carries masculine cologne underlaid with ritual herbs no ordinary noble would recognize. My nostrils flare, drinking in information my body processes before my mind can name it.

May the Raven's sight guide these eyes.

Lord Rivin Blackthorne enters the hall with casual authority that parts the crowd before him. Tall, with dark hair swept back from features carved with elegant care, he moves naturally. Each step conveys the certainty of a man who never questions his right to occupy any space he enters.

My mouth fills with copper taste though no crimson has been spilled. Every muscle tightens with anticipation while heat spreads through my lower body, a response I neither fight nor indulge. The body knows what fills it with desire, whether steel or flesh.

I permit myself a moment of hunger for what the Raven has marked for sacrifice. My body responds to his strong jaw and elegant features with unexpected fire. Life quickens through my flesh as I imagine tracing those lines with touch, with lips, with blade. There's a dark pleasure in knowing I'll learn every inch of his flesh before delivering him to Mordreth's embrace.

Women gravitate toward him immediately, drawn by forces beyond ordinary attraction. Men shift their posture to accommodate his presence, showing subtle deference in their stance. Power radiates from him like heat from flame.

I sip wine while watching how the gathering reorganizes itself around his presence. Lord Neverell approaches with effusive welcome, clasping Blackthorne's hand with both of his own. The gesture appears friendly but reveals deeper truth as Neverell's posture shows submission disguised as fellowship.

Blackthorne moves through the crowd charmingly, his laughter carrying across the room with rich and compelling tones. He touches selected guests briefly, placing a hand on a shoulder here, brushing fingers across an arm there. Each contact leaves its recipient glowing with pleased significance. He bestows attention like precious gifts, creating obligation with seeming generosity.

A servant passes with wine whose scent reminds me of communion wine, dark as spilled crimson, served during ritual darkness. I breathe it in, letting it center my intent. Memories flash of lips stained red, of bodies moving in ceremonial forms within the Sanctuary's vaulted ceilings, of whispered prayers and flesh marked with holy symbols.

"Fascinating, isn't he?" A woman's voice flows over me like warmed honey, cultured and knowing. Lady Mereswen, wife to a royal advisor, follows Blackthorne with her eyes across the room. "Like watching a wolf move among lapdogs."

"You know him well?" I keep my tone merely curious while heat spreads through my veins.

She laughs softly. "Everyone knows Blackthorne, darling. Few know him well." Her painted lips curve with private memory. "His gatherings are quite... memorable, for those fortunate enough to receive an invitation."

"Private gatherings?" My pulse quickens, life singing with anticipation of the hunt.

"For those with particular interests." Her eyes assess me with new appreciation. "Intellectual pursuits beyond what society readily embraces. Arcane wisdom. Mysteries from the darkness." She sips her wine, leaving a red stain on the crystal rim. "Though I wouldn't mention such things in certain company."

The information settles like blessed wine on my tongue. Mother Superior's intelligence proves true in my bones. Blackthorne moves beyond ordinary society into territories touched by shadow, recruiting those drawn to forbidden wisdom much as the Sisterhood selects those with potential. His calling serves profane ambition rather than divine will.

Yet the pattern doesn't align perfectly with Mother Superior's assessment. There's an unexpected intensity to Blackthorne's focus when discussing artifacts with selected nobles, a genuine passion under the social veneer. Not the hollow charm of a man seeking only power, but the fervor of one truly seeking knowledge. The glimpse of authenticity stirs an unwelcome curiosity in my chest.

"How does one receive such invitations?" I allow subtle interest to color my voice.

Mereswen's smile sharpens. "One catches his attention. Though I warn you, Lady Ravencrest, once caught, it's difficult to escape."

She drifts away as another guest claims her attention. I remain positioned near the windows, my body instinctively learning Blackthorne's rhythms. I feel his patterns in my flesh. The weight he places on his right foot when emphasizing a point becomes a vulnerability my muscles memorize like a lover's touch. The slight tilt of his head when listening with genuine interest rather than polite attention marks moments of true engagement. The angle of his smile when pleased versus when merely conforming to social expectation reveals the man under the mask.

The gathering breathes around me like a living creature. Conversations rise and fall rhythmically as lords and ladies speak of crops and weather with their mouths while their eyes negotiate power and advantage. Their scents mingle, expensive perfumes, sweat, desire and fear and ambition, creating a complex aroma my senses interpret instinctively.

I position myself near a marble column, angling my body to appear engaged with a vapid duchess while maintaining focus on Blackthorne's location. He has moved to a small grouping of men clustered near the grand fireplace whose posture suggests conversation beyond ordinary social exchange.

I drift closer, positioning myself beside a large floral arrangement that partially obscures my presence while allowing their words to reach my ears.

"...shipment arrived from Nocthys border yesterday." Blackthorne's voice carries controlled excitement under a casual tone. "The writings confirm what we suspected about the ceremonial binding."

"Dangerous territory, Rivin." An older lord lowers his voice with concern. "The royal advisors watch border traffic closely since the last... incident."

"Their understanding remains limited by conventional thinking." Blackthorne dismisses the concern with elegant confidence. "The shadow essence responds differently when prepared according to the traditional methods. The golden effect manifests only under specific conditions."

Golden flecked eyes. My skin burns with recognition. My blade opened Brother Elias's throat when those same flecks provided evidence of shadow corruption that justified his execution. Blackthorne pursues the same forbidden wisdom that condemned the apostate to judgment.

Divine intent floods my veins with liquid fire as certainty burns away doubt. My hands tingle with the memory of blade meeting flesh, of crimson baptizing my skin. Soon they will know a different sacrament through touch that leads to ultimate judgment.

And yet, I find myself drawn to the hunger in Blackthorne's voice. What forbidden knowledge could be worth such a risk?

The passion in his words speaks to a quest beyond mere power. For a moment, the question heats my life force before I push it aside. The Raven's judgment doesn't require understanding, only obedience.

"Your previous demonstration proved compelling." A third man speaks, younger, with hungry ambition evident in his tone. "When will the next ceremony occur?"

"Patience, Lord Trevaine." Blackthorne's smile carries genuine amusement. "The holy change requires exquisite preparation. The moon reaches its perfect phase in two weeks' time. Those deemed ready will receive an invitation."

Their language confirms every suspicion. Blackthorne leads a cult trafficking in shadow corruption. His Vessels of the Void use perverted forms of knowledge reserved only for the chosen. Each word from his lips justifies the judgment that awaits him.

Their conversation shifts to safer topics as others approach. I withdraw carefully, moving through the gathering with renewed calling. Lady Ravencrest makes appropriate social connections while under the pleasant exterior, my body sings with the promise of the hunt, of holy connection through crimson and shadow.

The night progresses in measured time. Servants refill wine glasses, musicians play compositions that stir no emotion, and lords and ladies form and dissolve conversational groups like clouds reshaping in changing winds. Through it all, I maintain focus on Blackthorne's position without obvious attention.

His gaze sweeps the gathering occasionally, reading the room with predator's instinct. Twice his eyes pass over me, registering my presence without particular interest. This disregard serves my calling perfectly. He perceives only another widow seeking social position while the blade within remains overlooked.

I continue gathering intelligence through seemingly innocent conversation. Three more mentions of Blackthorne's private gatherings emerge from carefully guided discussion. Each reference carries similar undertones. Exclusive intellectual gatherings mask darker realities. Invitations become both coveted and feared. Participants change after their experiences in ways they struggle to articulate.

As the gathering reaches its peak, I position myself near the refreshment table where Blackthorne has paused alone, examining a small sculpture displayed on a side table. The piece depicts a raven with wings outstretched, carved from black stone that drinks light rather than reflecting it. The Raven's sigil rendered in profane material can't be an accident. The symbol before his judgment's target feels like confirmation, like divine permission whispering over my skin.

I stand close enough to observe without engaging directly. At this distance, new details emerge. The subtle pattern embroidered on his formal jacket resembles ritual markings I've seen in forbidden manuscripts within the Sanctuary's locked archives. His signet ring bears symbols that would mean nothing to ordinary nobility but speak volumes to one trained in shadow lore.

Most telling, under his cologne lingers the unmistakable scent of shadow-oil. It slides beneath the civilized notes of sandalwood and citrus like a serpent through grass. Fainter than what Sisterhood rituals employ, diluted or altered, but unmistakably there, making my skin prickle with recognition. The scent triggers memories of ceremonies, of life spilled in service. My mouth waters with involuntary response, tongue remembering the taste of blessed communion.

Blackthorne turns suddenly, as if sensing observation. His eyes, those gray irises ringed with unusual darkness, study me with intensity that seems to reach past skin and bone to deeper truths. An energy passes between us in that moment as one predator recognizes another. My skin heats under his gaze, life rushing to my face, to my breasts, to places I refuse to acknowledge.

I lower my gaze with false modesty, offering the slight smile appropriate from a widow no longer in deep mourning yet maintaining proper reserve. When I look up again, his attention has returned to the sculpture, though a new focus lingers in his posture.

This first contact, invisible to witnesses yet significant to cat and mouse, begins the ritual, though he mistakes its nature.

I withdraw before a direct conversation becomes necessary. Tonight brings observation only, as the hunt progresses through careful stages. Rush the mouse and it escapes, approach patiently and it delivers itself willingly to judgment.

Lord Hargrove finds me as the gathering begins to thin. "Did you enjoy the evening, Lady Ravencrest?"

"Illuminating." The word tastes of truth on my tongue. "Luridian society proves most intriguing."

"I noticed you observing Lord Blackthorne with some interest." His tone carries carefully disguised jealousy under a social polish. "His reputation with ladies of quality remains... complicated."

"I observed many interesting souls this evening." The lie tastes bitter but necessary. "Each face tells its own story to those willing to see past masks." I smile with Lady Ravencrest's practiced charm while the assassin watches from behind my eyes.

The conversation shifts to safer topics as his carriage returns me to Crescent Court. Night embraces the city in velvet darkness while stars pierce the sky like blade points. The moon hangs heavy, approaching fullness that will bring Blackthorne's next ritual and draw me closer to my calling.

Liora waits despite the late hour, her eyes soft with concern that catches me unprepared. No one has looked at me with such genuine care since before the Sisterhood claimed me. The sensation burns strangely in my chest.

"You needn't have waited, Liora." My voice emerges softer than intended as Lady Ravencrest's armor slips after hours of performance.

"I wanted to ensure you returned safely, my lady." She helps remove my cloak, her touch sure yet gentle over my shoulders.

"Some gatherings continue until dawn, leaving guests vulnerable on the return journey."

Her genuine concern unsettles a force long dormant as my breath catches with unfamiliar heat.

"The evening proved entertaining and informative." I move toward the stairs, Liora following quietly. "I met many of Luridian's prominent families."

She nods attentively as she follows me up the staircase. "Did you make favorable connections, my lady?"

"Several that may prove useful." I pause at my chamber door, flesh remembering tonight's observations, mind already planning the next stage of the hunt. "The royal gallery opening approaches soon. Lord Hargrove has offered to make introductions."

"An excellent opportunity." Her hands fold before her simple dress. "Shall I prepare the midnight blue gown with silver threading for that occasion?"

"Yes. Though we have time yet to decide." I feel fatigue spreading through my body, the night's performance drawing on reserves I didn't know I possessed. "Thank you for waiting, Liora, but please don't feel obligated. I'm quite capable of preparing for bed unassisted."

"Of course, my lady." She curtseys naturally. "Rest well. I'll return in the morning with breakfast."

She withdraws with quietness, leaving me alone with the night's revelations. In my chambers, I remove Lady Ravencrest's elegant attire, folding midnight silk with care. Under the formal gown, my body remains a daughter of the Raven, each muscle honed for divine calling, each scar a testament to life spilled in righteous service.

I kneel before the hidden altar concealed behind a false panel in the wardrobe. The small raven effigy gleams in darkness, carved obsidian drinking what little light reaches it. Seven ritual candles surround it in the pattern of the Void Crown constellation that guides the Sisters' midnight prayers.

My hands strike flint to steel. Sparks leap in darkness as the candles ignite one by one, their flames stretching toward the ceiling. The scent of blessed wax fills my lungs, carrying memories of countless nights spent in similar devotion.

I touch the ritual scars on my inner wrist, seven marks for seven aspects of the dark. "Through silence and shadow, through sacrifice and surrender, let this servant bring your mercy."

The prayer sinks into my flesh, burning away distractions accumulated during hours of social performance. My heartbeat steadies within my breast. One. Two. Three. Four. Five. Six. Seven. The holy count brings clarity, brings calling, brings certainty flowing back through my veins.

Tonight confirms everything Mother Superior revealed. My body recognizes the truth of it. Blackthorne pursues wisdom reserved only for the chosen. His cult changes initiates through shadow corruption marked by golden flecked eyes. The private gatherings, the moon phase ceremony, the writings from Nocthys all align with her warnings. My flesh remembers Brother

Elias's life baptizing my face, remembers the golden flecks dying in his eyes as Mordreth's judgment flowed through my blade.

My flesh tingles with divine calling. Judgment approaches with each carefully placed step toward the final act. The Raven's Kiss awaits in its wooden box, patient as death itself. When the moment ripens with holy timing, Blackthorne will receive mercy through lips rather than blade.

I extinguish the candles with moistened skin, feeling each flame die over my touch. Small pain centers attention. The altar returns to darkness as I close the hidden panel, sealing its calling within ordinary furnishings.

Sleep comes slowly despite exhaustion. My body remembers the scent of shadow-oil clinging to Blackthorne's skin, the penetrating assessment in gray eyes ringed with unusual darkness, and the controlled power in his movements. Memory mingles with anticipation, creating restlessness within me.

The hunt proceeds exactly as designed. First observation complete, next comes a "chance" encounter, then a careful cultivation of interest. Each step brings judgment closer to fulfillment, brings my blade closer to his throat, brings my kiss closer to his lips.

The mouse and the cat only ever have one outcome.

7

ENCOUNTER

The gallery opening draws Luridian's nobility like carrion birds to fresh death. Lord Hargrove's carriage deposits me before the Royal Museum's columned entrance, where torches cast dancing shadows across marble steps. My burgundy silk gown flows like liquid shadow, the fitted bodice adorned with jet beading that catches torchlight like drops of black blood. The off-shoulder design bares my collarbones and the elegant slope of my neck, cream skin against wine-dark fabric, while the skirts pool around me in rich waves of burgundy and garnet, parting just enough when I walk to hint at the midnight silk beneath.

Ten days have passed since my arrival at Crescent Court. Ten days of Lady Ravencrest establishing herself within acceptable social circles. Tonight marks my formal introduction to the circles that matter. Tonight, I begin hunting Lord Blackthorne in earnest.

"Lady Ravencrest." Hargrove offers his arm with theatrical gallantry, his silver hair gleaming under torchlight. "You honor us with your presence this evening."

"The honor is entirely mine, Lord Hargrove." I rest my gloved hand along his sleeve, feeling the steady pulse beneath expensive fabric. "Luridian's artistic treasures have earned quite a reputation beyond our borders."

The museum's interior overwhelms with grandeur. Soaring ceilings painted with mythological scenes. Marble floors polished to mirror brightness. Crystal chandeliers casting prisms of light that fragment and multiply across every surface. Nobles in their finest attire cluster around displayed artworks, their conversations creating a din of cultured voices and clinking crystal.

My eyes catalog everything with predatory focus. Exit routes. Guard positions. Potential weapons concealed among decorative elements. The habits of a lifetime assert themselves even as Lady Ravencrest smiles and nods at appropriate intervals.

"The centerpiece exhibition features artifacts recovered from Nocthys expeditions," Hargrove explains, guiding me deeper into the crowded gallery. "Quite controversial, really. Many believe such items shouldn't be displayed publicly."

My pulse quickens at the mention of Nocthys. "How fascinating. What manner of artifacts?"

"Sculptures. Ceremonial implements. Items of... unclear purpose." His voice drops slightly. "Some say they emanate an unnatural chill, though I suspect such claims represent overactive imagination rather than supernatural influence."

We approach a roped-off section where guests cluster with morbid fascination. Behind velvet barriers stand display cases containing objects that make my skin prickle with recognition. A chalice carved from what appears to be black bone. Masks with eye holes that seem to track movement. Ceremonial daggers whose edges gleam despite their obvious age.

Air stills in my throat as I recognize symbols etched into several pieces. Not Mordreth's ravens, but forces older. Powers that predate the Sisterhood's teachings yet speak to the same primal darkness. The artifacts hum with barely contained power, their presence creating pressure within my skull like an approaching storm.

"Remarkable craftsmanship," I murmur, studying a silver pendant shaped like intertwining serpents. The piece draws my gaze with magnetic intensity, its surface seeming to shift in the flickering light.

"Indeed. Though I confess their appeal escapes me entirely." Hargrove's discomfort shows in his rigid posture. "Beautiful perhaps, but cold. Lifeless."

Not lifeless. Sleeping. Waiting for those who understand their true nature.

"Lady Ravencrest?"

The voice behind me carries cultured authority wrapped in silk. I turn, feeling the weight of destiny settling across my shoulders like a well-worn cloak. Lord Rivin Blackthorne stands three feet away, magnificent in formal black attire that emphasizes his imposing height. Dark hair swept back from features carved with elegant grace. Storm-gray eyes that study me with the intensity of a predator recognizing potential prey.

"Lord Blackthorne." I offer my hand, watching his pupils dilate as his gaze drops to the curve of my décolletage before returning to my face. "Lord Hargrove speaks of you often."

He takes my fingers, pressing lips to my knuckles in a kiss that lingers longer than propriety dictates. His mouth feels heated against my glove, the contact sending unexpected fire spiraling through my veins. When he straightens, his eyes hold mine with uncomfortable intensity.

His gaze travels over me with scholarly interest—cataloging the midnight fall of my hair, the way my height requires him to look down only slightly, the deliberate grace in my movements. I see him file away these details as he would any intriguing artifact.

"The pleasure is entirely mine, Lady Ravencrest." His voice flows like aged whiskey, smooth with underlying fire. "Your reputation precedes you, though I confess the reality exceeds even the most generous descriptions."

"You flatter me, my lord." I withdraw my hand slowly, allowing my fingertips to trail across his palm. The gesture appears accidental while being entirely deliberate.

"I speak only truth." His gaze never wavers from mine. "Beauty combined with intelligence creates a most compelling combination."

Hargrove clears his throat, clearly uncomfortable with the charged atmosphere developing between us. "Lord Blackthorne, I was just showing Lady Ravencrest the Nocthys collection. Perhaps you could share your expertise regarding these pieces?"

"I would be delighted." Blackthorne's smile reveals perfect teeth that somehow suggest hidden sharpness. "Few appreciate the true artistry represented in these works."

He moves closer, close enough that I catch his scent. Expensive cologne layered over musk earthier, more raw. The combination makes my pulse quicken despite my training.

"This pendant, for instance." His fingers hover near the silver serpents without quite touching the display case. "Most see mere decoration. Those with deeper understanding recognize the symbolism. Life and death intertwined. Light and shadow dancing in eternal balance."

"Balance suggests equality between opposing forces," I observe, testing his response. "Do you believe light and shadow possess equal power?"

His eyes sharpen with interest. "An excellent question. Most assume light represents strength while shadow embodies weakness. But consider—without darkness, how would we recognize illumination? Without shadow, how would we define form?"

"Philosophy disguised as art appreciation," Hargrove mutters, clearly out of his depth.

"The most profound truths often hide behind beautiful facades," Blackthorne replies without breaking eye contact with me. "Wouldn't you agree, Lady Ravencrest?"

"I find honesty often wears the most elegant masks." The words carry multiple meanings, each one crafted to intrigue rather than satisfy.

"Indeed." He steps closer, close enough that his sleeve brushes mine. "Perhaps you would join me for a more private examination of the collection? I could share insights unavailable in such... crowded circumstances."

The invitation arrives exactly as planned, yet his closeness creates complications I hadn't anticipated. Heat radiates from his body, making my skin feel flushed under silk and stays. My training screams warnings about becoming too close to the target, but the mission requires exactly such intimacy.

"I would find that most educational." My voice emerges breathier than intended.

"Excellent. Shall we begin with the ceremonial implements?" He gestures toward a section containing items that make my assassin's soul sing with recognition. Blades designed for ritual rather than warfare. Chalices meant to hold offerings other than wine.

We move through the gallery with Hargrove trailing behind like a reluctant chaperone. Blackthorne's knowledge proves extensive and deeply personal. He speaks of the artifacts with the reverence others reserve for religious texts, his passion evident in every observation.

"This dagger," he says, stopping before a blade whose handle bears symbols I recognize from forbidden Sisterhood manuscripts. "The metal was forged using techniques lost to modern smiths. Note how the edge seems to drink light rather than reflect it."

I lean closer, genuinely fascinated despite myself. The weapon calls to instincts in my blood, its presence creating sympathetic vibrations in the concealed blades I carry. "It's beautiful."

"Beauty born of purpose. Every curve serves function. Every symbol carries meaning." His voice drops to a whisper meant only for my ears. "True artistry emerges when form and function achieve perfect harmony."

"You speak as one with personal experience."

"I collect pieces of similar craftsmanship." His hand hovers near my elbow, not quite touching yet close enough that I feel the heat of his palm. "Perhaps you would appreciate seeing them in less... institutional surroundings."

"I would be honored."

The words emerge before I can consider their implications. My mission requires getting close to Blackthorne, gaining his trust, positioning myself for the fatal kiss. Yet his manner suggests depths I hadn't expected. Not merely the corrupt aristocrat Mother Superior described, but a man with genuine passion for occult knowledge.

Dangerous thoughts. Complications that threaten mission focus.

"Then it shall be arranged." His smile carries promise wrapped in silk. "I'll send an invitation within the week."

The remainder of the evening passes in a blur of introductions and carefully orchestrated conversations. Blackthorne never strays far from my side, his presence creating a charged atmosphere that makes other guests give us subtle space. I collect information with each exchange, mapping the social connections that bind Luridian's elite.

Yet my awareness keeps returning to the man beside me. The way his fingers brush mine when passing wine glasses. How his eyes follow my movements with predatory appreciation. The heat that builds between us with each shared glance across crowded rooms.

By evening's end, I've achieved every goal I set for tonight's mission. Contact established. Interest reciprocated. Future meeting arranged. The foundation laid for whatever intimacy the Raven's Kiss requires.

So why do I feel as though I'm the one being hunted?

Only when the evening concludes do I allow myself to recognize the mission's first success. The carriage returns me to Crescent Court through streets gleaming silver in moonlight. Inside my chambers, I remove the elegant attire with reverent care, each garment having served its purpose in the night's ritual.

Liora waits despite the late hour, a single candle casting gentle light across her patient features. She rises from the chair by the fireplace as I enter, and her expression, soft concern mixed with quiet welcome, eases a tension I didn't realize I carried.

"Did you enjoy the gallery, my lady?" She moves to help with the elaborate gown, working the fastenings deftly.

"It proved most illuminating." The truth flavors my words. "The Nocthys collection particularly."

I feel rather than see her hesitation, the slight pause in her movements as she processes my words. "They say those pieces carry darkness within them, that the shadows of Nocthys consume light even after leaving their kingdom."

In the mirror, our eyes meet. The candlelight catches the amber flecks in her gaze, and I find myself holding that contact longer than necessary. "And what do you believe, Liora?"

"I believe darkness takes many forms, my lady." Her voice drops to a more intimate tone, meant only for this space between us. "And not all are visible to ordinary sight."

The wisdom in her words catches me off guard. My pulse quickens as she begins removing the pins from my elaborate hairstyle. Each touch of her hands on my scalp sends unexpected warmth through me, not the electric charge of Blackthorne's practiced seduction but a gentler touch, more dangerous in its sincerity.

"You speak as if from experience," I observe, watching her face in the mirror.

Her hands still for a moment. "My brother—Daven Tanner—believed in seeing beyond the ordinary, my lady. Before he..." The sentence trails away, but her meaning is clear.

"Before he disappeared?" I turn slightly, breaking the proper positioning but needing to see her face directly.

She nods, eyes downcast. "Four months ago. The city guard says he ran off, but I know better. Daven Tanner wouldn't leave without word. Not when mother needs us both."

The pain in her voice creates an echo in my chest. Without thinking, I reach up to cover her hand where it rests on my shoulder. The contact sends warmth flooding through me, so different from the cold purpose that usually guides my actions.

"I'm sorry," I say, meaning it in ways that surprise me.

She looks at our joined hands with obvious wonder before gently extracting hers to continue her work. But I feel the slight tremor in her hands now, the awareness that wasn't there before.

"Thank you, my lady." Her voice has roughened slightly. "Most don't... that is, it's kind of you to care."

"Kindness has little to do with it." The admission emerges without permission. "You serve me well. Your troubles affect your service, which affects me."

It's a lie wrapped in truth. Her troubles affect me for reasons that have nothing to do with service and everything to do with the way lamplight catches in her hair, the gentle strength in her hands, the quiet dignity she maintains despite loss.

She resumes removing pins, but now each touch carries weight. I watch her in the mirror, the concentration on her face, the careful way she handles each strand of my hair as if it were precious. When she picks up the silver brush, our eyes meet again.

"Your hair is beautiful, my lady," she says softly. "Like ink and starlight woven together."

Heat rises in my cheeks at the poetic compliment. "Pretty words from a handmaiden."

"True words," she corrects gently, beginning to brush with long, soothing strokes. "My mother always said we should speak beauty when we find it, store it up for darker days."

"Your mother sounds wise."

"She is." A small smile touches her lips. "Though she'd box my ears for speaking so freely to a lady."

"Then it stays between us." I find myself smiling back, a real expression that feels foreign on my face. "What else would earn her disapproval?"

"Oh, many things." Her voice warms with affection. "Reading instead of mending. Bringing home injured birds. Dreaming of gardens instead of good marriages." She pauses, meeting my eyes in the mirror. "Speaking of impossible things as if they might come true."

The weight in that last statement hangs between us. Her hands slow in my hair, brush moving in absent rhythm as tension builds in the space between our bodies.

"Not all impossible things stay that way," I hear myself say.

She stills completely. In the mirror, I watch emotions chase across her face. Surprise, hope, fear, yearning, before she carefully schools her expression back to appropriate service.

"No, my lady," she agrees quietly. "Sometimes the world surprises us."

She sets down the brush, moving to braid my hair for sleep. Each touch now feels deliberate, weighted with awareness.

When she secures the braid with a silk ribbon, her touch ghosts across the nape of my neck, so light I might have imagined it.

"There." Her voice catches slightly. "Will you need anything else tonight, my lady?"

You. Stay. Talk to me about impossible things.

"No," I say instead. "Rest well, Liora."

She curtseys, moving toward the door. But at the threshold, she pauses, looking back. "My lady?"

"Yes?"

"Thank you. For... for listening. About my brother." Her eyes hold mine across the room. "It means more than you know."

After she leaves, I sit before the mirror, touching the braid she wove with such care. Her scent lingers, lavender and clean linen, honest things that ground me after a night of performance and deception. My reflection shows a woman I don't recognize, one whose eyes have softened from their usual sharp focus.

This is dangerous. More dangerous than Blackthorne's seduction or shadow cults. Because this, whatever this is, feels real in a way my life of sacred purpose never has.

Mordreth grant me strength to see this mission through. Let not my flesh weaken when my blade must strike true.

Yet as I extinguish the candle and slide between cool sheets, it's not Blackthorne's storm-gray eyes I see in the darkness. It's brown ones that catch amber in lamplight, watching me with understanding I've never known before.

The hunt has begun in earnest. But increasingly, I wonder who is truly the predator and who the prey.

8

CULT

The Lower City breathes differently than the heights where nobility dwells. Here, air carries the honest stink of unwashed bodies and rotting food rather than perfumed lies. Narrow streets wind between buildings that lean into each other like drunken conspirators. My lungs resist the sour thickness, but my body remembers similar alleyways from missions long past. Death smells the same in every kingdom.

I've spent three days since the gallery encounter preparing for tonight. I've traced maps of the Lower City until every alley burned into memory. Each night closed with prayer before Mordreth's altar, seeking guidance for this hunt.

I adjust the rough-spun cloak covering my hunting attire. The wool scratches along my neck, a welcome discomfort after weeks of silk on my skin. Under the disguise, leather armor embraces my body like an old lover. Each buckle, each strap sits exactly where they should. The weight centers me in ways fine gowns never could.

Mordreth guide your servant through shadow's test.

The tavern door stands before me, weathered wood stained dark with years of grime. The sign above reads "The Broken Crown," marking an establishment where desperation drowns itself nightly in cheap ale. From within comes the sound of a poorly tuned fiddle competing with drunken voices. My hand pushes on splintered wood, and the door yields with reluctance.

Heat and noise assault me immediately. Bodies press into each other in the cramped space, their combined warmth coating my skin with invisible film. The smell fills my nostrils next. Spilled ale mingling with sweat. The corner reeks of piss where drunks relieve themselves when the privy seems too distant. Woodsmoke rises from the hearth where some unidentifiable meat turns on a spit. Behind it all lingers the metallic scent of blood from a recent fight.

My eyes adjust to the dim light as I count fifteen patrons not counting the barkeep. I note the main door behind me and a service entrance near the bar. Three windows line the walls, too small for all but the most desperate escape. Four tables sit occupied, three by men drinking alone, one by a group sharing a pitcher of brew that smells like rotten fruit.

I select an empty table near the wall, positioning myself to watch the entire room while appearing to seek solitude. The bench creaks ominously beneath me. Grime sticks to my palm when I touch the table's surface.

A serving girl approaches, her youth hidden beneath exhaustion that has settled into the creases around her eyes. "Ale or spirits?" Her voice carries the rough edge of someone who shouts to be heard over the nightly din.

"Ale." I place two copper coins on the table. "And information."

She eyes the coins, calculating. "Ale's worth one copper. Information depends on what you're after."

I add another copper. "Disappearances. Young men from the Lower City."

Fear replaces weariness in her posture. Her voice drops. "That's worth more than copper, stranger. That's worth staying alive."

I slide a silver piece beside the copper. Her eyes widen slightly as silver represents several days' wages for someone of her station. "A name to start with. Someone who's lost someone."

She takes the silver with swift practiced ease, the coin vanishing into hidden pockets. "Tanner family. Lost their son four months back. Mother works in the textile district. Sister still searching." She leans closer, her breath sour with poor teeth. "Though if you're smart, you'll leave it alone. Those who ask about the missing tend to join them."

Tanner. The name hits me like a knife between ribs.

Liora.

Her family name burns across my skin. The connection between my mission and her missing brother makes my breath catch. My chest tightens with an emotion I refuse to name.

Mordreth weaves his will through every thread.

The serving girl returns with ale that smells like brew fermented in an unwashed boot. I lift it to my lips, letting the sour liquid touch my tongue without swallowing. The performance matters more than the drink itself. To sit untouched in such a place invites unwanted attention.

I listen. Years of training help me separate meaningful conversation from ambient noise. Certain words catch my ear. "Ceremony." "Gold eyes." "Shadow blessing." Each fragment confirms what Mother Superior told me.

A man at the bar speaks most openly, his heavy-set frame marked by a beard streaked with gray and hands bearing the scars of metalwork. His voice carries the loose confidence of someone three drinks beyond caution. "Marked, they were. Every one. Golden flecks in their eyes before they vanished. My Gerren included. Started with those meetings in the old temple district. Came home spouting nonsense about ancient power and worthy flesh."

The barkeep leans closer to him. "Keep your voice down, Kallen. You'll find yourself gone too, talking like that."

Kallen spits on the floor. "Let them come. What more can they take from me? My boy's gone. My wife follows a ghost through our home. What's left to fear?"

I drain another careful sip of ale and set my mug down with deliberate sound. The noise draws Kallen's eyes to me. Recognition flickers across his face though we've never met. The shared look of loss creates its own language. I angle my body to invite approach while maintaining the illusion of someone drinking alone.

He takes the bait. His heavy frame lumbers toward my table, ale sloshing over the sides of his mug. "You're new." His voice carries no accusation, merely observation. "Looking for someone?"

"Perhaps." I gesture to the bench across from me. "As are you, it seems."

He settles his weight onto the bench, which creaks in protest. "Not looking anymore. Knowing's different from looking. I know where my boy is. Just can't reach him."

"Tell me."

Kallen studies me with eyes reddened by drink and grief. "Why do you care, stranger?"

I lean forward, allowing sorrow learned from watching others to shape my features. "My sister's son. Nineteen. Disappeared three months ago. Golden flecks in his eyes before he vanished."

His face transforms with bitter recognition. "Same as my Gerren. Same as two dozen others from the Lower City." He leans closer, lowering his voice. "Started with meetings at the abandoned temple in the eastern ward. Talk of ancient wisdom. Power for those worthy. My boy brought home writings sometimes. Strange symbols that burned your eyes to look at too long."

My blood quickens through my veins. "This temple. Where exactly?"

"End of Tanner's Row where it meets the old eastern wall. Been abandoned since the Fading Plague twenty years back." His eyes dart around the tavern, suddenly cautious. "But listen, stranger. Don't go alone. Three fathers went looking together last month. None returned."

"I simply wish to see where my nephew spent his final days." The lie flows naturally from practiced lips.

Kallen's laugh holds no humor. "Final? That won't be the worst part. They're not dead, not exactly." His voice drops further, forcing me to lean in. The smell of cheap ale washes over me. "Sometimes they're seen. Twisted. Eyes gone completely gold. Moving like their bones don't fit right. Serving *him*."

"Him?" The question barely disturbs the air between us.

"The noble with the shadow touch. Blackthorne." The name emerges as barely a whisper. "Prances around the court playing lord while feeding our children to whatever darkness he serves."

Mother Superior was right. My hand twitches with the need to touch steel. Blackthorne's corruption reaches beyond aristocratic circles, claiming souls from all levels of society.

I rise, placing another silver coin on the table before him. "For your help. And for Gerren."

He traces the coin's edge without taking it. "If you find anything. If you learn what happened to them."

"I'll find you here?"

He nods. "Most nights. Drowning while I can still remember how to swim."

The night embraces me as I leave the tavern. The moon hangs heavy in the sky, approaching fullness. Stars pierce the darkness above, distant witnesses to mortal suffering below. My breath forms white clouds that dissipate in the cold air.

I move through streets that grow narrower with each turn. Buildings press closer together, blocking moonlight and creating depths deep enough to hide violence. My hand rests on the knife concealed under my cloak, steel on my palm providing comfort.

Tanner's Row emerges before me, sending a shiver along my spine. Liora lived here. Her brother walked these same cobblestones before darkness claimed him. I remember her touch in my hair this morning, gentle and careful. Did those same hands once reach for her brother in play or comfort? The thought twists in my chest.

The abandoned temple rises at the street's end. Once grand, now crumbling. Stone gargoyles guard empty windows, their features worn to haunting suggestions. The main entrance stands partially collapsed, wooden doors hanging crookedly from rusted hinges.

I circle the building, counting windows and noting possible entrances and exits. The structure whispers to my senses. A dark presence pulses within those walls, calling to the shadow-oil in my veins from countless rituals. My skin prickles with recognition.

A side entrance appears more intact than the main doors. I test the handle, which yields with surprising ease. The hinges move silently, well-oiled despite the building's apparent abandonment. Regular use, not occasional exploration. Interesting.

Inside, darkness enfolds me. My eyes adjust quickly, trained through years of moving through shadow. The scent tells me everything before vision confirms it. Shadow-oil hangs thick in the air, its familiar sweetness corrupted by something wrong. Copper tang of fresh blood weaves through clouds of incense that burns too hot, too bright. The herbs smell similar to what the Sisterhood uses but twisted, as if someone tried to copy a sacred recipe from memory and got the proportions wrong. The bitter undertone makes my throat close with revulsion. A mockery of our rituals.

First lesson of stealth. Breathe through your nose. Silent. Controlled.

I move through empty corridors where moonlight struggles through broken windows. My footsteps make no sound on stone floors covered with years of dust and debris. The building's layout unfolds before me. Main worship chamber ahead. Smaller rooms branching off to either side. The stairway leading to upper levels partially collapsed.

Voices reach me from deeper within the temple. Men speaking in hushed tones. My body moves instinctively toward sound with each step measured, each movement controlled by years of training. I press close to the wall beside a doorway, listening to the conversation beyond.

"The preparations must be flawless. Lord Blackthorne was explicit." The voice carries aristocratic refinement wrapped in ceremonial solemnity.

"The alignments match what the manuscripts describe. Three days until perfect convergence." This voice sounds younger, eager. "The chosen show promising developments ahead of schedule."

"Marden has completely altered. His eyes are fully golden now." A third voice, deeper than the others. "Lord Blackthorne believes he may be ready to receive the final blessing during the ceremony, though the true culmination awaits the next lunar cycle."

I ease my head around the doorframe, a fraction of movement that exposes one eye to the chamber beyond. Three men stand around a stone altar, their fine clothing marking them as nobility despite the dark robes covering their attire. On the altar rests an open manuscript, its pages illuminated by candles arranged in a pattern I recognize with chilling clarity. The Void Crown constellation.

Bile rises in my throat. The pattern belongs to Sisterhood rituals alone. Its presence here feels like a violation. My grip tightens around my knife, the pressure grounding my fury into purpose.

A fourth figure kneels in the corner, head bowed. Their posture seems wrong, as though the bones beneath have shifted. When they lift their head, I see eyes that glow amber in the candlelight. The entire iris transformed to luminous gold.

Marden. Fully remade. Ice flows through my veins despite the temple's heat.

I withdraw silently, continuing my exploration of the temple's lower level. Each chamber reveals further evidence of Blackthorne's work. Circles carved into stone floors. Altars stained with substances that gleam faintly in darkness. Symbols etched into walls that match forbidden teachings I've glimpsed in the Sanctuary's locked archives.

A narrow stairway leads downward, descending under the temple into older foundations. The air grows colder with each step, carrying the metallic scent of freshly spilled blood. My hand finds the second knife concealed at my back, drawing comfort from steel in my palm.

The chamber below opens into a space that stops my breath. Cold radiates from the walls like a living thing, making my skin prickle beneath my leathers. A vast ritual circle dominates the floor, intricate patterns carved into stone and filled with substances that gleam like wet obsidian, their surfaces rippling though no air moves in this tomb-like space. The smell hits me next. Old blood and newer fear, shadow-oil so concentrated it makes my eyes water. Around the circle stand seven stone pillars, each bearing carvings that hurt my eyes to examine directly. The symbols twist in my vision, seeming to move when viewed from peripheral awareness.

But what freezes my blood are the cages lining the walls. Seven iron enclosures large enough to hold human occupants. Three contain huddled figures whose features remain obscured in shadow. From one comes sounds between sobbing and prayer, the words indistinguishable but the desperation unmistakable.

My body tenses, instinct urging immediate action. These captives could taste freedom through my blade. Yet training prevails over impulse. Their liberation would alert Blackthorne to outside awareness of his operation. The mission requires patience. They will find release when Blackthorne meets judgment.

Reluctantly, I withdraw from the chamber, memorizing every detail for future redemption. The layout. The guards glimpsed during exploration. The patterns of movement within the temple. Each observation sharpens my purpose.

A hidden doorway behind a fallen statue leads to what appears to be an administrative chamber. Desks and shelving units contain stacks of manuscripts and ledgers. I trace bindings, noting titles in languages both known and forbidden. Records of initiates arranged by date. Detailed notes about physical changes as shadow corruption progresses.

Then I find it. A journal bearing Blackthorne's personal seal, a raven in flight over a mountain peak. The symbol's similarity to our own raven sends anger burning through my veins, a theft of what belongs to Mordreth alone.

9

— • —

CORRUPTION

I open the journal, pages turning under my touch. The entries confirm every suspicion and exceed them in horrifying detail. Blackthorne documents rituals combining corrupted Sisterhood practices with forbidden shadow magic. His writing reveals genuine passion warped toward unholy ends. More disturbing than simple malevolence would be.

One entry dated three weeks ago catches my attention.

Lady Ravencrest intrigues me from afar. There's depth behind those violet eyes that reminds me of ancient descriptions of shadow-touched priestesses. I must arrange an introduction. Perhaps she could understand my work in ways others cannot.

My heart pounds in my ribs. Blackthorne noted me before our "chance" encounter at the gallery. His interest preceded my approach, creating uncomfortable questions about who truly initiated our connection. How amusing that the hunter believes himself the predator when my blade already hovers near his throat.

Deeper in the journal, I discover a map marking locations of disappearances throughout the Lower City. Each point corresponds with lunar cycles and shadow strength measurements. One location burns into my vision. A small house on Tanner's Row marked with a date four months past. Liora's brother.

My throat tightens as I think of Liora preparing my bath yesterday, her quiet humming as she worked. Did she hum for her brother too? Did she search these same streets calling his name after he vanished? The thought makes my skin feel too tight.

Voices from above interrupt my examination. Cultists arriving for some midnight gathering. I return the journal to its place, ensuring no evidence of my presence remains. Information gathered. Must return to Crescent Court for proper consideration.

I move toward exit routes mapped during entry, keeping to depths that embrace me like old friends. My body remembers the temple's layout perfectly. Three cultists pass within arm's reach, never sensing my presence as I press flat to a wall, becoming one with darkness.

Their conversation reaches my ears in fragments.

"...preparations for the ceremony..."

"...Lord Blackthorne expects at least three more to complete the change..."

"...shadow essence growing stronger near the border..."

I file each word away, building understanding of the cult's immediate plans.

The side entrance appears ahead, moonlight bleeding through cracks around its frame. Freedom awaits beyond. My hand reaches for the door when a new sound freezes my movement.

A cultist enters from outside, his frame silhouetted in the night sky. Behind him walks another figure whose gait shows the same wrongness I observed in Marden. Golden eyes gleam in darkness as they pass, neither noticing my presence concealed in darkness to their right.

The door stands open behind them, offering a clean escape. I move silently toward freedom, sliding through the opening without disturbing air around me.

Then glass crunches under my boot. A sound like thunder in the silent night.

Both cultists turn immediately. The normal one reaches for a blade at his hip. The golden-eyed figure makes a sound no human throat should produce.

"Intruder!" The cultist's shout shatters the night's peace.

My blade finds his throat with desperate urgency. Steel slides through flesh with fatal certainty, opening vessels that yield his life in a rush of scarlet. The heat flows over my hand as light fades from his eyes, his expression frozen in eternal surprise.

Mordreth receives his soul.

The warped figure lunges with inhuman speed. Its body twists at impossible angles, joints bending backward as it propels itself toward me. Elongated claws swipe through air where my head had been a heartbeat earlier, close enough that I feel wind from their passage on my cheek.

Movement behind me. I pivot as the creature behind me bends at angles that hurt to watch. Another cultist rounds the corner, torch in hand. The flame shows his face clearly. Young, barely past twenty, brown eyes wide with shock.

My throwing knife embeds in his face. The torch drops, flame sputtering against damp stone. He screams once. High. Frantic. Then my second blade finds his heart and the sound cuts off like someone slammed a door.

Two bodies. Four seconds. The mathematics of murder.

Something moves in the deeper darkness. Not human movement. Wrong. Joints bending backward. Too many angles.

The creature emerges into torchlight and the air suddenly feels too thin. Golden eyes in a face stretched too thin. Fingers extended into claws that scrape stone. It wears the remnants of human clothing, but the body beneath has been remade. Improved, the whispers would say.

Corrupted.

Liora's eyes are brown. This thing's eyes are gold. Not him. Can't be him.

It doesn't walk. It flows. Like water finding the fastest path downhill. One moment it's twenty feet away. The next moment, claws rake across my ribs. Leather parts like paper. Hot lines of pain bloom instantly. I twist away but it follows, moving in stutters that make my eyes water trying to track it.

My blade finds flesh that feels wrong. Too soft in places, too hard in others. Black blood sprays, smelling of rot and copper and something sweet like overripe fruit. The creature doesn't scream. It laughs. The sound makes my teeth ache.

We dance. That's what the Sisterhood would call it. But there's no grace here. Just two things trying to unmake each other in the dark.

It gets inside my guard. Claws puncture leather at my shoulder, sliding between plates meant to turn steel. The pain is immediate and wrong. Not just torn flesh but something else. Poison. Corruption. The wound burns cold.

Move. Deal with the toxin later. Move or die.

I slam my forehead into its face. Cartilage crunches. Black blood explodes from what used to be a nose. The thing staggers back, hands going to its ruined face.

My blade opens its throat in a smile that nearly takes the head off.

It drops but doesn't die.

The body thrashes. Limbs bend in directions that make geometry scream. Black blood pools, then starts moving. Crawling back toward the body like it has opinions about being spilled.

"Fuck." The word tears out of me. "Fuck fuck fuck."

I grab the shadow-oil from my belt. Three drops on the blade. The metal drinks it eagerly, edge going black as the void itself.

The creature's still trying to heal when I take its head properly. The blessed blade parts corrupted flesh with a wet sound like tearing silk. The body convulses once more, then stills.

This time it stays dead.

My shoulder throbs. The corruption spreads, visible black veins spider-webbing under torn leather. Each heartbeat pushes it deeper. I pour shadow-oil directly on the wound, hissing at the burn. Clean pain, at least. Better than the alternative.

I kneel beside the corpse. Something about the bone structure makes my stomach drop. The cheekbones. The shape of the jaw beneath all that corruption. Details that transformation couldn't fully erase.

Liora's eyes are brown. Her brother's were too.

My hands start to shake. If this thing was him—

No. Can't think about that now.

Footsteps echo from deeper in the temple. Many feet. Moving fast. Time to go.

I run. Not gracefully. Not like a Sister should. Just a wounded animal fleeing into the dark, leaving blood and bodies behind. The Lower City swallows me, another predator returning to its den.

My ribs scream with each breath. Something's cracked. Maybe broken. The creature hit harder than anything human should. Black veins spread from my shoulder wound despite the shadow-oil. Each step sends fire through my side.

Crescent Court appears after an hour of careful movement through increasingly refined neighborhoods. The transition from Lower City squalor to aristocratic elegance passes under my feet like a physical manifestation of Luridian's divided society. Such pretty facades hiding rot beneath, not unlike the nobles themselves.

I enter through the servant's entrance, using the key kept hidden for such purposes. The house stands silent and dark. Sleep claimed its inhabitants hours ago. Not even Liora waits up at this hour, thinking of her lady attending some late aristocratic function rather than hunting in Lower City darkness.

My chambers welcome me with silence. I remove the rough-spun disguise, folding each piece with ritual care despite the night's violence. Blood stains my skin, embedding itself under fingernails and in the creases of my knuckles. The sight normally comforts me, but tonight it brings only questions.

The bathing chamber holds water prepared earlier and kept warm by heated stones under the copper tub. I sink into its embrace, watching blood and grime turn clear water pink. The heat soothes muscles tightened by combat and tension. I trace bruises already forming along my ribs, mapping damage with clinical detachment.

Clean again, I kneel before the hidden altar, seven candles burning in their pattern. Blood-cleaned palms press together in prayer's position. Tonight's discoveries burn behind my eyes. The temple's practices. The captured souls. The journal entries confirming Blackthorne's corruption. The map marking Liora's brother among the taken.

"Mordreth guide your servant." My voice barely disturbs the night air. "The darkness grows beyond boundaries. Corruption spreads through unworthy hands."

The prayer feels hollow tonight. Each discovery, each connection between Liora's suffering and Blackthorne's judgment follows patterns I can't fully grasp. The thought of her brother dying by my blade makes my stomach turn, even if death was mercy for what he'd become.

I extinguish the candles with moistened fingertips, feeling each flame die on my skin. Small pain brings focus, but not enough to chase away unbidden thoughts.

Sleep comes reluctantly despite exhaustion. I lie awake, the weight of what I've learned pressing on my chest. The face of the creature burns behind my eyelids, its features carrying the ghost of Liora's bone structure. What would I tell her if the thing I killed tonight was truly her brother? How would she look at me if she knew?

Morning will bring Liora to my chamber. Her soft touch will brush my hair. Her quiet voice will ask about my evening. She'll be unaware I've walked the streets of her childhood, seen the house where she grew up, perhaps ended what remained of her brother. My stomach twists at the thought of her touch in my hair, so similar to the corrupted hands I fought mere hours ago.

I turn onto my side, wincing as bruised ribs protest the movement. Blackthorne's next ceremony looms on the horizon. My path should be clear, but Liora's face keeps appearing in my mind. The way she looked up at me yesterday morning, concern in her eyes when she noticed my distraction. The soft humming under her breath as she arranged my gowns. The story of her brother was told with quiet dignity despite obvious pain.

I've never struggled with a mission before. Never questioned the hand that guides my blade. But tonight, the creature's golden eyes flash in my memory, overlaid with Liora's gentle gaze. Both pairs of eyes haunt me equally.

Let Liora remain ignorant of tonight's events. Let her continue hoping while I continue hunting. Maybe it wasn't her brother. Maybe the resemblance was a coincidence born of exhaustion and shadow-oil fumes. But if it was him...

The thought follows me into uneasy dreams where golden eyes weep black tears and Liora's hands pull steel from her brother's throat.

10

DANCE

Morning light falls across my chambers, caressing the burgundy silk gown that awaits tonight's royal ball. The dress breathes against the bed where Liora arranged it, a battle garment of different design but equal purpose. Its color reminds me of blood just before it dries, rich with promise and significance. My fingertips graze the silver embroidery that flows like liquid metal across rich fabric, skin remembering the weight of steel even as it anticipates silk.

Nearly a month in Luridian. Tonight's royal ball offers the perfect stage to deepen my connection with Blackthorne. After our encounters at the gallery and smaller gatherings, this grand event provides opportunity for more intimate conversation.

I have spent three days planning my next approach to Blackthorne. Three days watching Liora move through my chambers quietly, unaware of what I discovered in the Lower City. Three days of feeling secrets burn within my chest while her gentle touch styles my hair.

"These pearl combs will complement the silver embroidery beautifully." Liora's voice brushes my neck as she secures another pin. Lavender rises from her skin as she leans closer, the scent lodging in my memory beside crimson and shadow-oil.

My body remains perfectly still as she works, the control born of years where movement invited correction. The bruised ribs from my Lower City investigation have faded to dull yellow-green, Liora's herbal poultices working their quiet magic over the past days. She hasn't asked how I acquired such injuries, though I've caught her studying the healing marks when she thinks I'm not watching. Her touch whispers across my scalp, so different from ritual preparation before missions. No prayers accompany her movements, yet something reverent lingers in her care.

"There." Satisfaction warms her voice. "A style worthy of a royal gathering."

The mirror reflects a woman I recognize but don't know. My violet eyes stare back from Lady Sera Ravencrest's face, dark hair arranged in elaborate coils adorned with pearls and silver wire. The refined elegance conceals the weapon inside, just as the gown will hide knives strapped to my thighs tonight.

"You seem focused on tonight's gathering, my lady." Liora's voice carries careful neutrality as she adjusts a pearl pin in my hair. "More than usual preparation."

"The royal ball offers opportunities beyond mere social connection." I watch her face in the mirror, measuring how much truth to share. "Certain introductions could prove... valuable."

Her hands pause momentarily in my hair. "Lord Blackthorne will attend tonight." It's not a question.

The name hangs between us, weighted with unspoken understanding.

Coldness freezes in my veins. Her perception cuts deeper than expected, exposing the intent I've worked to conceal.

"Court gossip travels faster than royal decrees, my lady." Her touch smooths the silk robe across my shoulders, practical yet strangely intimate. "The servants speak of your conversation at the gallery. Of how Lord Blackthorne watched you when you departed."

The knowledge that others observe my hunt sends warnings prickling along my spine. I curl my fingers into the polished wood, seeking solid comfort while masks shift unexpectedly.

"Gossip provides a poor foundation for truth." My voice hardens, edge slipping past control.

Liora steps back, proper distance restored. "Forgive me, my lady. I spoke out of turn."

The sudden space between us feels wrong. Cold. Hollow loss spreads through me as she withdraws. I count three heartbeats before I find words that taste true.

"Your concern honors your service, Liora." The formal acknowledgment feels inadequate next to the genuine care she's shown these strange weeks.

Her smile returns, warming the air between us. "I only wish for your happiness and success in Luridian."

The sincerity in her voice sends heat rushing through my skin. This care without end, this attention without blood debt leaves me defenseless where blades and poison never could.

"The royal ball provides a perfect opportunity to further establish your position," she continues, moving toward the wardrobe smoothly. "Lady Mereswen mentioned the queen herself might attend."

My focus sharpens at the name. Mereswen. Close to Blackthorne. Knows his secrets. Shares them when it serves her aims.

The burgundy gown rises between us as Liora lifts it with careful grace. Silk catches light like blood in a holy offering. The fabric whispers its intent to trained ears, to announce Lady Ravencrest as worthy of Blackthorne's attention.

"I will keep my ears open for any word of your brother while among nobility tonight," I say, the promise gentler than my usual vows. "Their conversations often reveal more than they intend."

Hope transforms her face, stripped of pretense and protection. The naked faith in her eyes burns my skin. Something vital shifts inside me.

"Thank you, my lady." Her voice barely disturbs the air between us. "That would be more than I could hope for."

Her gratitude tastes bitter. The memory of the creature from the temple, with those same eyes corrupted by gold, flashes unbidden through my mind. The thought twists something vital within my ribs, an ache without name or remedy.

The gown slides over my body like a second skin, heavy with intent and promise. Each layer transforms me further from blade to widow. Silk petticoats whisper across my legs with every movement. The corset reshapes my breath into shallow patterns that dizzy my senses after years of warrior's deep breathing. The burgundy overskirt conceals the weight of knives pressed to my thighs, cold steel warming on flesh. My body remembers both roles, the killer and the seductress, finding power in each.

Liora works carefully, securing each button, adjusting each fold with artistic care. Her touch remains proper yet somehow intimate, a paradox that confuses senses trained to categorize contact as either threat or opportunity.

"There." Her voice carries satisfaction as she steps back. "You look magnificent."

The mirror shows a stranger wearing my face. Lady Sera Ravencrest stands draped in burgundy silk that catches light like freshly spilled blood. Silver embroidery traces patterns reminiscent of holy symbols, though none would recognize their meaning beyond the Sanctuary's walls. My hair rises in elaborate coils adorned with pearls that gleam in darkness. The woman reflected appears both dangerous and vulnerable, powerful and exposed.

I am perfect for tonight's intent. Mordreth shapes his instruments according to need.

"Lord Hargrove will be delighted." Liora smooths an invisible wrinkle from the skirt, her touch lingering on the rich fabric.

My lips curve into a smile that feels surprisingly natural. "Lord Hargrove serves merely as an introduction. It's Lord Blackthorne I must impress."

The admission falls between us, more truth than this strange relationship typically allows. Liora's eyes widen slightly, but she offers no judgment, only a small nod of understanding that warms cold spaces within my chest.

"Your wounds still need healing," she observes, eyes moving to my bandaged shoulder. "This evening will strain your strength."

"I have remedies." I move to my trunk, unlocking a hidden compartment. Inside rests a small wooden box containing vials of liquid darker than night. The concoctions come from the Sanctuary's apothecary. Divine medicines reserved for missions where pain must be temporarily mastered.

I uncork one vial, the bitter scent filling my nostrils with memories of midnight rituals and blood offerings. The liquid burns cold down my throat, spreading numbing fire through damaged tissue.

"This will hold the pain at bay for several hours," I explain, seeing concern in her eyes. "Though I'll pay for the relief later. The body merely borrows strength it doesn't possess."

"Be cautious with Lord Blackthorne." Her voice lowers, weighted with genuine concern. "Men like him see beauty as something to possess, not cherish."

The warning touches something unexpected within me. I reach out, briefly touching her palm resting on the gown. The contact burns like fire, cleansing and dangerous.

"I understand dangerous men better than most." Truth slips through defenses weakened by her care.

Her eyes hold mine, an unspoken message passing between us. For one heartbeat, the space separating servant from mistress, hunter from innocent, shrinks to nothing. Then reality reasserts as a clock chimes somewhere in the house.

"Your carriage will arrive shortly." She withdraws, proper distance restored.

As if summoned by her words, hoofbeats sound on cobblestones outside. Lord Hargrove, punctual as death. The thought brings a smile to my lips that Liora can't understand.

Liora helps secure a velvet cloak around my shoulders, her touch brushing my neck with whispered intimacy. "Return safely, my lady. The shadows grow deeper after sunset."

Her voice suggests deeper meaning than social pleasantries. My skin warms at the simple concern, a sensation both foreign and intoxicating.

"I shall." The promise tastes true on my tongue, though what awaits beyond tonight's dance remains hidden in darkness.

Lord Hargrove's carriage gleams black in the fading day. Fresh-polished brass catches the last sunlight with blinding intensity. Inside, velvet cushions the color of dried blood await, catching my gown in perfect complement as I settle across from my escort.

"Lady Ravencrest." Hargrove's eyes move over me with appreciation that leaves my skin untouched. His silver hair gleams in the last daylight, an odd contrast to the hungry youth in his gaze. Another old man who believes wealth entitles him to beauty's company. "You look absolutely enchanting this evening."

"You're too kind." The words flow from practiced lips while my mind focuses on the night's true hunt.

The carriage lurches forward, wheels striking cobblestones with rhythmic violence. Hargrove speaks of the ball, of nobles whose names drift past my ears without landing, of restoration efforts funded by the royal family. I respond with phrases crafted to sound interested while my senses map our route through Luridian, marking alternative paths should retreat become necessary.

My fingertips brush the smallest knife concealed within my skirts. The blade's touch grounds me like a whispered prayer.

"The royal family acquired several new pieces for their collection," Hargrove continues, oblivious to my divided attention. Perhaps he's used to women dreaming of escape while he speaks. "Some from Nocthys, I believe, though such acquisitions grow increasingly difficult with the border tensions."

My attention sharpens at the mention of the shadow kingdom. "Nocthys artifacts at a royal ball? How fascinating."

Hargrove's face tightens with sudden caution. "Certain influential nobles maintain connections despite official restrictions. Lord Blackthorne in particular has developed quite a collection of shadow-touched items."

The name falls between us like a sacrificial blade. "I encountered some of his collection at the gallery. His knowledge seemed extensive."

"Indeed." His tone suggests more than mere scholarly interest. "Blackthorne's academic pursuits extend to practical applications that some find... unconventional."

The carriage slows as we approach the royal palace. The building rises from the street like a mountain of quarried stone, three stories of marble and glass illuminate the darkening sky. Guards in royal livery stand at attention by massive doors thrown open to receive guests. Ladies in vibrant silks and gentlemen in formal attire flow into the entrance like a river of wealth and power, decadent and oblivious to the power that moves among them.

Hargrove assists me from the carriage, his gloved touch cool on my skin. My body shifts balance instantly, Lady Ravencrest's graceful movements replacing the predator's stance buried under silk and manners.

"Remember, the queen herself may attend," Hargrove murmurs as we approach the entrance. "Should she acknowledge you, a simple curtsy and 'Your Majesty' will suffice."

I nod with appropriate appreciation for his guidance. The palace guards study each guest with trained eyes, their posture revealing military discipline underneath ceremonial attire.

I catch one watching my approach with particular attention, his gaze settling briefly on my face before moving to the next arrival.

I file this away for later. Should escape prove necessary, I now know which throat would need to be opened first.

The ballroom opens before us. Marble floors stretch under soaring ceilings filled with fading frescos depicting legendary battles and mythological scenes. Chandeliers drip light onto polished surfaces and gilt frames that can't hide the slow decay underneath aristocratic splendor. The air fills my lungs with beeswax candles, expensive perfumes, and the dusty breath of tapestries that line the walls.

My eyes sweep the gathering with trained observation. Fifty-seven nobles already present. Three visible exits plus two servant passages partially concealed behind heavy curtains. Guards positioned at intervals that suggest concern for the art rather than the guests. Each face burns into my memory, categorized by threat and opportunity.

"Lady Ravencrest, allow me to make some introductions." Hargrove leads me toward women draped in jewels that could feed a village for a year. "The Countess Mereswen has expressed interest in meeting our newest neighbor."

The Countess extends her hand gracefully, rings flashing fire in the excessive light. "Lady Ravencrest. How delightful to finally meet you properly."

"The pleasure is mine, Countess." I accept her grasp briefly, noting the strength in her grip that belies her decorative appearance.

"I understand you've developed an interest in our kingdom's art collections." Her painted lips curve in a smile that never reaches her eyes. "Particularly the more... esoteric pieces."

My skin warms with subtle warning. "Beauty takes many forms. Some reveal themselves only to those who truly look."

Her laugh tinkles like broken glass. "How delightfully phrased. You must meet Lord Trevaine. He shares your appreciation for the unconventional."

Introductions proceed with ritualistic care. Names and titles wash over me while my body records impressions for later judgment. The Baron whose gaze lingers too long on my throat, already imagining how it might taste under his lips. The merchant's wife whose accent betrays origins far humbler than her current status, eyes darting constantly for threats to her precarious position. The royal advisor who watches conversations with calculating eyes rather than participating, storing secrets like a raven hoards shiny objects.

I play my role perfectly. Lady Sera Ravencrest emerges from my lips, discussing cultural differences between Valmeria and Luridian with just enough detail to seem knowledgeable while remaining vague enough to prevent specific questioning.

I hunt for my true prey throughout these conversations, senses alert for his particular scent and presence. Nobles cling to each other like drowning men grasping floating debris, desperate to believe their importance will save them from the waters rising underneath this crumbling palace.

"The collection expanded considerably under Queen Elissandra's patronage," the Countess explains, her voice carrying the bored expertise of one discussing comfortable subjects. "Though some acquisitions proved controversial."

"How so?" I sip champagne that tastes of summer fruit and expensive breeding.

"The Nocthys artifacts in the eastern gallery." Her voice lowers conspiratorially. "Some believe shadow-touched items bring misfortune. Superstitious nonsense, of course, but the whispers persist."

The Baron beside her leans closer, drawn by gossip's gravity. "Speaking of shadows, did you hear about the merchant district? Another attack last night. Third one this week."

My awareness sharpens at this unexpected intelligence. "Shadow attacks?"

"Dreadful business." He shudders theatrically. "Witnesses speak of darkness that moves like living things, leaving victims cold and pale. The city guard claims they're investigating, but what can steel do against shadows?"

The Countess waves dismissively, though something flickers behind her eyes. "The authorities insist they're unrelated incidents. Random manifestations. Though I admit, the increase in frequency is... concerning."

"And yet you mentioned shadow-touched artifacts." I keep my tone light, curious rather than probing. "Surely that's mere coincidence?"

"If you're interested in such things..." She stops suddenly, her attention shifting beyond my shoulder. Her expression transforms subtly, pleasure mixing with dangerous deviousness. "Ah, speaking of controversial tastes. Lord Blackthorne has arrived."

The air in the ballroom shifts like a living thing. The temperature seems to rise a degree, shadows in the corners deepening despite the blazing chandeliers. My skin prickles with awareness before I turn, the body recognizing an apex predator before the mind processes the threat.

Raven God guide my hunter's eyes.

I turn.

There's something different about him tonight, or perhaps this is simply Blackthorne unleashed in his natural habitat. The formal black evening wear fits him like armor, emphasizing broad shoulders and a lean waist that speaks of discipline. Silver threads through his temples catch the light, and those storm-gray eyes with their dark rings survey the room with the lazy confidence of a man who owns everything he sees.

But it's how he moves that steals my breath. Where other nobles mince and posture, Blackthorne flows through the crowd with controlled power. Each gesture deliberate yet natural. The shadows seem to cling to him, creating pools of intimate darkness wherever he pauses. Women turn to watch him pass, fans fluttering faster. Men straighten unconsciously, responding to an alpha they don't consciously recognize.

My breath catches despite years of training. His presence fills the room, demanding response. Hunger rises unbidden in my flesh. My body responds with appropriate appreciation, flesh warming, senses heightening. I welcome these sensations as tools, weapons as deadly as any blade when properly wielded.

"Quite the presence, isn't he?" Mereswen's voice carries knowing delight. "He arrived late, as always. Says punctuality is for those who fear missing something."

I compose my features to show mild curiosity rather than the heat spreading through me. "He seems remarkably confident."

"Confidence earned through survival." Her painted lips curve. "His young wife died in his arms, you know. Shadow madness took her mind first, then her body. They say he held her for hours after she'd gone cold, whispering promises to the darkness."

The image forms unbidden. Blackthorne cradling a woman's body, making vows to shadows that listen. An unwelcome pang strikes beneath my breastbone.

"Since then, he's been... different. More focused. More dangerous." She watches him greet a cluster of younger nobles, noting how they hang on his every word. "He could have any woman in this room, many have offered. But he seems to be hunting for a specific type."

My skin warms at her implication. "You speak as though you know him well."

"Oh my dear, everyone knows Blackthorne." Her eyes glitter with meaning. "Few know him well."

The orchestra begins a new composition, the opening notes flowing through the chamber skillfully. Couples move toward the center of the ballroom, forming patterns as old as the dance itself.

"I should return to Lord Hargrove." I offer the Countess a smile designed to linger in memory. "Thank you for the fascinating conversation."

"Of course." She touches my arm briefly, the contact light yet significant. "Do seek out the Nocthys display if you have the opportunity. I suspect you'll find it... illuminating."

11

PARTNERSHIP

I move through the crowd carefully, positioning myself where Hargrove might naturally find me while maintaining awareness of Blackthorne's location. For the next hour, I navigate the gathering with meticulous care. My path appears random to observers while following a course mapped with predator's intention.

I position myself before a large painting in the eastern gallery where smaller clusters examine displayed treasures. The canvas shows a mountain landscape at twilight, shadows writhing across valleys of darkened snow with unnatural vitality. The longer I stare, the more the darkness appears to pulse with intelligence, swirling in patterns that suggest consciousness inhabiting void. In one corner, a village's windows gleam with golden light, slowly being consumed by encroaching blackness that seems to reach toward the viewer with hungry intent.

My hands itch to touch the painted surface, to verify whether power truly resides within or merely the artist's skill. The black pigment gleams with unusual luster, catching light while somehow darkening the space around it. Mordreth's touch lingers in these strokes, though the painter likely never recognized the divine hand guiding his brush.

"A remarkable technique, isn't it?" His voice flows over me like consecrated wine, deep and cultured. "The artist captured the living quality of Nocthys shadows perfectly."

My skin tightens at his approach, a flush rising unbidden under burgundy silk. My heart quickens as I maintain my pose of artistic contemplation.

Our eyes meet properly since our last encounter. His gaze holds both calculation and genuine interest, the intense focus making the strange darkness surrounding his gray irises seem to pulse slightly in the candlelight.

"Living quality?" I allow genuine curiosity to color my words. "An unusual description for shadows."

His smile transforms his face, creating creases at the corners of his eyes that speak of authentic feeling rather than practiced charm. "In Nocthys, shadows behave differently than elsewhere. They respond to certain stimuli, almost like sentient beings." His gaze holds mine with unexpected intensity. "Lady Raven-crest. I had hoped to encounter you this evening."

"Lord Blackthorne." I offer my hand with the perfect blend of social polish and reserved dignity. "How pleasant to see you again."

His hands close around mine with gentle pressure that shoots fire through my body. The touch lasts long enough to establish connection, brief enough to maintain propriety. "You look absolutely magnificent this evening. That shade of burgundy suits you perfectly."

"Most kind." My voice emerges warmer than intended. "I confess I was drawn to this gallery specifically to see these shadow-touched works you mentioned at our previous meeting."

"And what do you think of them?" His attention focuses entirely on me, creating the illusion of privacy despite the crowded space.

"Fascinating." Truth flavors the word. "They seem to capture darkness as substance rather than absence."

His eyes light with genuine pleasure, aristocratic polish momentarily replaced by academic fervor. "Exactly! Few recognize that distinction immediately." He leans closer, voice dropping to an intimate whisper. "The brushwork technique originated in Nocthys's eastern provinces before the border disputes. The pigment contains actual shadow essence."

I watch his transformation with interest. For that brief moment, the nobleman vanishes, replaced by a scholar who has spent years in devoted study. Then, noticing my observation, he straightens and the aristocratic mask slips back into place, though his eyes retain their passionate gleam.

The orchestra begins a waltz, the opening notes signaling formal dancing. Blackthorne's eyes move briefly to the forming pairs before returning to mine.

"Would you honor me with this dance?" He extends his hand, having crossed the space between us with fluid motion.

My body responds before conscious thought, anticipation flowering within me. "With pleasure."

His fingers close around mine, and the contact sends heat shooting through my entire body. His grip is larger than expected, engulfing mine completely. Not the soft palm of a mere nobleman but calloused in specific places, from holding a sword, from working with dangerous materials. The knowledge burns into my memory.

He guides me to the dance floor with perfect confidence, his other palm settling at my waist. The touch brands through silk to skin underneath, spanning from my ribs nearly to my hip. The possession in that spread contact makes my breath catch.

Guide this hunt to its holy conclusion. Let pleasure serve mercy's intent.

"You're trembling." His voice rumbles near my ear as we begin to move. "Are you cold?"

"Quite the opposite." The honesty slips out before I can stop it.

His grip tightens fractionally at my waist, approval and warning combined. "Careful, Lady Ravencrest. Honesty can be dangerous in rooms like this."

We move together with shocking synchronicity. Where other partners require adjustment, Blackthorne anticipates my movements as I anticipate his. Combat training repurposed for courtly dance, two predators circling in elaborate patterns. His lead is firm without forcing, dominant without domineering.

"You dance like you were born to it." His thumb moves on my waist, the smallest motion that sends waves of heat through my core. "Yet you hold yourself like someone who knows how to fight. Fascinating contradiction."

My pulse hammers through my throat. He sees too much. "Perhaps you're imagining things, Lord Blackthorne."

"Perhaps." He spins me out, then draws me back closer than before. For a moment, our bodies align completely, chest to chest, his thigh between mine through layers of silk. "Or perhaps I recognize a kindred spirit."

The contact lasts a heartbeat before propriety demands distance, but my body thrums with the imprint. His scent surrounds me, sandalwood and shadow-smoke, leather and spice that makes my mouth water.

"Tell me," he continues, voice dropping to an intimate register that excludes the world beyond our orbit, "what does a Valmerian widow want with shadow artifacts?"

"Knowledge." Truth makes the best lies. "Understanding. The same things that drive your own interests, I imagine."

His eyes darken, pupils dilating. "Dangerous assumptions, my dear. My interests run deeper than mere academic curiosity."

We turn again, bodies moving in perfect synchronization. The waltz carries us in sweeping circles across polished marble. From the corner of my eye, I notice other dancers giving us space, attention drawn to our movement. The knowledge sends satisfaction curling through my chest. The more witnesses to our connection, the more natural our growing intimacy will appear.

"Some suggest that appreciation for shadow artifacts indicates a natural affinity." His eyes study mine with focused intensity. "That certain souls resonate with shadow essence without prior exposure."

The statement borders on religious discussion, venturing into territory reserved for divine knowledge. My senses heighten with both warning and excitement. "An interesting theory. Do you subscribe to it?"

His palm presses slightly firmer at my waist, fingers spreading in a gesture both proprietary and testing. "I believe certain individuals are born with capabilities others can't comprehend. That power recognizes itself across divides others find insurmountable."

My body responds without permission, a pleasant shiver racing along my spine. We turn again, the movement bringing us closer, his chest nearly touching mine before the dance separates us. Under expensive cologne and cedar lies darker notes, memories of divine chambers and midnight rituals.

"You speak from personal experience, Lord Blackthorne?" My voice emerges husky, intimate despite the public setting.

His smile transforms his face, creating creases at the corners of his eyes that speak of genuine feeling rather than practiced charm. "Perhaps I recognize a kindred spirit, Lady Ravencrest."

We turn again, and he guides us toward the open balcony doors with subtle pressure. The transition feels inevitable, like water finding its course. The night air hits my heated skin, a relief and a torment.

"The depth appeals to me." I meet his gaze directly, letting him see the predator behind the widow's mask for just a moment. "Surface understanding has never satisfied."

Something shifts in his expression, hunger sharpening to intent. His grip at my waist pulls me closer, propriety abandoned in the shadow of the balcony. "You're playing a dangerous game, Lady Ravencrest."

"Am I playing?" The question hangs between us, weighted with meanings neither of us fully acknowledge.

He studies me for a long moment, thumb tracing absent patterns on my waist that make coherent thought difficult. "No," he finally says, voice rough. "I don't think you are."

The music swells behind us, but we've stopped dancing. We stand too close, his body caging mine at the balcony rail. The heat of him surrounds me, and I have to tilt my head back to maintain eye contact. This close, I can see the flecks of charcoal in his gray eyes, the way his pupils have blown wide with interest.

"I should return you to Lord Hargrove." The words say one thing, his body says another, not moving an inch.

"Should you?" My voice comes out breathier than intended.

His free palm rises, fingertips ghosting along my jaw without quite touching. The almost-contact makes my skin ache. "What I should do and what I want rarely align, Lady Ravencrest."

"Sera," I breathe, surprising myself. "When we're alone, call me Sera."

His breath shudders between us. "Sera." He tastes my name like expensive wine. "You're going to be trouble, aren't you?"

Before I can respond, he steps back, proper distance restored so suddenly I sway. His grip steadies me, firm, controlled, maddening.

"I'll send a proper invitation tomorrow." His thumbs brush my palms before releasing me entirely. "My gatherings require... preparation. Mental fortitude. Are you certain you're ready for what you might discover?"

The challenge in his voice makes my blood sing. "I've never shied away from difficult truths."

"No," he agrees, eyes scanning my face like he's memorizing it. "I don't believe you have."

Lord Hargrove's voice breaks the spell, calling from the doorway. Blackthorne bows, correctly formal yet somehow making the gesture feel intimate.

"Until next time, Sera." My name on his lips is a promise and a threat.

He leaves me on the balcony, my body still humming from his presence. When I press my palm to my waist, I swear I can still feel the heat of his touch through the silk.

"I see you've met Blackthorne." Hargrove's tone carries jealousy under polished manners. His fists flex at his sides, the gesture of a child denied a desired toy. "He tends to seek out newcomers to society."

"He proved quite knowledgeable about the collection." I keep my voice neutral. "A refreshing quality in a gentleman."

Lord Hargrove's expression tightens before smoothing into polite agreement. "Indeed. Though his interests sometimes run toward the unusual."

The evening continues according to plan. I meet the Marquis of Essendal as promised, making connections that reinforce Lady Ravencrest's social position while maintaining awareness of Blackthorne's location throughout the gathering. Twice more our eyes meet across the crowded space, brief acknowledgments that build anticipation for future encounters.

Only when the evening concludes do I allow myself to recognize the mission's progress. The carriage returns me to Crescent Court through streets gleaming silver in moonlight. Inside my chambers, I remove the elegant attire with careful attention, each garment having served its role in the night's ritual.

Liora waits despite the late hour. "Did you enjoy the ball, my lady?" Her fingers work methodically, removing the pins from my elaborately styled hair.

"It proved most illuminating." Truth flavors my words. "The Nocthys collection particularly."

Her touch pauses momentarily. "They say those pieces carry darkness within them, that the shadows of Nocthys consume light even after leaving their kingdom."

I meet her eyes in the mirror. "And what do you believe, Liora?"

"I believe darkness takes many forms, my lady." Her fingers resume their gentle work. "And not all are visible to ordinary sight."

Something shifts within me at the wisdom in her simple words, so different from Blackthorne's cultivated knowledge, yet holding truth he might never grasp. Her touch on my scalp awakens something unknown, not the electric fire Blackthorne sparked but something gentler, warmer, truer.

"Thank you, Liora. That will be all for tonight." After she leaves, I prepare for bed, but find rest elusive.

Sleep comes slowly despite exhaustion. My body remembers the exact timbre of Blackthorne's voice, the exact pressure of his hands on my waist, the particular scent that clung to his skin.

The first dance executed perfectly. The invitation extended exactly as predicted. Each step brings judgment closer to fulfillment.

The waxing moon marks three weeks since my arrival in Luridian. Three weeks of careful cultivation, of foundation laid with measured patience. The facade of Lady Ravencrest grows more comfortable with each passing day, like a second skin rather than borrowed flesh.

Liora's gentle touch each morning reminds me of a simplicity I've never known, while evening gatherings with nobility pull me deeper into Blackthorne's orbit. Time serves Mordreth's aims, each day bringing the final judgment nearer like the moon approaching fullness.

Each movement brings my lips closer to delivering mercy.

12

FEAST

Blackthorne's estate rises from manicured grounds outside the city proper. Stone walls surround gardens that gleam silver in moonlight. The main house presents a facade of graceful elegance, three stories of pale stone with windows that glow from within like golden eyes.

My time in Luridian has passed in careful steps, each one bringing me closer to my target. The weeks of patient observation and planned encounters have built a foundation for tonight. The darkness wanes as the moon thins, and with it comes deeper infiltration, closer connection to my prey.

The carriage slows, wheels crunching on gravel as we approach the entrance where Blackthorne awaits.

The hunt moves forward. The blade is in a different form, but the divine rite remains unchanged.

The door opens before I reach it. A manservant in black livery bows deeply, his posture suggesting training beyond household service. My eyes catch the slight bulge beneath his jacket where a weapon rests. Not ordinary staff but protection disguised as propriety. I file this observation away for later use.

"Lady Ravencrest." His voice carries the perfect balance of deference and dignity that marks superior service. "Lord Blackthorne awaits you in the eastern salon."

My skirts whisper against marble floors as I follow him through corridors designed to impress. Paintings line the walls, their subjects predominantly nocturnal landscapes and shadow-touched scenes. Each piece speaks of wealth guided by genuine appreciation rather than mere display.

The servant stops before double doors of polished wood carved with intertwining vines. "Your guest has arrived, my lord."

The doors open to reveal a room that steals my breath. The eastern salon stretches before me, walls lined with books interrupted by tall windows that capture the rising moon. A fireplace large enough to consume a small tree dominates one wall, flames casting dancing light across rich furnishings. The ceiling arches overhead, painted with constellations that seem to move when viewed from the corner of my eye.

Lord Blackthorne rises from a chair near the fire, his tall frame silhouetted against flames. He wears formal attire that emphasizes muscular shoulders and narrow waist, black and silver creating striking contrast against his skin. My body responds with immediate heat, blood rushing within me.

"Lady Ravencrest." He crosses the room smoothly. "You honor my home with your presence."

He takes my hand, and this time there's no pretense of mere courtesy. His lips press against my knuckles with deliberate pressure, the contact lasting long enough to make my breath catch. When he lifts his head, his storm-gray eyes hold mine with an intensity that makes the vast room feel suddenly intimate.

"You came." The words carry weight, as if my arrival settles some internal wager.

"Did you doubt I would?" I allow a hint of challenge to color my response.

"Never doubt. Only... hope." His thumb brushes across my knuckles before releasing my hand, the gesture so subtle I might have imagined it. "Most find excuses to avoid private dinners after witnessing my interests at public gatherings."

"I'm not most people, Lord Blackthorne."

"No." His voice drops half an octave, sending pleasant shivers down my spine. "You certainly are not."

He guides me toward seating arranged before the fire, his palm at my elbow. Even through layers of silk, his touch radiates unnatural heat. Not the divine cold of Mordreth's blessing but heat that makes my skin ache for more contact.

"Wine?" He moves to a side table where a decanter waits, the liquid within so dark it seems to absorb light. "From vineyards on Nocthys's western border. The soil there produces flavors impossible to replicate elsewhere."

"You seem to have a talent for acquiring the impossible." I settle into the offered chair, noting how he's arranged them.

Close enough for intimate conversation, angled to let firelight play across our faces.

"Persistence and patience." He pours elegantly, the wine moving like liquid shadow into crystal glasses. "Most worthwhile things require both."

When he offers me the glass, our fingertips brush. This time I'm certain the contact is deliberate, his touch trailing along mine just long enough to send heat spiraling through my body.

The wine's scent fills my senses before I taste it. Complex, dark, with undertones that remind me of midnight rituals and forbidden ceremonies. The first sip coats my tongue with flavors that shift and change. Berries give way to spice, then an essence metallic like blood, finally settling into a warmth that spreads through my chest.

"Divine." The word escapes without calculation.

His eyes darken with pleasure. "You taste the shadow essence. Most find it... unsettling."

"I find things that unsettle others tend to be the most interesting."

He laughs, a rich sound that transforms his features from dangerously handsome to devastatingly so. "Careful, Lady Ravencrest. Such admissions might give me ideas."

"What sort of ideas?" The question emerges breathier than intended.

He leans forward, elbows resting on his knees, bringing him close enough that I can see the individual flecks of charcoal in his gray eyes. "The sort that would scandalize proper society. The sort that involve sharing more than wine and conversation."

My pulse races, but I hold his gaze. "Perhaps I'm tired of proper society."

"Perhaps you are." He studies me with that focused intensity that makes me feel stripped bare despite my layers of silk. "Tell me, Sera—" He tastes my name like the wine, savoring it. "What do you really want? Not the prepared answer about seeking new surroundings after loss. The truth."

The question cuts deeper than expected. For a moment, I glimpse the man behind the cultured facade. Someone who understands wearing masks, who recognizes a kindred spirit in deception.

"Understanding," I answer honestly. "Knowledge that goes beyond what's permitted. Power that doesn't come from birth or marriage but from within."

His expression shifts, hunger sharpening his features. "And if I told you such things were possible? That the shadows you appreciate in art could offer so much more?"

"I'd ask what price such gifts demand." My voice remains steady despite my racing heart.

"Everything." The single word falls between us with the weight of prophecy. "But for those willing to pay, the rewards are beyond imagination."

He rises abruptly, offering his hand. "Come. Dinner awaits, and I find myself eager to share more than just a meal with you."

His eyes darken, pupils widening. "We share more than I initially hoped, Lady Ravencrest."

The manservant appears with silent grace, announcing dinner without interrupting the tension building between us. Blackthorne offers his arm to escort me to the dining room. My palm rests against the fine fabric of his sleeve, feeling muscle beneath that speaks of activities beyond aristocratic leisure.

The dining room continues the theme of opulence. A table that could seat twenty has been arranged for intimacy, two places set at one end with silver service gleaming in candle flame. Windows line one wall, revealing moonlight that competes with the fire's glow.

He seats me himself rather than leaving the task to servants, his touch warm through silk as he adjusts my chair. The small courtesy carries possession in its caress, sending pleasant shivers across my skin. My body responds with genuine appreciation while my mind remains fixed on intent beneath pleasure.

Servants appear with the first course. The plating transforms simple soup into artistic offering, a pool of liquid midnight garnished with violet petals and silver-leafed herbs I recognize from the most sacred ceremonies. Steam rises like incense smoke, carrying scents that make my pulse quicken. The black porcelain bowl feels warm against my palms, its surface painted with constellations that seem to shift in the candlelight. The aroma fills my lungs with unexpected complexity. Rich, earthy mushrooms mingle with star anise and something darker, a whisper of shadow-oil so diluted it exists more as memory than flavor.

The intimate table setting makes the vast dining room feel like a private chamber. Candlelight flickers across his features as he watches me taste the soup, his attention making every bite feel like a seduction.

My spoon slides through liquid darkness, bringing warmth to my lips. Flavor explodes across my tongue with rich earth and forbidden herbs and a force that awakens memories of consecration rituals. Heat spreads through my body from throat to belly to limbs, a pleasant fire that sharpens senses rather than dulling them.

"You're not eating," I observe, noting his barely touched bowl.

"I find myself satisfied by watching you enjoy what I've provided." His voice carries notes that make the simple statement sound indecent. "There's a particular pleasure in introducing someone to new experiences."

"Is that what this is? An introduction?"

"Among other things." He finally takes a bite, and I find myself mesmerized by the movement of his throat as he swallows. "Tell me, what did you think of the shadow truffle soup?"

"The black truffles grow only in forests bordering Nocthys." Blackthorne watches with hungry attention. "They absorb qualities from the soil that transfer subtle properties to those who consume them."

"Exquisite. Though I suspect it contained more than just rare mushrooms."

His smile is slow, dangerous. "Perceptive. The preparation includes herbs that grow only where shadow has touched the earth for centuries. They... enhance certain sensitivities."

As if to prove his point, I become hyperaware of everything. The whisper of silk against my skin, the warmth radiating from his body across the small distance between us, the way shadows seem to deepen and pulse in my peripheral vision.

"You're trying to seduce me." The accusation comes out more breathless than accusatory.

"Am I?" He leans back in his chair, studying me with those storm-gray eyes. "And if I were, would you object?"

"That depends on what kind of seduction you have in mind."

"Every kind." The admission is bold, delivered with a confidence that sends warmth spiraling through my core. "Your mind first. It's exquisite, the way you grasp concepts others fear to contemplate. Your trust next. I want you to believe that what I offer is not corruption but evolution. And finally."

He lets the sentence hang, but his eyes complete it eloquently.

"Bold words for a second private meeting," I manage.

"Time is more fluid than most believe. I knew within moments of meeting you at the gallery that you were different. Special." He pauses, vulnerability flickering across his features. "I've been searching for someone like you for longer than you could imagine."

"Someone like me?"

"Someone unafraid. Someone who sees darkness as possibility rather than threat. Someone who might understand why I do what I do."

The conversation has veered into dangerous territory, but I find myself leaning closer rather than retreating. "And why do you do it?"

For a moment, his mask slips entirely. Raw pain flashes across his features before being carefully controlled. "Because the light failed me when I needed it most. Because the shadows offered answers when the gods remained silent. Because power, real power, comes from understanding forces others fear to acknowledge."

"You speak from experience." I keep my voice gentle, sensing the wound behind his words.

"My wife." The two words carry years of grief. "She was everything light and good and pure. And it didn't save her. The shadows took her mind first, made her see things that weren't there. Or perhaps were there, just hidden from the rest of us." His fists clench on the table. "I held her as she died, promising I would understand what killed her. That I would master what destroyed her."

"I'm sorry." The sympathy is genuine, despite everything.

"Don't be. Her death led me to truth. The shadows didn't kill her—ignorance did. Fear did. If we'd understood instead of fled, if we'd embraced instead of rejected..." He stops himself, reining in the passion that threatens to overwhelm his control. "Forgive me. I don't usually speak of such things."

"I'm honored you shared it with me."

Each course that follows continues the pattern. Foods I've never encountered served with explanations of their unusual properties. Wine poured from bottles with labels in languages even my training can't decipher. Every flavor is designed to heighten awareness, to push senses beyond ordinary limitations.

Throughout the meal, our conversation ventures into territories far beyond social pleasantries. Blackthorne speaks of lost traditions forgotten by modern kingdoms, of shadow properties studied by scholars before religious restrictions limited research, of power available to those willing to venture beyond conventional boundaries.

"The modern understanding of shadow as corruption represents perhaps the greatest tragedy of our age." His voice carries genuine passion that transforms his features. "Our ancestors recognized it as merely another form of energy, neither inherently destructive nor benevolent."

"Yet golden eyes mark those who dabble too deeply." The observation slips out before I can contain it, too close to mission rather than persona.

His expression sharpens with sudden interest rather than suspicion. "You're remarkably well-informed for someone who recently arrived in Luridian."

My heart pounds while I maintain an outward calm. "One hears whispers even in the highest circles. Servants talk. Nobles speculate."

"Indeed." He studies me with renewed focus. "And what do these whispers say?"

"That the city grows more dangerous. Shadow attacks in the merchant district. Citizens found pale and cold." I pause, watching his reaction. "Some blame your interests for attracting such darkness."

His laugh is rich and unexpected. "Ah, the shadow manifestations. Yes, I imagine they would blame me." He swirls his wine thoughtfully. "Tell me, Sera, what do you think causes darkness to move of its own accord?"

"I couldn't begin to guess."

"Wild shadow." His voice takes on a teaching quality. "Shadow energy without conscious direction. Like lightning seeking ground, it attacks whatever draws its attention. The city guard claims they're random incidents, but the pattern suggests otherwise."

"You've studied these attacks?" The question emerges with genuine curiosity.

"I study all manifestations of shadow." He leans forward, intensity sharpening his features. "These incidents prove what I've long suspected—shadow energy grows stronger in our world. The untrained see only danger. But properly channeled, properly understood..." He trails off, meeting my gaze. "The physical manifestation represents merely one aspect of shadow attunement. In its early stages, properly managed, it offers heightened awareness rather than corruption."

Our eyes meet across candlelight. The admission confirms Mother Superior's intelligence while revealing an unexpected perspective. Blackthorne believes his practices can control corruption rather than merely causing it. The distinction burns in my memory, neither justifying his heresy nor fully condemning his intent.

"Forgive my boldness," I say, allowing my voice to soften vulnerably. "But your knowledge exceeds academic interest."

His laugh carries genuine amusement. "Perceptive as well as beautiful. A dangerous combination." He refills my wine glass, the vintage darker than what we began with. "I've spent years studying shadow properties and their applications. My collection includes texts rescued from destruction during the Great Purge when the Church of Solanus systematically eliminated shadow research."

The servant clears our final course, leaving us with crystal glasses filled with midnight wine and conversation balanced on propriety's edge. Blackthorne watches me over the rim of his glass, candlelight catching in his eyes with unusual intensity.

He looks at me then with such intensity I feel pinned to my chair. "You're dangerous, aren't you? Behind that flawless facade of the proper widow."

My heart stops, but I force a smile. "Whatever makes you think that?"

"Because I recognize a predator when I see one." He rises, moving around the table fluidly. "The question is, what are you hunting?"

He stops behind my chair, his grip resting on the back, caging me without touching. I can feel the heat of him, smell that intoxicating mix of sandalwood and shadow-smoke.

"Perhaps I'm hunting the same thing you are," I whisper. "Understanding. Truth. Power."

"Perhaps." His breath stirs my hair as he leans closer. "Or perhaps you're hunting me."

My pulse stumbles. Has he guessed? But when I turn to look up at him, there's no suspicion in his eyes. Only heat and hunger and an emotion that might be hope.

"Would that be such a bad thing?" I ask.

"That depends on what you plan to do when you catch me." His palm moves to my shoulder, thumb brushing the exposed skin above my neckline. The touch is light, barely there, but it sends fire racing through my veins.

"Lord Blackthorne—"

"Rivin." His voice is rough. "When we're alone, call me Rivin."

"Rivin." His name tastes dangerous on my tongue. "We should be careful."

"Should we?" His touch moves from my shoulder to cup my jaw, tilting my face up to meet his gaze. "I've been careful for years. Controlled. Contained. And where has it gotten me?"

"Alive," I point out, though my voice wavers as his thumb traces my cheekbone.

"Existing isn't the same as living." He releases me abruptly, stepping back. "Forgive me. The wine and your presence make me forget myself."

I rise on unsteady legs, turning to face him. "Perhaps forgetting yourself isn't always wrong."

"Would you care to see some of my collection?" The invitation carries multiple meanings, all serving my ultimate mission.

"I would be honored." My body leans forward, drawn by the promise of forbidden knowledge and the next stage of the hunt.

13

— · —

REVELATION

He rises fluidly, offering his palm rather than his arm. The gesture crosses formal boundaries while maintaining plausible deniability. My fingers slide against his grip, the contact sending liquid heat through my body. His skin feels warmer than human flesh should, suggesting shadow-energy simmers just under the skin.

He leads me through corridors I memorize for potential escape routes. Our path takes us deeper into the estate's eastern wing, where windows facing Nocthys capture moonlight that seems to behave strangely, pooling in corners rather than spreading evenly. The air grows cooler with each step, carrying a subtle scent I recognize from temple rituals. Incense mingled with shadow-oil and an essence metallic like blood freshly spilled.

My senses heighten with each step, wine and exotic food and Blackthorne's presence combining to create a state of hyperawareness. The knife against my thigh presses reassuringly against flesh that remembers its ultimate mission. My fingertips remain loosely entwined with his, neither capturing nor captured.

We stop before a door different from others we've passed. Heavy wood banded with iron, bearing carvings that seem to move when viewed indirectly. No light escapes around its edges despite illumination that must exist beyond.

"My private collection." Blackthorne's voice lowers with reverence that feels genuine rather than affected. "Few have seen what rests behind this door."

He produces a key from within his jacket, the metal catching moonlight from a nearby window. The lock accepts it with a sound like distant thunder. The door opens to darkness that breathes against my face with a living presence.

Blackthorne steps through first, his grip maintaining connection with mine as though concerned I might flee. Light blooms as he touches a crystal sconce near the entrance. The illumination spreads through the chamber without behaving as light should, casting shadows toward the source rather than away, pooling in corners as though drawn to darkness rather than dispelling it.

The collection room makes my breath catch. Shelves line walls interrupted by display cases containing objects that pulse with subtle energy. I see books bound in materials I recognize from forbidden archives, objects that drink light rather than reflecting it, and paintings whose subjects seem to move when not directly observed.

In the center stands a circular table of polished obsidian, its surface etched with constellations that match neither the ceiling in the salon nor any star patterns I learned during astronomical training. Around it seven chairs wait like supplicants, their high backs carved with symbols that hurt my eyes when I try to focus directly on them.

"Breathtaking." The word emerges with genuine appreciation. The collection exceeds my expectations in both scope and significance.

"Years of effort." His voice carries pride warmed with genuine enthusiasm. "Some pieces acquired through conventional means, purchases from private collectors, estate sales of noble families that had fallen into disgrace. Others required more... creative acquisition methods."

He guides me through the collection, explaining pieces with knowledge that flows from dedicated study rather than surface understanding. The entire room radiates energy my body recognizes from Sanctuary rituals, from shadow-oil blessed beneath the Raven's gaze, from ceremonies performed at the confluence of astronomical alignments.

We pause before a glass case containing a small obsidian medallion. The artifact draws my eye despite more elaborate pieces nearby. Its design bears a striking resemblance to symbols used in Sisterhood rituals. A raven in flight over seven stars arranged in a pattern from sacred texts.

"This particular piece came from a temple excavation near the Nocthys border." Blackthorne watches my reaction with careful attention. "Archaeological evidence suggests it predates the current religious structures by several centuries."

My fingertips itch to touch it, to verify whether power truly resides within or merely suggestion born of shape and origin. The glass between us feels like the thinnest of barriers, propriety's final protection against forbidden knowledge.

"It's beautiful." Truth spills from my lips. "The craftsmanship suggests ritual significance rather than decoration."

"Precisely." His approval heats my skin. "Most observers see only aesthetic value. The true ritual purpose requires deeper understanding."

He produces a key from his waistcoat, opening the case with reverent care. "I suspected from the beginning that you might be one of the rare few who could appreciate its true nature."

The medallion rests on velvet, seeming to pulse with internal rhythm. This close, I feel its pull more strongly, like recognition singing through my veins.

"Touch it." His words drop to that commanding register that makes my knees weak.

"Is it safe?"

"Nothing worthwhile ever is." He lifts the medallion, holding it between us. "But I'll catch you if you fall."

The promise in those words makes me reach out despite every warning screaming in my head. My fingertips brush the cold stone.

Fire and ice explode through my veins simultaneously. The room tilts, golden light flooding my vision. Primordial whispers fill my mind in a language I shouldn't understand but do. Power surges through me, intoxicating and terrifying in equal measure.

She who stands between worlds.

Mordreth guide your servant through heresy's flame.

My knees buckle, but strong arms wrap around my waist before I can fall. I'm pulled against a solid chest, feeling Blackthorne's heart pounding against my back, his breath harsh against my ear.

"Extraordinary." His voice is rough with awe. "I suspected, but to see it confirmed changes everything."

I turn in his arms, still unsteady from the medallion's impact. His face is inches from mine, those storm-gray eyes blown wide with a mix of triumph and wonder.

"What was that?"

"Proof." His hand cups my jaw, thumb brushing my lower lip. "You're not just sensitive to shadow, Sera. You're connected to it in ways most can only dream of."

"Connected how?" The question emerges as a whisper.

"Your bloodline carries the old gifts. The ability to work with shadow rather than face it." His thumb continues its maddening path across my lip. "Do you have any idea how rare that is? How long I've searched for someone like you?"

"Someone like me?"

"Someone who can stand at my side as an equal." The words are fierce, possessive. "Not a student or acolyte, but a true partner in understanding."

He releases me abruptly, stepping back. The loss of his warmth leaves me bereft, still trembling from the medallion's touch.

"Some families carry latent abilities that manifest under the right conditions," he continues, his voice filled with reverence.

He moves closer again, his breath fanning across my neck. "The Ravencrest line from Valmeria was known for such gifts before religious purges eliminated most carriers."

My cover story turns on me. He reads significance into a name I selected for its obscurity. My skin prickles with warning.

"My family never mentioned such abilities." Truth within deception.

"Of course not." His fingers trace the curve of my neck, the contact possessive. "Speaking of shadow gifts meant death during the Purges. Families learned to hide their nature, suppress their abilities, forget their heritage. But lineage remembers what minds are trained to forget."

The implications settle like lead in my belly. If he believes my false bloodline grants inherent power, when time reveals no such gifts... My mission tilts toward an impossible deception.

"You're trembling." His tone roughens with concern that sounds genuine. "Have I frightened you?"

"Overwhelmed, perhaps." I allow vulnerability to color my words. "So much revealed in one evening."

"And so much more to discover." He moves deeper into the collection, and I follow on unsteady legs.

"This changes everything," he says, stopping before a glass case containing an age-darkened tome. "I was going to ease you into our practices, but someone with your gifts deserves the full truth."

He opens the case, withdrawing the leather-bound book. When he sets it on the obsidian reading table, I notice the constellation pattern etched into its surface. The same seven stars from the medallion.

"Come here." It's not a request.

I move to stand beside him, hyperaware of his hand on my waist. He opens the tome, revealing pages covered in diagrams I recognize from my training but twisted, reimagined in ways that make my stomach tighten.

"The Church teaches that shadow corrupts absolutely." His tone takes on a teaching cadence, but his hand finds my waist, thumb tracing absent patterns that make concentration difficult. "But the old masters understood differently. Shadow can transform or preserve, corrupt or enhance, depending on how it's channeled."

He turns pages, showing progression charts. "Look here. Early manifestation can be guided, shaped, even reversed if necessary. The corruption only becomes irreversible after a certain threshold."

"A threshold?" My words catch as his hand tightens on my waist.

"Time enough to master the change rather than be mastered by it. With correct guidance, of course."

"And you provide such guidance?"

"Among other offerings." He turns me to face him, backing me against the table's edge. "I could teach you, Sera. Show you wonders beyond imagination. Power beyond comprehension."

"At what cost?" My hands press against his chest, feeling the rapid beat of his heart.

"Everything." His honesty is brutal, beautiful. "Your old life, your old limitations, your old fears. But what you'd gain would eclipse any loss."

His hands frame my face again, and this time when he leans in, I don't pull back. His lips hover a breath from mine.

"The next gathering approaches." His words ghost across my mouth. "The moon will be nearly full, the veil at its thinnest. You'll see visions that will challenge everything you believe."

"I'm not afraid."

"You should be." But he's smiling as he says it, a dark, promising expression. "The ceremonies can be... physically demanding."

The implications in his tone make warmth gather in my center.

He guides me from the collection room, shadows seeming to reach toward us as we leave. The door closes with finality that sends a shiver along my spine.

The journey back through the estate passes in charged silence. At the entrance, his carriage waits to return me to Crescent Court. He helps me inside himself, his hands lingering at my waist.

"Until the gathering." His lips brush my knuckles in parting. The contact burns like a brand. "I'll send proper instructions tomorrow."

"I look forward to deeper understanding." The words taste of truth despite their duplicity.

His smile promises pleasures and knowledge in equal measure. "So do I, Lady Ravencrest. More than you can possibly imagine."

The carriage pulls away, leaving me with skin still tingling from his touch and mind racing with new revelations. The medallion test confirmed what Blackthorne suspected. I carry some natural affinity for shadow work. The knowledge should terrify me. Instead, it raises questions about my selection by the Sisterhood that I'm not ready to face.

More immediately concerning, the next gathering will test my supposed bloodline gifts.

The mission proceeds, but on paths I never anticipated walking.

14

— · —

ARTIFACTS

The carriage bears me away through streets wrapped in gathering darkness. I press my trembling hands to lips that still tingle from undelivered kisses, skin that burns from touches that skirted propriety's edge. The medallion's fire still races through my veins, golden light leaving afterimages when I close my eyes.

She who stands between worlds.

The words echo in my mind, not in Blackthorne's voice but in something older, deeper. The obsidian medallion had recognized me, awakened something within my blood that the Sisterhood never named. Natural affinity for shadow, not through corruption but through birthright.

The mission tilts on a blade's edge. Blackthorne sees what he wishes to see. A woman of shadow-blessed lineage drawn to forbidden knowledge. When that illusion shatters on reality, when my humanity reveals no special gifts beyond what training provides...

Grant wisdom to navigate deception's maze. Let Thy servant's purpose remain pure despite body's weakness.

The prayer rises automatically, seeking divine guidance through heresy's attractive lies. Yet part of me wonders at truths hidden in Blackthorne's words. Lineage remembering what minds forget. Gifts suppressed through fear.

The Sisterhood found me in ruins. No family name. No history. Only potential Mordreth's servants recognized.

Questions I've never dared express whisper through my thoughts. Why me among the orphans? What drew Mother Superior's eye? What if these questions hold answers I'm not prepared to face?

I press my hands to my lips, trying to hold onto the sensation of his nearness, the promise in his words about the next gathering. The medallion's fire still races through my veins, its revelation about my supposed bloodline gifts creating new complications for my mission.

The thought of returning to his collection should fill me with purpose for the hunt. Instead, anticipation burns beneath my skin. What else might he reveal? What other tests await?

I crush the wondering under trained discipline. My purpose comes from divine selection, not inherited power. The Raven's Kiss waits for lips that serve justice, not shadow's seduction.

Crescent Court appears through the carriage window, lights burning in upper windows despite the late hour. The sight sends unexpected warmth through my chest growing cold from the medallion's aftereffects.

The driver assists me from the carriage with professional courtesy, unaware of the turmoil beneath my composed exterior. My legs shake slightly as I climb the steps, the medallion's touch having drained more strength than I anticipated.

Inside, the house embraces me with familiar silence. Yet as I reach the second floor, soft light spills from beneath my chamber door. My hand moves instinctively to the knife at my thigh before recognition settles. Liora waits within.

The door opens to reveal her rising from a chair near the fireplace, concern evident in every line of her body. She's changed from her servant's attire into a simple night robe, honey-brown hair loose around her shoulders. The informal appearance suggests she's been waiting for hours.

"My lady." She moves toward me with natural grace. "Forgive me for waiting. I wanted to ensure your safe return."

"You needn't have waited, Liora." My voice emerges gentler than intended.

"I wished to." Her fingers work at my cloak's fastenings, careful yet practiced. "I know you can protect yourself, but even the strongest among us deserve someone waiting to welcome them home."

Her sincere attention awakens something I thought I'd buried with my childhood. Not the vulnerability I expected, but a hunger for connection I never knew existed.

"I've prepared a bath for you," she says, guiding me toward the bathing chamber. "The evening must have been taxing."

Steam rises from water scented with lavender oil. The copper tub gleams in candlelight, flames reflected in the rippling surface. The sight promises comfort after hours of performance and mission.

"Was the evening enjoyable?" She helps remove the sage-blue gown, working the buttons with ease.

"Revelatory." The word carries more truth than I should share. "Lord Blackthorne's knowledge of art and history is extensive."

"And his home?" Her touch slides silk from my shoulders, the material whispering against skin that still remembers his caress at the small of my back.

"Impressive. His collection particularly." The admission flows naturally, though I leave out details. "Rare artifacts from several kingdoms, including Nocthys."

Her movements still momentarily at the mention of the shadow kingdom. "They say Nocthys objects carry darkness within them. That shadows behave strangely in their presence."

The observation cuts closer to truth than she could know. My skin warms with the memory of darkness moving with intelligence across Blackthorne's floor. "An interesting perspective."

"More than perspective, according to some." She helps me into the bath, and the water shocks against my cooled skin, sharp enough to make me gasp. Each inch I sink deeper pulls tension from my muscles like poison from a wound. Rose petals drift across the surface, their silk edges catching against my skin in fleeting kisses. The copper walls radiate warmth into my spine as I settle back, finally allowing my body to soften. For this moment, I can stop performing. "My brother mentioned similar things before he disappeared. Said certain objects seemed to breathe when no one was watching directly."

Ice slides through my veins despite the fire's warmth. "You never mentioned such details before."

Her eyes darken with memory. "It seemed too fantastical to share with a lady of your station. The ramblings of a boy caught up in stories."

"Yet now you mention it." My voice remains gentle while my heart pounds against my ribs.

"The look in your expression when you returned." She looks away, suddenly uncertain. "You looked as though you'd seen similar manifestations."

Her insight stuns me. I reach for her hands without thinking, gripping her smaller fingers with sudden urgency. "Liora, if your brother spoke of such things, who listened? Who showed interest in his observations?"

Hope and fear war across her features. "He attended gatherings in the Lower City. Discussion groups, he called them. Led by scholars who spoke of hidden wisdom forgotten by modern society." Her voice lowers. "After several meetings, a noble took interest in him specifically. Offered special instruction for those showing particular... sensitivity."

Blood chills beneath my skin. "This noble. Did your brother ever name him?"

She shakes her head, frustration tightening her features. "Only that he lived outside the city proper. That his home contained wonders beyond imagination." Her fingers grip mine with surprising strength. "Do you think..."

I can't lie while her hand grasps mine with desperate hope. Neither can I speak the full truth that would shatter that same hope with finality. "It's possible Lord Blackthorne knew your brother. The description matches his estate and interests."

Joy transforms her face, stripped of pretense and protection. The naked faith in her eyes burns against my skin. My chest tightens with guilt as memories of the temple flash through my mind. The golden-eyed creature wearing remnants of human clothing, moving with inhuman grace before my blade granted mercy.

"If there's any connection, I'll find it." The promise emerges gentler than my usual vows, weighted with emotion beyond the mission.

"Thank you, my lady." Her voice carries reverence that feels undeserved against the knowledge I withhold. "That would mean everything to me."

She helps wash my hair, her fingertips working through strands with gentleness, applying soap with circular motions that send pleasant shivers down my spine. Each touch feels like a revelation—not the efficient grooming I've known, but something that makes me understand why poets write of simple intimacies. Her hands move with a tenderness that has nothing to do with my station and everything to do with the woman beneath the title.

"My mother always said a woman's hair is her second weapon." Her voice flows soft as the water streaming between her fingers. "The first being her mind, of course."

"Wise words." I close my eyes as her hands massage my scalp. "Your mother sounds like a remarkable woman."

"She was. Raised two children alone after my father died in the mines." Pride and grief mingle in her tone. "Taught us dignity has nothing to do with station."

Her touch guides my head back, rinsing soap away with careful movements that shield my eyes from stinging. Water cascades over my scalp, carrying tension with it. My body yields to her gentle caress with a trust that should alarm me.

The bath continues as she tends to me with quiet devotion, her hands gentle as they help cleanse away the evening's performance. Each movement flows naturally, her gaze averted for modesty yet attention fully focused on my comfort. The thoughtfulness in these small gestures warms emotion in my chest.

"Be careful with Lord Blackthorne, my lady." Her voice lowers, weighted with honest worry. "Men like him see beauty as an object to possess, not cherish."

The warning touches vulnerability within me. My palm reaches out, briefly touching her cheek. "I understand dangerous men better than most."

The contact burns between us, her skin warm against my fingertips. For one heartbeat, the space separating servant from mistress, hunter from innocent, shrinks to nothing. Her eyes widen slightly, surprise and an unnamed emotion moving across her features before propriety reasserts itself.

"My lady," she whispers, color rising in her cheeks.

The bath concludes too soon, warm towels enveloping my body as Liora helps me from the copper embrace. She guides me to sit at my vanity, beginning to work the pins from my elaborate hairstyle. Her fingertips brush against my scalp with each removal, the simple touch more intimate than Blackthorne's artful seduction.

"You seem troubled tonight," she observes, meeting my eyes in the mirror. "More than just fatigue from social performance."

The perceptiveness in her gaze threatens my carefully maintained composure. How does this servant see through masks that fool trained nobles?

"Lord Blackthorne showed me things tonight that challenge what I believed possible." The admission slips out before wisdom can stop it. "Artifacts that respond to touch. Knowledge that suggests accepted truths might be incomplete."

Her hands still in my hair. "The medallion?"

I turn sharply, causing several pins to scatter across the floor. "How could you know about that?"

Fear flickers across her features before she masters it. "I... I've heard rumors. Servants talk. They say Lord Blackthorne possesses a medallion that burns with cold fire when certain people touch it. That it reveals those with old blood, old gifts."

My heart races. How much does she know? How much has she guessed about my true nature?

"And if someone responded to such an artifact?" I ask carefully. "What would the rumors say then?"

She resumes her work on my hair, movements gentle despite the tension between us. "That they carry power in their bloodline. That shadows recognize them as kin." Her voice drops to barely above a whisper. "That they're either blessed or cursed, depending on who tells the tale."

"Which do you believe?"

"I believe," she says slowly, "that power itself is neither good nor evil. It's what we choose to do with it that matters."

The wisdom in her words strikes deeper than expected. I catch her hand where it rests on my shoulder, holding it against my skin. "You speak as one who's seen both sides of power."

"I've seen enough to know that those who claim absolute morality often cause the most harm." She squeezes my shoulder gently. "And that sometimes those deemed dangerous are simply different."

I turn to face her fully, studying her features with new understanding. "What are you, Liora?"

"Someone who recognizes another soul carrying secrets too heavy for their frame." She kneels beside my chair, bringing us to eye level. "Someone who sees past Lady Ravencrest to the woman underneath. Someone who..." She pauses, color rising in her cheeks.

"Someone who?" I prompt gently.

"Someone who cares more than wisdom suggests I should." The words emerge in a rush. "When you return from these gatherings, you carry shadows on your skin. Not corruption. Something else. Like you've been marked by forces I can't name."

I should deny it. Should maintain the comfortable distance between lady and servant. Instead, I find myself cupping her face in my hands, thumbs tracing her cheekbones with devastating gentleness.

"What if I told you these forces call to me?" The question emerges without permission. "That I feel pulled toward purposes I don't fully understand?"

"Then I'd ask if you chose them back." Her eyes search mine. "If what marks you comes from your will or another's."

The question cuts to the heart of doubts I've carried since childhood. Did I choose the Sisterhood, or did they simply claim me? Is my devotion genuine faith or careful conditioning?

"I don't know anymore," I admit, the honesty burning my throat. "Tonight changed things. Revealed possibilities I never considered."

She rises, pulling me to my feet with surprising strength. "Then let me show you something."

15

CHOICES

She moves to the window, gazing at the garden below. "Sometimes I wonder what truly separates light from shadow. Whether the divisions we're taught are as absolute as they claim."

"You speak of dangerous thoughts," I say, though without condemnation.

"Perhaps. But I've seen too much to believe in simple answers." She turns back to me. "Those deemed corrupt often showed kindness. Those claiming righteousness often caused harm."

"The world is rarely as clear as we're taught," I admit.

"No, it isn't." She moves closer, studying my face. "Which is why I trust what I see in you more than what others might say about you."

The heresy in her words should appall me. Instead, they resonate with truths I've avoided. The Sisterhood serves Mordreth's shadow, but is that service truly different from Blackthorne's corruption? Both command death. Both demand transformation. Both promise power through submission to darkness.

"You're dangerous," I whisper.

"So are you." She smiles, sad and knowing. "The difference is, I've made peace with my nature. You're still fighting yours."

She moves away, gathering the scattered pins from the floor. Her absence aches more than it should. When she returns to finish my hair, her touch carries new intimacy. Not servant tending mistress, but one gifted soul recognizing another.

"Lord Blackthorne seemed quite taken with you," she observes quietly. "The servants at the estate send word of his interest."

I close my eyes, remembering the intensity of his gaze, the way the medallion had responded to my touch. "He showed me things tonight that I'm still trying to understand."

"Be careful with such men." She continues working on my hair, her touch gentle and soothing. "They rarely reveal their mysteries without expecting something in return."

"Blackthorne believes something similar." The admission tastes bitter.

"A truth spoken by evil lips remains true." She finishes with my hair, stepping back. "The question is what you'll do with that truth."

I study my reflection in the mirror. Without the elaborate style, I look younger, more vulnerable. More human. The woman staring back seems caught between worlds. Not quite the assassin I was, not yet whatever I'm becoming.

"I have a duty," I say, though the words lack conviction.

"To whom?" Liora asks gently. "To those who shaped you, or to your own conscience?"

"There's something between us." The words tumble out desperate and unplanned. "Something I never expected and don't understand."

"I know." She moves behind me, hands resting lightly on my shoulders. "I feel it too."

"It complicates everything." I close my eyes, unable to hold her gaze even in reflection.

"Or simplifies it." Her reflection meets mine in the mirror. Her thumbs stroke small circles on my shoulders, a gesture meant to comfort that only heightens my awareness of her. "When we strip away duty and expectation, what remains?"

"I don't know." The lie tastes bitter. But I do know. What remains is this—her touch on my shoulders, her presence in my space, her light balancing my shadow. "I've never wanted anything for myself before. Never thought beyond the next day, the next social obligation."

She's quiet for a moment, her hands stilling on my shoulders. When she speaks, her voice is barely above a whisper. "And now?"

"Now I think about impossible things." I cover her hands with mine. "Things I have no right to want. A different life. Freedom to choose."

She makes a soft sound, caught between hope and sorrow. "We all dream of impossible things sometimes."

"Do we?" I turn to face her, our hands still joined. "Or do we learn to stop dreaming?"

"Never stop." Her voice is fierce. "Even if they remain only dreams."

The intensity of her words moves something inside me. I pull her closer, our foreheads touching. "Some dreams are dangerous to hold too tightly."

"Then we'll take what moments we can." Her breath warms my lips. "Store them up against whatever darkness comes."

This moment demands an intimacy we've only danced around before. Instead of words, we simply hold each other. Her arms wrap around my waist while mine encircle her shoulders. We fit together perfectly, light and shadow finding balance.

"You're troubled by more than just what you've learned," she says after long moments. "There's something else weighing on you."

"Lord Blackthorne has shared knowledge that could help people." I choose my words carefully. "But using it would m ean... complications."

"Because of your obligations?" Her voice is gentle. "Or because the source troubles you?"

"Both." I pull back to look at her. "How do we judge the value of knowledge separate from its source? Can truth be tainted by the one who speaks it?"

"Truth is truth," she says simply. "What matters is how we choose to use it."

"Even if obtaining it requires... compromise?"

She studies me with those perceptive eyes. "You're facing a choice. Between what you feel you must do and what you believe is right."

The accuracy of her observation steals my breath. "How did you—"

"Because I see the conflict in you." She touches my cheek gently. "Whatever you're struggling with, remember that rigid paths rarely lead to wisdom."

The logic in her argument undermines years of absolute thinking. Kill the heretic. That's always been the way. But what if the heretic holds keys to redemption?

"I have... obligations," I say weakly.

"From whom? The ghosts of your past that still control your choices?" Her perception cuts through pretense. "The same ghosts that would condemn the sick rather than attempt healing?"

Each question strikes deeper than the last. Mother Superior's face rises in my mind, cold, certain, absolute in her judgments. Would she use reversal knowledge if she possessed it? Or would she suppress it to maintain the Sisterhood's monopoly on defining corruption?

"It's not that simple," I protest.

"Isn't it?" Liora moves to the window, gazing at the garden. "Sometimes the most difficult choices are between two rights, not right and wrong."

"You speak as if you know what I face."

"I know you're torn." She turns back to me. "Between duty and conscience. Between what you've been told and what you've discovered. Such conflicts leave marks."

The perception in her words unsettles me. She sees too much, understands too well.

"Some paths once chosen can't be abandoned," I say softly.

"Perhaps. Or perhaps we tell ourselves that to avoid the harder choice of change." She returns to me, hands finding mine again. "Whatever you decide, make it your choice. Not one dictated by others."

The question carries weight beyond words. She's asking me to choose between duty and possibility, between predetermined path and unexplored future.

"I don't know if I can." The admission burns. "The bonds on me run deeper than simple promises. There are... consequences I can't escape."

"Then fulfill your obligations in ways that serve life rather than death." Her thumbs trace circles on my palms. "You're clever, resourceful, able to see possibilities others miss. Find another way."

Another way. The concept feels foreign yet tantalizing. All my life, I've followed straight paths laid out by others. What if branching from those paths led somewhere better?

A knock at the door interrupts my spiraling thoughts. We spring apart instinctively, proper distance restored between lady and servant.

"Enter," I call.

Phillips appears, looking apologetic. "Forgive the late hour, my lady. A message arrived marked urgent."

He offers a sealed envelope on a silver tray. The black wax bears Blackthorne's raven symbol. My pulse quickens as I break the seal.

My dearest Sera,

Tonight's revelation changes everything. Your response to the medallion confirms what I've long suspected. You are exactly who I've been seeking. Not just sensitive to shadow, but born to walk between worlds.

The royal garden party will soon provide the perfect setting for your introduction to my inner circle. Such events offer unique opportunities for those ready to see beyond society's masks.

I find myself counting the hours until I see you again. Until we can explore the full depth of your remarkable gifts.

Yours in shadow and light, Rivin

My hands tremble slightly as I fold the letter. A royal garden party. The perfect stage for deeper infiltration.

"Thank you, Phillips. That will be all."

He withdraws, leaving us alone with the weight of what approaches.

"Soon," Liora murmurs. "Time to prepare, at least."

"Time for many things." I burn the letter in the fireplace, watching Blackthorne's words turn to ash.

"Whatever comes next, we'll face it when it arrives." She moves toward the door, pausing with her hand on the handle. "Rest well, my lady. I'll ensure you're not disturbed."

The formal words carry weight far beyond their meaning. Our eyes meet across the room, and in that gaze lies everything we cannot yet say. Everything we cannot yet be.

For a moment, I think she might turn back. The air between us thrums with unspoken possibility. But then she slips from the room, leaving me alone with the dying fire and the memory of her touch.

"Stay," I whisper after the door closes.

The word hangs in the empty air, a confession I couldn't voice while she stood before me. My hand reaches toward where she stood, fingers closing on nothing.

What am I doing? This feeling, this ache in my chest, serves no divine purpose. Yet I cannot escape the memory of her touch, the way she sees through every carefully constructed facade to the woman I've never had the chance to be.

I sink onto the bed, pressing my palms against silk sheets that feel too cold without her warmth nearby. For the first time since the Sisterhood claimed me, I wanted something beyond duty.

I wanted someone.

16

CITY

Six weeks in Luridian. The wound from the temple has closed but shadow corruption still fights beneath new skin.

My infiltration of Blackthorne's inner circle proceeds as planned. Dinner at his estate, viewing his collection, each encounter building toward judgment's climax.

Yet the full picture eludes me like shadows slipping between my fingers.

The Lower City breathes with rot and desperation. I inhale deeply, savoring the stink after too many days swimming through aristocratic perfume. Sweat. Piss. Smoke from cheap coal. The sour tang of too many bodies pressed too close together. My nostrils flare, separating scents not just as hunter tracking prey but as someone seeking a particular face among many, the brother whose absence leaves shadows in Liora's eyes.

Through your darkness guide my steps, Raven Lord. Not just for your will, but for her peace.

Buildings lean toward each other like dying penitents, creating tunnels where sunlight never reaches. Water drips from rotting eaves, each drop carrying filth from the levels above. The cobblestones under my feet gleam black with substances best left unexamined. My boots stick slightly with each step, the ground reluctant to release me.

I pull the rough-spun cloak tighter, its coarse weave a stark contrast to the silks I've grown accustomed to wearing. The disguise transforms me back into what I truly am, a hunter moving through shadows rather than a widow dancing through ballrooms.

Morning mist clings to the cobblestones slick with refuse. The sun struggles to penetrate the haze of cook fires and factory smoke. Blackthorne's collection room lingers in memory, my fingers still burning with the touch of forbidden texts. The familiar rhythm of mission preparation flows through my blood, yet something different beats beneath it now. Liora's gentle questions about her brother. The way her voice softened when speaking of him. The hope she refuses to surrender despite months of absence.

If Mother Superior's intelligence remains incomplete concerning these disappearances, it may be flawed in other areas. My blade must strike true, yet...what if truth lies beyond our teachings?

The market square sprawls before me, a maze of rickety stalls and desperate commerce. Fishmongers haggle over catches pulled from polluted harbors. Butchers hang scraps that wealthier districts would reject. The scents mingle into something alive, a hungry beast that claws its way into my lungs. I taste blood and brine along with rotting vegetables and human sweat, all of it honest in a way the perfumed Upper City never permits.

I move through the crowded lanes with deadly intent. My body flows between bodies, touching none, noticed by few. The rough fabric of my disguise marks me as unremarkable. I become just another form among the many scraping survival from Luridian's cruelty.

"Fresh news from the Temple Quarter!" A paper boy's voice cuts through the market noise. His small frame perches atop a crate, sheets of cheap newsprint clutched in dirty hands. "Three more missing last night! City guard increases patrols!"

The crowd shifts nervously at his words. Bodies press closer together, unconsciously seeking safety in numbers. Fear permeates the market like rot through a fruit. I drift closer, observing the faces around me. They all know someone who's vanished. Children. Siblings. Neighbors. They speak of it in hushed tones when they believe no one listens.

I drop a coin in the boy's cup, taking a paper I don't need. "Your voice carries well for one so small."

His spine straightens with pride despite hollow cheeks that speak of too many missed meals. "Have to be heard above the crowd, miss. Papers don't sell themselves."

"The missing. Do you know where they were last seen?"

Wariness replaces pride. His eyes dart to my face, then away. "Depends who's asking."

I drop another coin, heavier than the first. His eyes widen at silver where copper usually lands.

"Someone looking for patterns. Someone who might stop more disappearances." *Someone who promised a handmaiden to learn the truth.*

The boy studies me with eyes far older than his body. "They take the ones who listen." His voice drops so low I must lean closer. "At the meetings. Near the old Teller's Bridge. They talk about ancient wisdom, secret powers. Then people start changing. Eyes first. Then they vanish."

My breath catches. Eyes changing. Just like Liora described when speaking of her brother's last days.

"Who leads these meetings?"

He shrugs, but fear tightens his shoulders. "Nobody knows. Not for certain. But they say he comes from the Upper City. Nobility slumming for souls." His gaze darts past my shoulder. "That's all I know. Take your paper and move along. People are watching."

I drift away, tucking the paper under my arm. The boy's warning buzzes in my ears. *People are watching.* Not the city guards, who barely patrol these streets. Another force hunts here. Eyes that report to hidden masters. The darkness has spread deeper through Luridian's layers than even Mother Superior realized.

The textile district lies three streets east. I navigate narrow alleys where sunlight never reaches the ground. Rats scurry from my footsteps, their claws scratching over stone. Water drips from overhangs, black with filth from upper stories. The stench intensifies here. Human waste and chemical dyes create an almost solid presence on my skin.

Tanner. Liora's mother works the looms here. I find myself seeking her not just for intelligence but to see the face that might reflect her daughter's features. To understand the root from which Liora's strength grows. The mission and more personal desires intertwine within my chest, creating tension where clarity once ruled.

The textile factory rises before me, a smoke-belching monstrosity that devours light and spits darkness. Workers stream through narrow doors, their shifts changing with the bells. Women mostly, with arms thin but strong from pulling threads and lifting bolts of cloth. Their faces wear the same tired resignation I've seen in every kingdom I've visited. The poor remain the same, only the architecture crushing them changes.

I join the flow, allowing bodies to carry me inside. The noise hits me first. Hundreds of looms clacking in perfect rhythm. Voices shouting over the din. Overseers barking orders that turn workers into extensions of the machines. Then the smell reaches me. Chemical dyes burn my nostrils. Sweat from bodies working beyond endurance. Dust and fiber fill lungs until they surrender.

I move along the walls, watching faces, searching for one that might carry Liora's features. The shared bone structure of the family. The curve of a cheek or the angle of a brow that my fingers have memorized while she dressed my hair.

Why does her face come to me so clearly now? These thoughts serve no divine calling, yet I cannot banish them.

The name reaches me first, shouted across the room by an overseer with a face like spoiled meat.

"Tanner! Station seven needs more thread!"

My eyes track the call to a woman moving between looms. Small, like Liora, but bent with years of labor. Her hands move with swift practiced movements, delivering spools where needed. She pushes graying hair from her face with a gesture so similar to Liora's that a cold fist grips my heart. The family resemblance burns through years of hard work etched into her skin.

I wait until she moves toward a side room where supplies are stored. No one notices another body slipping through the door behind her. The small room offers brief respite from the factory's roar. Shelves lined with thread spools and mechanical parts surround us. I pull the door closed, reducing the noise to a distant rumble.

She turns, startled by unexpected company. Her eyes widen with brief fear before hardening into the wariness of someone long accustomed to life's cruelties.

"I don't know you." Her voice carries the same accent as Liora's, but rougher, worn by years of shouting over machinery.

"I'm looking for information about your son."

Her body stiffens like a rabbit sensing a predator. "Daven's been gone for too long. There's nothing to tell that ain't been told a hundred times."

"I know about the meetings. The golden eyes. The changes before he disappeared."

Bitterness twists her mouth. "Then you know more than the city guard cared to learn." Her eyes narrow. "Who are you? Another cultist come to promise I'll see him again if I just attend your gatherings?"

"No. Someone looking to end the disappearances." The mission's words come automatically, but an unexpected addition follows. "Someone who promised Liora I would search for answers."

Her expression changes at her daughter's name, suspicion mixing with surprise. "You know my Liora?"

The question requires care. "She serves in my household. She speaks often of her brother."

Mrs. Tanner's shoulders relax slightly. "That girl refuses to give up hope. Still believes her brother could be found." A sad smile touches her lips. "Always was stubborn, even as a child."

An emotion in her description of Liora creates an unfamiliar heat in my chest. I force my focus back to the hunt.

"She gets that from you, I think." The words emerge without planning, too personal for the conversation but true nonetheless.

Mrs. Tanner studies me with eyes that hold Liora's perceptiveness under years of harder living. "You care for her." It's not a question.

"She serves me well." The deflection sounds hollow even to my ears.

"That's not what I meant." She steps closer, voice dropping. "I see how you speak of her. How your face changes when you say her name. Be careful with my girl's heart, my lady. It's already been bruised by loss."

The warning hits like cold water. My disguise should be flawless, yet this factory woman sees through it to feelings I've barely acknowledged myself.

"I would never intentionally—" I stop, unsure how to finish. Never intentionally what? Hurt her? Too late. My very presence in her life is built on deception. Love her? The word feels foreign in my mind, yet it fits too well around the shape of what grows between us.

"Intentions matter less than actions," Mrs. Tanner says, not unkindly. "Liora sees the best in people. Always has. She'll give her whole heart without realizing it's happening, and by then it's too late to take it back."

I think of last night, the way Liora's hands lingered in my hair, the weight of unspoken things between us. "Perhaps it's already too late."

An emotion in my voice must convince her, because her expression softens. "Then be worthy of it. That's all any mother can ask."

She turns back to her work, effectively dismissing me. But as I reach the door, she calls out one last time.

"My lady?"

I pause without turning.

"Daven used to meet them near the old Teller's Bridge. Third night of each week, when the moon was dark. The gatherings might still happen there."

Information freely given, a mother's blessing in the form of intelligence. I nod once and slip away, carrying the weight of her trust alongside my mission's burden.

"What happened to Daven before he disappeared?"

A long silence stretches between us. Factory noises press upon the door, demanding her return. Finally, she reaches under her collar, withdrawing a small cloth pouch on a leather cord.

"Found this in his room after he vanished." She unties the pouch, revealing a small obsidian stone carved with a symbol that makes my skin prickle with recognition. Seven stars around a central void. "He said a noble gave it to him. Said it would help him see beyond ordinary sight."

I resist the urge to touch it, remembering the medallion's fire in Blackthorne's collection. "Which noble?"

"Never said a name. Just called him 'the benefactor.'" She wraps the stone again, hiding it away within her clothes. "Daven changed after he started carrying it. Could see in darkness better than daylight. Said darkness sometimes moved when nothing cast them." Her voice breaks slightly. "His eyes started showing gold flecks. Like little stars appearing in the brown."

The description matches every account of early shadow influence. If the temple creature was indeed her son, my blade delivered the only mercy possible.

An unexpected thought intrudes. *What if Blackthorne's texts spoke truth? What if early corruption could be reversed?* The possibility that I might have killed Liora's brother unnecessarily sends cold tendrils crawling up my spine.

"Your daughter still searches for him."

Pride and grief battle in her expression. "That girl refuses to give up hope. Spends her coin on useless herbwomen and fortune tellers. Looking for any sign of him." Her eyes soften. "Got herself that position just to search among better classes. Thinks nobility might know details we don't."

She speaks truth I can't share. The knowledge would bring no comfort.

"Did Daven leave anything else behind? Notes about meeting places? Names of others who attended with him?"

She hesitates, then reaches into her pocket. "This address. Found it sewn into his jacket lining. Never showed the guards. Didn't trust them to care."

The paper slip bears an address near Teller's Bridge. The same area the paper boy mentioned. My hands accept it, memorizing the location before returning it.

"Don't go there alone." Her voice hardens with unexpected concern. "Others have tried. None returned."

"I can protect myself."

Her eyes move over me, seeing more than my disguise suggests she should. "Perhaps you can at that." The factory bell rings, demanding her return. "If you find anything... if you learn what happened to my boy..."

"I'll ensure Liora knows." The promise comes unbidden, driven by motives beyond mission parameters. Her gratitude cuts deeper than expected.

She nods once, a mother's grief momentarily overwhelmed by intent, then slips back into the factory's chaos. I follow moments later, moving past the current of bodies toward freedom and air that doesn't taste of chemicals and despair.

The journey back to Crescent Court passes in a blur of unwelcome thoughts. Liora's mother sees what trained assassins might miss, the way my carefully constructed walls crack when her daughter is near. If a factory worker can perceive it, who else might notice?

More concerning, do I care if they do?

The thought terrifies me more than any shadow cult or divine judgment. I've been shaped for death, honed into an instrument of holy intent. There's no room in such a life for gentle hands and honest hearts. No space for impossible things that might come true.

Yet as Crescent Court rises before me, I find myself eager to return. Not to the mission or the next phase of the hunt, but to her. To see if Liora's eyes still hold that mix of hope and fear I saw in the mirror last night.

17

HUNT

The address burns in my memory, but before I venture into the Lower City's dangers, practical matters demand attention.

Liora appears in my doorway carrying fresh bandages, her expression carefully neutral. "Your shoulder needs checking before you venture out again."

"I'm well enough." But I'm already moving to the chair, unable to refuse her care.

She works in silence at first, unwinding yesterday's dressing. Her touch pauses at the healing edges. "It's better. Whatever you did at the temple, your body fights it remarkably well."

"And you?" I watch her face in the mirror. "How do you fight what troubles you?"

Her hands still. Since our growing closeness, she's been quieter, watchful. "I tend the garden. Plant things that might help others someday." Her eyes meet mine in the glass. "My mother says healing work is just hope given form."

"Your mother sounds wise."

"She asked about you." Liora's voice drops. "Said the lady I serve seems kind. Said kindness is rarer than gold in noble houses."

The weight of her words, what her mother sees, what Liora herself sees, presses through my chest. "I'm not kind, Liora."

"No?" She secures the fresh bandage gracefully. "Then what do you call searching the city for answers about my brother?"

My throat tightens. "Practical. Your distress affects your work."

Her smile is sad and knowing. "Of course, my lady." She steps back, professional distance restored. "Will you need anything else before you go?"

You. Always you. "No. Thank you."

At the door, she pauses. "Be careful today. The lower districts... people vanish there even in daylight."

"I know how to handle myself."

"I know you do." Her grip tightens on the doorframe. "That's what worries me."

After she leaves, I dress for the hunt ahead. The address burns in my memory as I navigate toward the Lower City. My steps carry me northwest, toward where Teller's Bridge spans one of Luridian's narrower canals.

Guide me not just to finish my mission, but to bring peace to those deserving mercy. Does Liora deserve this truth? Or would knowledge only wound deeper?

The neighborhood deteriorates with each street. Empty windows, watching children, shadows that swallow light. The address leads to a narrow building wedged between a boarded tavern and an alley. The structure looks abandoned but my skin prickles with awareness. Someone uses this place regularly.

A crash from the alley freezes my blood. Voices drift toward me as three figures emerge from the building's hidden entrance. Two men flank a third between them, the center figure staggering like a puppet with tangled strings. Cultists bring another victim for their unholy ceremonies.

My hands twitch toward steel. The urge to strike burns hot through my skin, but patience serves the hunt better. These soldiers lead to generals. Knowing truth matters more than immediate blood.

The cultists never hear me coming.

I follow them through Lower City streets that stink of piss and desperation. Three of them. Robes hidden under common cloaks but the shadow-oil scent gives them away. That sweet-rot smell that clings to those who've touched what they shouldn't.

They duck into an alley. I count ten breaths, then follow.

The first one's taking a piss against the wall. Perfect.

My blade punches through his kidney. In and twist. His scream dies in a gurgle as I open his throat with the return stroke. Blood paints the alley wall. He drops, cock still in hand, piss mixing with the red pooling around him.

One.

"Marcus?" The second turns. Sees me. Sees his friend. His mouth opens.

My throwing knife fills it.

The blade enters under his tongue, travels up through palate, finds brain. His eyes cross trying to see what's killing him. I step in close, catch him as he falls. Lower him quiet to the stones.

Two.

The third is smarter. Already running.

I let him get twenty feet. Let him think escape is possible.

The knife takes him between shoulder blades. He goes down hard, face scraping stone. I walk over, taking my time. He's trying to crawl, legs not working right. Spine's probably nicked.

"Please," he gasps. Blood bubbles from his mouth. "Please, I have children—"

I put my boot on the knife hilt and push. Feel it grind through vertebrae. He stops talking. Stops moving. Stops.

Three.

I retrieve my blades. Wipe them on their robes. The entrance they were heading for is obvious now. A grate in the alley floor, bars bent wide enough for a body to squeeze through. The metal's etched with symbols that hurt to look at.

The leader was carrying something. I search his body, finding a leather pouch tucked inside his robes. Inside, folded documents bear Blackthorne's seal.

I unfold them in the dim alley light. A registry of names, dates, stages of transformation. My eyes scan the list until they freeze on one entry.

Daven Tanner. Age 19. Stage Three. Serving as guardian at eastern temple.

The words blur as understanding crashes through me. Liora's brother, not just taken but transformed. Made into one of those golden-eyed creatures I've already encountered. My throat tightens with the weight of knowledge I can never share.

Voices echo, more cultists alerted by their missing brothers. I pocket the documents and fade into the shadows, leaving three corpses to tell their own story.

The return to Crescent Court takes indirect paths through sleeping streets. Each step carries the burden of truth. Liora searches for a brother who no longer exists in any form she would recognize. The creature he became might already be dead by my blade, or still haunts some darkened temple, waiting.

A dark ritual network runs deeper than expected. The cult's ceremonies continue across lunar phases, maintaining ongoing recruitment and transformation. Those showing sensitivity receive tokens that accelerate their claiming. The changed serve as guardians, their humanity surrendered to collective will.

Most concerning, someone believes I carry natural affinity for shadow. My invitation into inner circles comes not merely from attraction but recognition of supposed shared nature.

*Did Mother Superior know? Did she select me for sensitivity she recognized but never named?

Crescent Court welcomes me with appropriate silence. I enter through the servant's passage, moving with a ghost's stealth to my chambers.

Liora.

The name resonates differently now. Her brother transforms from abstract concept to flesh-and-blood tragedy. The thought creates an unfamiliar ache.

I kneel before my weapons laid out on black cloth, tracing Mordreth's symbol across my chest. "Through shadow we see truth. Through blood we honor the covenant." The trusted prayer feels hollow where it once rang with certainty.

Let my blade bring true mercy, whether through death or knowledge that prevents unnecessary killing. Let me understand what separates our sacred shadow from their corruption. Let me bring Liora peace, not merely vengeance.

The mission remains clear, yet somehow changed. Not just Mordreth's will made manifest through my hand, but complexity, with Liora's gentle presence woven through its sacred calling.

Tomorrow brings answers, perhaps. Tonight brings questions that burn through my skin, heated not just by sacred calling but by the unexpected desire to bring genuine peace to eyes that have shown me only kindness.

18

—·—

RITUAL

T he night after the gallery attack pulls me back to the abandoned temple. Blackthorne's words about a ceremony haunt my thoughts, and I must witness what darkness he orchestrates in shadow. My wounds protest each movement, but the mission demands intelligence before judgment.

Inside the temple, darkness wraps around me like a comfortable cloak. The air grows heavier with each step, carrying blood scent mingled with corrupted incense and ritual herbs. I taste the sweet undercurrent of transformation on my tongue, metallic yet somehow enticing.

My recent surveillance has revealed Blackthorne's pattern. His ceremonies grow in power with each lunar phase, building toward a convergence when the moon hangs full again.

Guide my steps through shadows others fear to walk.

Voices drift through narrow passages. Aristocratic tones echo off walls never meant for such sounds. I press into the cold stone, letting darkness embrace me until my pulse slows to a hunting rhythm.

The ritual chamber spreads before me as I peer through a collapsed section of wall. Seven black pillars rise toward a ceiling hidden in shadow. Torches cast inconstant light that reveals the chamber's central feature. An obsidian altar carved with the Void Crown constellation stands at the center, the exact pattern I saw within Blackthorne's private collection.

Robed figures surround the altar while three initiates kneel before it. Each person showcases a different stage of the shadow's ravaging of mortal form.

The first appears mostly human. A young woman with honey-blonde hair trembles with anticipation rather than fear. Golden flecks spark within otherwise ordinary eyes. Her face tugs at my memory. I recognize her from one of the gatherings where nobles pretend at ordinary society. Her youth strikes me unexpectedly. She can't be much older than I was during my first offering to Mordreth.

The second has progressed further into defilement, with hands unnaturally long under skin that absorbs light rather than reflects it. Her eyes have transformed to liquid gold with vertical pupils.

The third barely retains human shape, a form caught between worlds with bones visible through midnight skin that ripples with strange patterns. Only occasional shudders suggest anything human remains inside the unholy vessel.

A tall figure enters from a side passage. Despite his elaborate mask, I recognize Blackthorne immediately from the controlled power in his stride.

"Tonight we strengthen our connection to the shadow's blessing." His voice fills the chamber with commanding authority. "These chosen ones demonstrate the path we walk together."

He approaches the first initiate, placing his hand upon her head with unsettling gentleness. "Amara receives her blessing beautifully. The shadow already recognizes her natural affinity."

Pride warms his voice as he speaks to watching cultists. "She will advance further when the shadow grows stronger."

I feel my stomach tighten at how recently this girl entered his web. Her trembling doesn't come from fear but from excitement. She believes she's been chosen for magnificence.

I need a better vantage point. My body flows through shadow toward an observation chamber connected to the main ritual space. From behind a partially collapsed wall, I see what remained hidden before. A small altar stands apart from the main ceremony with items arranged in ritual care. I see herbs bound with silver thread, gleaming crystals that catch torchlight at specific angles, and vials filled with liquids that shimmer with internal radiance.

My pulse quickens. I recognize these components from the Raven's Tongue manuscript. The cultists possess ancient knowledge that might undo early shadow possession. They maintain the means to reverse the unholy claiming of human vessels.

Ice spreads through my veins with unwelcome revelation. If reversal exists, why have we condemned so many souls unnecessarily? Brother Elias met his end by my blade for the same affliction now beginning in this young woman's gaze.

My hands remain certain when my heart falters.

This thought brings no comfort. If Mother Superior knows of these reversal possibilities and chooses to withhold them, what aims does such secrecy serve?

Blackthorne moves to the second initiate. "Elise continues her journey toward perfection." He gestures to her altered hands. "The shadow reshapes her body to receive its gifts."

He traces the air above her head. "Transformation brings pain, but her sacrifice leads to greater ends."

The words burn in my ears with unwelcome recognition. His phrases echo Sisterhood teachings about divine trials. His corruption mimicking true devotion creates a more perfect blasphemy.

I study his expression as he examines the initiate's changing form. Under the ceremonial performance, I glimpse genuine intellectual curiosity. His eyes catalog every detail with researcher's care, his hands occasionally noting observations in a small journal. Power hunger drives him, but so does scholarly fascination.

The third figure sits motionless under Blackthorne's touch. "Korvin nears completion." A note like genuine sorrow colors his voice. "Three cycles of the moon since his first blessing. Soon, his journey reaches its culmination."

My eyes linger on what remains of Korvin. Once a man, now a vessel for the unholy. His shudders come at irregular intervals, like someone fighting for control of their own body and losing.

Two cultists speak near my hiding place, unaware of hunter's ears trained to catch whispers.

"This ain't what they promised us," one whispers. "Thought we'd control the shadows, not the other way around."

"Depends on the person," the second murmurs. "Some fight it better than others. Poor Korvin's still in there somewhere, watching through eyes that ain't his anymore."

"What happens when they're... fully changed?"

"Still conscious. Trapped inside while the shadow pulls the strings. Like being buried alive in your own flesh."

Horror prickles across my skin. Consciousness persists after transformation. The transformed become prisoners within their own desecrated bodies.

I finally understand why my blade offers true mercy. Death frees souls from bondage within twisted flesh. Yet the young woman, Amara, still stands at the threshold of corruption. Her desecration has barely begun. The possibility of reversal changes everything.

Focus. Judgment comes through intent, not distraction.

The ritual continues with sickening clarity. Their chants pervert the prayers I learned at Mother Superior's knee. Blood spills in patterns that mirror our execution ceremonies. Each desecration sends anger burning through my veins.

When the ceremony concludes, Blackthorne removes his mask. Sweat glistens on his forehead from channeling energies beyond his comprehension.

"Our preparations advance as expected," he tells a lieutenant whose robe bears markings of higher rank. "Our enemies would stop us if they understood what approaches."

"The church increases patrols," the lieutenant replies. "Many have noticed the disappearances."

"They suspect common criminality," Blackthorne says with a dismissive wave. "Nothing more. Their priests can't conceive of true transcendence."

The gathering disperses swiftly. I remain motionless within shadow until silence confirms opportunity. The main chamber stands empty, yet sounds from nearby corridors suggest twisted sentinels patrol.

The side altar contains the ritual components I've sought since discovering the possibility of reversal in Blackthorne's texts. I examine each element carefully. Crushed obsidian powder arranged in exact measurements, vials of quicksilver mixed with darker liquid, and most crucially, a binding agent created from distilled moonlight caught in crystal.

I discover a journal containing fragmentary notes on theoretical reversal attempts, mostly failed experiments and desperate speculation rather than proven methods. These notes suggest a four-week threshold, confirming my suspicions.

The young woman Amara might still be saved with this knowledge.

I feel an unusual urge to help her, a sensation entirely separate from my mission. The possibility of saving rather than ending life stirs dormant instincts within me.

I must find where the twisted ones wait. The passage narrows as I progress, forcing my body lower. The air grows thick with the cloying scent of defilement.

The chamber door seals behind me. Seven figures emerge from shadow. Not men anymore. Haven't been for months. Their golden eyes track me with predator focus.

Seven of them. One of me. The Sisterhood would call these good odds.

The first one moves weirdly. Shoulders rotating backward. Spine bending like rope. It crosses twenty feet in a heartbeat, claws already swinging for my throat.

I drop. Roll. Come up with steel moving.

The blade catches it mid-leap. Momentum does the work. It splits from groin to sternum, organs spilling like party favors. Black blood hits my face, tastes like copper and ash.

Six.

Two more rush while their brother's still falling. They move together, practiced. Hunting pack tactics. One high, one low. Trying to bracket me.

I throw myself backward. My back cracks against stone but I'm already rolling. Claws spark against floor where my head was. I come up between them, both blades working.

Left blade hamstrings the first. Right blade opens the second's throat.

The hamstrung one drops, leg folding wrong. I stomp its skull on the way past. Bone gives way like eggs under boots. Brain matter splatters, gray and black and moving.

Four.

Pain explodes across my back. Claws rake spine to shoulder blade. Leather parts. Skin follows. I can feel air on exposed muscle.

I spin, blade extended. It takes the creature's arm off at the elbow. The limb hits the floor, fingers still grasping. Black blood pumps from the stump in rhythmic spurts.

The thing doesn't scream. Just stares at where its arm used to be like it's confused.

I put steel through its face. The blade punches out the back of its skull with a wet pop. It drops, twitching.

Three.

My shoulder's wrong. Corruption from the wound spreads fast, black veins visible under torn skin. Every movement tears the wound wider. Blood runs down my back, pooling in my boots.

The remaining three circle. Learning. They've seen what direct assault costs.

One feints left. I pivot to track it.

Mistake.

The second hits me from behind. We go down hard, its weight crushing air from my lungs. Claws sink into my wounded shoulder. I scream. Can't help it. The pain whites out everything.

Teeth find my neck. I twist, offering shoulder instead. Fangs punch through leather and muscle. It locks on like a dog, shaking its head. Tearing.

My left arm goes numb. Blade drops from nerveless fingers. *Move or die here.*

I slam my head back. Connect with something soft. It loosens its bite, hissing. I roll, bringing my knee up hard. Feel ribs fold inward. It falls off me, clutching its chest.

I'm up. Right blade still in hand. Shoulder screaming. Left arm dead weight.

The third guardian flanks while I'm struggling to stand. Its claw takes meat from my thigh. I stumble. Nearly go down. *No. Not like this. Not to these things.*

The one I kicked is getting up. Ribs already healing. They all heal too fast. Need to make the damage stick.

Shadow-oil.

I fumble the vial one-handed. Upend it over my blade.

The flanking guardian strikes again. I let it come. Take the hit to get inside its reach. Claws puncture my side, sliding between ribs.

Worth it.

My blade finds its heart. The shadow-oil ignites corrupted flesh from within. Blue flame races through black veins. It screams, really screams, as holy fire consumes it from inside out. *Two.*

I rip my blade free, taking chunks of burning meat with it. The guardian collapses, body eating itself.

The one with healed ribs charges. No tactics now. Just rage.

I sidestep. Barely. My leg gives out mid-movement. We both go down, tangled. Its weight pins my sword arm. Claws find my throat.

Can't breathe. Vision graying.

My free hand finds my boot knife. Three inches of sharp mercy. I punch it through the thing's temple. Twist.

Bone crunches. Brain matter leaks. It goes limp.

I shove the corpse off. Gasp air that tastes of blood and shadow-oil. Everything hurts. Shoulder's dead. Leg won't hold weight. Blood pools beneath me, too much of it mine.

One left.

The final guardian stands ten feet away. Watching. It's different from the others. Older in its corruption. More complete in its transformation. It studies my wounds with intelligence the others lacked.

"Sisterhood," it says. The word comes out wrong through a throat not meant for speech. "Mother Superior sends another daughter to die."

It knows what I am. Who sent me. This thing was human enough to remember.

We stare at each other across blood-slicked stone. Predator and prey, though I'm no longer sure which is which.

It moves first. Not the stuttering rush of its brothers. Smoothly. Intently.

I raise my blade with my good arm. The shadow-oil has faded. Just steel now. Steel and whatever strength I have left.

We meet in the center of the chamber. Its claws catch my blade, metal screaming. We strain against each other, its strength against my training.

My wounded leg buckles. I go to one knee. It leans in, pressing advantage.

"You smell like her," it whispers. Breath hot on my face. "Like sister-blood. Like failure."

Rage gives me strength. I surge up, forehead cracking into its jaw. Teeth shatter. It staggers back.

I follow. Blade high. Swinging down with everything left.

The creature raises its arm to block. Steel meets corrupted flesh. And goes through.

Arm falls. Head follows.

The body stands for three heartbeats, confused. Then drops.

Zero.

I collapse beside it. Can't stand anymore. Blood loss makes the world soft at the edges. The shadow corruption spreads from multiple wounds, black veins mapping my skin like dark rivers.

Get up. Bandage the wounds. Find the reversal materials.

I crawl instead. Toward the altar where ritual components wait. Each movement costs. Blood trails behind me, marking my path in red.

The combat disturbs me. The creatures recognized me differently than they did their cultist handlers. The way their golden eyes tracked my movements held more than simple predatory focus. I sensed recognition in their gaze, as if shadow saw shadow.

Footsteps approach from the corridor. I force my body to move despite pain's protest, seeking exit beyond approaching cultists. A small archway reveals another passage, narrower and darker than those already explored.

The passage descends deeper under the temple. I find myself in a chamber unlike those above. A true sanctum buried under profane imitations. The ancient stone bears carvings predating the temple's construction. I recognize symbols of the original Void Crown, the Raven's Flight, and the Seven Aspects, all uncorrupted by church doctrine or cult manipulation.

A stone desk dominates the chamber's center. Papers and scrolls cover its surface, illuminated by a crystal that glows with internal light.

The maps spread across the desk show ritual sites throughout Luridian, positioned to create the Void Crown pattern across the city. Seven locations will host simultaneous ceremonies during the coming full moon ritual.

Other documents reveal Blackthorne's ultimate intent. The fully transformed will serve as doorways between the shadow realm and physical world. The gateways created during the ritual will allow passage from beyond mortal understanding.

My blood runs cold. This extends beyond individual corruption into threat to the world's structure itself. Blackthorne believes he controls this process, yet his own notes document unexpected developments beyond his comprehension.

A locked case yields to my blade. Inside lies a compendium of early-stage reversal attempts. The contents reveal desperate experiments rather than proven methods, with annotations documenting more failures than successes. The young woman Amara might still be saved, but these notes suggest significant risk.

The reversal ritual requires specific components in exact measures. Moonwater collected during waning phases, crystallized shadow-oil diluted with holy salt, and blood freely given by one with natural affinity. The proportions vary based on exposure duration, with efficacy dropping dramatically after the first lunar cycle.

So there is a window, small but real, when mercy might take forms beyond steel and death. The knowledge shatters everything I believed about Mordreth's will. If Mother Superior withheld this truth, what other mercy has been denied in favor of blood offerings?

My hands gather crucial pages despite growing weakness. The reversal attempts, ritual site maps, and ceremony details fold into a packet secured over my heart. My blood marks the paper, sanctifying knowledge with sacrifice.

My blood drips steadily onto the stone floor. My body feels increasingly distant as consciousness begins to fade. The wound at my shoulder pulses with each heartbeat, deeper than initially assessed. The claw wounds penetrated deeper than normal weapons would, creating a corruption that resists ordinary healing.

These wounds will take days to heal properly, but I can't afford such luxury. Blackthorne's convergence ritual comes soon.

Voices from the passage grow louder. My eyes search for another way out, finding a narrow opening partly hidden behind a fallen statue. The passage eventually opens to night air. Stars pierce velvet darkness overhead, watching my struggle with indifference.

City streets welcome me with empty silence. Each step requires separate will. Blood loss makes the world increasingly dreamlike, buildings wavering at the edges of my vision.

The packet of knowledge presses over my heart. My mind fills with what I learned. Transformation process. Reversal possibilities. Ritual sites marked for the coming ceremony.

Yet perfect knowledge now brings perfect doubt. My hands still serve judgment, but my heart questions its foundation. If the Sisterhood concealed reversal knowledge, does their judgment truly represent Mordreth's will?

Amara's young face flashes before my eyes. Still time to save her from transformation's horror.

Crescent Court appears through narrowing vision. Lights burn in upper windows despite the late hour. The sight sends unexpected warmth through my chest growing cold from blood loss.

My chamber door stands before me, salvation's promise behind solid wood. My hand reaches for the handle as dizziness threatens to overtake me.

As I push through the door, Liora's concerned face is the first thing I see, and relief washes over me.

19

VULNERABILITY

I wake to lavender and pain.

My consciousness returns slowly, revealing that I have lost two days to fever dreams and darkness while Blackthorne's plans progress unchecked. The scent of herbs reaches me first, their sweet fragrance mingling with the copper tang of blood.

My body awakens with steady pain, each heartbeat sending heat through the wound on my shoulder. The temple guardian's claw has left its mark in my flesh, a single deep gash rather than the scattered lacerations I anticipated in combat.

Painful, but not life-threatening.

Soft sheets cradle my battered form instead of cold stone. I recognize the weight of silk on my skin before my eyes even open, telling me I have reached Crescent Court safely. Despite all odds, I survived the temple.

When my eyelids finally part, golden morning light filters through partly drawn curtains. Movement at my bedside draws my focus. Liora rises from a chair, exhaustion etched in every line of her face. The sight of her eases the tension in my shoulders, her presence creating a moment of unexpected relief amid the pain.

"My lady." Her voice cracks. "You're awake."

Memory surges back with brutal clarity. The temple. The twisted guardians with golden eyes. My blades opening their corrupted flesh while black fluid sprayed across stone walls. The precious papers secured close to my heart as I dragged myself back through city streets, my blood marking each step of my journey.

I try to speak, but my throat feels lined with broken glass. She anticipates my need without being told, supporting my head with gentle hands as she brings water to my lips. The liquid slides down my throat, cool mercy over parched tissue.

Her touch trembles on my scalp, the slight vibration transferring into my skull. No one has ever touched me with such honest care, such naked concern. The sensation leaves me strangely defenseless.

"I found you collapsed outside your door." Fear makes her voice waver. "There was so much blood..."

I take inventory of my body without moving. Bandages wrap my shoulder and ribs, applied with skill. Pain pulses beneath clean linen with each heartbeat, the tempo slightly too fast, slightly too weak. My skin burns with lingering fever while my limbs feel weighted with stone.

"How long have I been unconscious?" The words scrape my throat raw.

"Two days." She fidgets with a bandage edge. "The fever broke last night. I thought—"

She doesn't finish, but I hear the words anyway. *I thought you wouldn't wake. I thought you would die.*

Two days wasted while corruption spreads through the city. Blackthorne moves closer to his goal with each hour I lie helpless.

My heart stumbles in its rhythm at the realization. Blackthorne's garden party approaches. My plan to draw him closer suddenly requires no pretense at all.

I push myself upward, ignoring how my vision splinters into fragments of light and shadow. Pain races through my shoulder like liquid fire, consuming thought and reason alike.

"The garden party," I gasp. "I must attend."

"Please don't." Liora's hands find my shoulders, surprisingly firm as she eases me back into the pillows. "You've lost too much blood. The corruption in this wound fights normal healing. You shouldn't even be conscious yet, let alone planning to attend an event."

"My body has endured worse," I insist, though the room still spins when I move too quickly. "I have medicines from the Sanctuary that will temporarily mask the worst symptoms. The opportunity is too important to miss."

Liora's face shows her disapproval. "Those kind of remedies always have a cost that comes later."

"A price I'm willing to pay," I whisper, the mission's urgency overriding my body's limitations.

Corruption.

The shadow-creatures' claws had carried darkness within them. The black fluid had burned cold on my skin, sinking deep into tissue. The memory makes me taste metal on my tongue.

"The papers." Panic surges through my weakened body. "From the temple. There was a packet..."

Relief softens her features. "Yes. Blood-stained but I found them." She retrieves a bundle from the bedside table. "I didn't read them, but I cleaned what I could."

The pages feel sacred under my fingertips. Knowledge worth every drop of spilled blood. My eyes find Liora's, studying her with new intensity. She found me wounded and bleeding. She tended injuries that would raise questions and said nothing. She preserved the documents rather than summoning authorities or serving her own curiosity.

"You didn't call for a healer." I measure each word carefully.

Her gaze drops to her hands, fingers twisting together in her lap. "I thought you might prefer discretion." A pause, weighted with meaning. "And I have experience with wounds. My father worked in the mines before he died."

Not the complete truth. I recognize the shape of partial honesty from years crafting my own. Yet her evasion feels different from deliberate deception, protection rather than manipulation.

"Thank you." The gratitude is genuine. "For your care. And your silence."

Her smile warms the coldness inside my chest, her presence stirring feelings I dare not name. "Rest now. I'll bring broth shortly to help restore your strength."

When she leaves, I force myself to examine the temple intelligence despite my vision swimming with each movement. The papers contain everything I risked my life to obtain. Ritual sites marked across Luridian in the Void Crown pattern, confirmation of Blackthorne's final ceremony during the approaching full moon, and disturbing details of the transformation process.

These are the pieces Mother Superior never revealed. The true scope of his blasphemy goes beyond individual corruption to the very fabric between worlds.

The door opens, Liora returning with a tray balanced carefully. Steam rises from a simple bowl, carrying the scent of chicken broth mixed with healing herbs. My stomach contracts with sudden, sharp hunger that reminds me how animal our needs remain despite sacred purpose.

She helps me sit upright, her touch gentle over my inflamed skin. The broth slides down my throat, each swallow returning a fraction of strength to my depleted body. The simple nourishment feels more sacred than communion wine after a kill.

"Lord Hargrove called twice inquiring after your health," she says as I eat. "I told him you suffered a mild fever and needed rest."

"And Blackthorne?" The question escapes before I can contain it.

Careless. Too eager. Remember your training.

Her eyes sharpen with suspicion. "A messenger brought this yesterday."

She retrieves an envelope sealed with black wax bearing the raven symbol I've seen throughout his collection. The sight sends a chill through me despite the warm broth in my belly.

I break the seal, unfolding heavy paper that carries his scent that makes my skin tingle traitorously.

Lady Ravencrest,

Your presence has been missed these past weeks. I trust your health improves swiftly. The royal garden party provides a perfect opportunity for your return to society. I shall look for you among the roses.

Until then, RB

A small obsidian disk falls from the envelope. The same symbol from the medallion in his collection, seven stars surrounding a central void. I tremble slightly as I lift it, the stone feeling unnaturally cool on my skin, drinking heat rather than reflecting it.

"What is it?" Liora eyes the token with unexpected wariness.

"An invitation." I set it on the bedside table. "To the royal garden party."

Her face pales visibly. "You can't seriously intend to attend. Your wounds. You're in no condition—"

"Will not prevent me from keeping this appointment." My voice hardens with purpose. "The mission proceeds despite my flesh's weakness."

The words slip out unintended. I watch understanding dawn in her eyes, another piece of the puzzle that is Lady Ravencrest clicking into place. Not just a wealthy widow with unusual interests, but more than a widow.

"May I speak plainly, my lady?" Her tone captures my attention. Fear mingled with resolve.

I nod once, curious what truth hides behind her careful facade.

"These gatherings... people from the Lower City have vanished after attending similar events. My brother included." Her fingers twist together in her lap, knuckles whitening. "The servants whisper about them. How guests arrive but fewer leave. How some who return seem... changed."

The shadow corruption. Blackthorne selects those with sensitivity from all social strata. He tests sacred blood across class boundaries.

"All the more reason I must attend," I say. "I may learn what might help us understand what happened to Daven."

Hope brightens her eyes, the emotion so fierce it burns on my skin. "Do you truly think so?"

I can't tell her everything.

I can't destroy the fragile hope she still carries.

I can't burden her with knowledge that would shatter her completely. That I may have delivered mercy to what remained of her brother with my own blade.

"I don't know." The half-truth tastes bitter on my tongue. "I found mentions of their methods for selection and transformation." I weigh truth versus comfort. "They believe early stages can be reversed within the first lunar cycle, but after that..."

"Reversed?" Her hands still on my bandage, hope and confusion warring across her features. "The private journal I found in Daven's room mentioned cleansing rituals. He wrote about cleansing rituals performed at specific moon phases."

She moves to a small pouch at her waist, withdrawing a folded paper. "He drew this symbol repeatedly in his final entries. It appeared in his eyes sometimes, he wrote, reflected when he looked in mirrors."

The paper reveals a seven-pointed star drawn with fevered exactness, matching the Void Crown constellation.

"Daven is far beyond that window, Liora." My voice softens with genuine regret. "But others might still be helped if we act quickly enough. And this symbol might help us understand what happened to him."

Liora's face transforms, emotions chasing across her features too quickly to name. Hope. Fear. Disbelief. Then raw pain that leaves her cheeks wet with tears she doesn't seem to notice.

Air freezes in her lungs. A small sound escapes her throat, not quite a sob. Then control reasserts itself, a resilience that mirrors my own training though born from different soil.

"But others might still be helped," she whispers.

"If we reach them in time." I leave the statement deliberately vague. "If we stop Blackthorne before his final ceremony."

If I deliver judgment as ordained, though not with the mercy she imagines.

The afternoon passes in careful preparation for the garden party. Liora helps me bathe, her touch gentle around bandaged wounds. The water stings where it finds broken skin, but the pain grounds me, reminds me of purpose and sacrifice.

She applies my make-up skillfully, creating color in my skin drained by blood loss, disguising weakness under careful artifice. She moves through my hair with quiet care, arranging dark strands to frame my features. Every touch contains softness I've never known in the harsh handling of the Sisterhood.

This gentleness should frighten me. I was taught that softness creates weakness. Yet her care strengthens me in ways I never expected.

The sage-blue gown she selects slips over my body, silk cool on heated flesh. Silver embroidery catches light like stars scattered across a twilight sky. The design allows for movement despite its elegant appearance, a battle garment disguised as aristocratic display.

"You look beautiful." Liora's voice carries genuine appreciation. "Though I still wish you wouldn't attend."

"Some obligations can't be avoided." I secure a knife to my thigh smoothly, the steel hidden beneath layers of silk. A poor substitute for my usual arsenal, but better than facing darkness unarmed. "No matter the personal cost."

"The carriage arrives soon." She straightens the gown's folds with care. "Lord Hargrove arranged it upon learning you recovered sufficiently to attend."

"Be careful tonight." Her voice lowers, weighted with genuine concern. "Whatever Lord Blackthorne offers, remember that beauty often disguises poison."

The warning touches rawness within me. My hand reaches out, brushing her cheek with gentleness. Her skin feels warm to mine, alive with simple humanity untouched by the shadow's taint.

"I understand poison better than most."

I am poison in its most refined form.

She leans almost imperceptibly into my touch, eyes closing briefly before they open to meet mine with startling directness. An unspoken truth passes between us at that moment. For one heartbeat, the space separating servant from mistress, hunter from innocent, collapses to nothing.

Then reality comes crashing back. She steps away, proper distance restored.

The evening finds me restless despite my weakened state. Each attempt to rest brings visions of the garden party, of Blackthorne's storm-gray eyes and the choices that await me in shadows and moonlight.

The garden calls to me with promise of space and air untainted by the chamber's close walls. Liora walks beside me, her presence both comforting and confusing after our closeness over the forbidden texts.

The night garden embraces us with cool air and the scent of roses. Moonlight transforms garden paths into a magical realm, shadows dancing between silver-touched leaves. We walk without speaking at first, but the silence feels full rather than empty.

"You were different today," Liora observes quietly. "When we studied those documents. More... present."

"Present?" I glance at her, noting how moonlight catches in her hair.

"Usually you're here but also somewhere else. Like part of you is always calculating, planning, preparing for danger." She pauses by a stone bench, hand trailing over its surface. "Today you were just with me."

The accuracy of her observation steals my prepared deflection. "You see too much."

"Or perhaps others see too little." She sits, patting the space beside her in invitation. "Will you tell me what weighs on you so heavily? Sometimes sharing a burden makes it lighter."

I sink onto the bench, careful to maintain proper distance even as every fiber of my being wants to close the gap. "If I could tell anyone, it would be you."

"But you can't." No accusation in her voice, just understanding. "There are things about you that don't fit, my lady. Calluses where a noblewoman wouldn't have them. The way you check every room's exits. How you hold yourself like someone expecting attack."

My heart skips. "And yet you say nothing to anyone."

"I told you when we met that I keep secrets." She turns to face me fully, moonlight turning her eyes to molten amber. "I don't need to know your truths. I just need to know if I can trust what's between us."

"Liora..." How do I answer that? How do I tell her that what's between us is the only true thing in my life of lies?

"I know our stations make this impossible," she continues before I can form words. "I know I'm foolish to even speak of it. But when you look at me, when you touch my hand, when you say my name like it's precious..." Her voice breaks slightly. "Is that real? Or am I simply another part of whatever role you're playing?"

The pain in her voice shatters my composure. I shift closer, taking her hands in mine despite every warning screaming in my head.

"It's the most real thing I've ever felt." The admission burns my throat. "You're not part of any role. If anything, you're the reason I'm forgetting how to play it."

Her hands tremble in mine. "Then why do I feel like I'm losing you to forces I can't see or fight?"

Because you are. Because in days or weeks, Blackthorne will be dead and I'll return to the Sanctuary, leaving Lady Ravencrest and everything she represents behind. The thought sends pain lancing through my chest.

"I wish I could promise you forever," I whisper. "I wish I could be the woman you deserve, someone simple and true, who could love you openly without shadows or secrets."

"I don't want simple." Her hands tighten on mine. "I want you, exactly as you are. Shadows, secrets, and all."

"You don't know what you're saying." My voice roughens with emotion. "I'm not... I've done things. I will do things. I'm not the gentle lady you think you see."

"No," she agrees. "You're a warrior wearing silk instead of armor. And I care for you more than I should, more than makes sense."

The words hang between us, weighted with meaning I'm not ready to name. My heart pounds so hard I'm certain she must hear it.

"You shouldn't," I breathe. "Liora, you shouldn't feel this way about me."

"Too late." A sad smile touches her lips. "I think I've been falling these past weeks, since you first looked at me like I was worth seeing. Like I was more than just hands to dress you and fix your hair."

"You are." The words tumble out desperate and true. "You're everything bright and good and real in a life full of darkness and deception. You're..." I stop, overwhelmed by the magnitude of what she's becoming to me.

"I'm what?" she prompts gently.

"Home," I whisper. "You're home in a way no place has ever been."

She makes a sound between a laugh and sob, pulling one hand free to cup my cheek. "Then stay. Whatever you're planning, wherever you think you have to go, stay with me instead."

The offer hangs between us, beautiful and impossible as moonlight on water. For a moment, I let myself imagine it.

Throwing off duty and destiny, choosing love over purpose. Building that small house by the sea she spoke of, tending gardens without walls, growing old beside her.

"I want to," I admit, leaning into her touch. "More than I've ever wanted anything."

"But?"

"But wanting isn't enough to change what I am." I turn my head to press a kiss to her palm, feeling her shiver. "There are chains on me you can't see, duties that bind tighter than any rope."

"Then let me help you break them."

"You can't. No one can." I pull back enough to meet her eyes. "But you've already helped more than you know. You've shown me what it feels like to be human instead of weapon. To be woman instead of instrument. Even if I can't keep it, I'll treasure knowing it was possible."

Tears track silver down her cheeks. "That sounds like good-bye."

"Not yet." I brush away her tears with my thumbs, cradling her face. "Not tonight. We still have time."

"How much?"

"I don't know." The honesty burns. "But whatever we have, I want to spend it memorizing you. The way your eyes change color in different light. How you hum when you think no one's listening. The way you see beauty in shadows where others see only darkness."

She laughs wetly. "That's because you taught me to look properly."

"No." I shake my head. "You always saw clearly. You just helped me remember how."

We sit in silence for a moment, hands entwined, breathing the same night air. Then, slowly, she leans closer.

"May I?" she whispers.

I know I should say no. Should maintain what little distance remains. Instead, I close the gap between us.

Our lips meet soft and careful, nothing like the passionate collision I expected. This is tender, almost reverent, a question and answer and promise all at once. Her mouth is warm on mine, tasting of mint tea and possibility.

When we part, we're both trembling.

"Whatever happens," she whispers over my lips, "remember this. Remember us."

"Always," I promise, knowing it's both truth and lie. Whatever the Raven's Kiss takes from me, this moment will burn bright in my memory until my final breath.

The carriage arrives punctually. My body protests each movement as I descend the stairs, weakness making every step a separate victory over gravity. Liora walks beside me, close enough to offer support disguised as companionship.

"Return safely." Her touch lingers at my cloak's fastenings, the contact conveying more than words. "They say strange things happen in those gardens after dark."

"I shall." The promise tastes true despite the danger that awaits. "Wait for me, no matter how late I return."

"Always." A single word weighted with so much meaning.

Why does that word feel like a vow neither of us fully understands?

20

— · —

GARDEN

Two months since arrival. The Midnight Festival fills Luridian's streets. The moon waxes toward fullness. Time grows short.

The journey passes in measured silence, each turn of the wheels bringing me closer to danger. Through the carriage windows, I glimpse festival crowds spilling from side streets. Revelers in masks and flowing robes, their laughter echoing off stone walls. Yet among the celebration, I catch glimpses of more purposeful movement. A hooded figure whispers to a young woman beside a fountain, slipping a token into her palm before melting back into the crowd. Two men I recognize from my Lower City surveillance guide a stumbling drunk toward a narrow alley.

Even during celebration, the shadow cult continues its recruitment. How many souls will they claim tonight while the city dances?

The royal gardens rise before the darkening sky, paths illuminated by lanterns that create pools of golden light amid deepening gloom. Nobles in finery stroll between flowering hedges and marble statues, their laughter carrying on the evening breeze.

Each step from the carriage sends fresh agony through my wounded shoulder, but I force my back straight, my expression composed. Weakness becomes a weapon tonight. Vulnerability transforms to bait.

My arrival draws expected attention, whispers following my path through the gardens. Lady Ravencrest, recovered from a mysterious fever. The widow whose grace and mystery have captured Lord Blackthorne's interest. Each gaze carries speculation I encourage with subtle performance, allowing my steps to falter slightly, my complexion to remain paler than usual under cosmetics.

The aristocracy plays at hunting, but they've never tasted true predation. Their gossip marks me as Blackthorne's potential conquest while I sharpen judgment's edge.

I find a stone bench near a reflecting pool where moonlight creates silver patterns on dark water. The perfect location for a wounded prey awaiting her hunter.

Conversation flows around me in currents of gossip and intrigue. I listen without appearing to hear, gathering intelligence while seeming lost in contemplation of night-blooming flowers. Mentions of Blackthorne surface repeatedly, his name carrying weight that stills other topics when spoken.

A servant passes close to my bench, balancing a tray of wine glasses. His whispered words to a companion drift to my trained ears. "Three nights until the grand ascension. Master says all preparations must be complete by then."

My pulse quickens. Three nights. That aligns with the full moon. Blackthorne's ultimate ritual approaches faster than anticipated.

"He's arrived," a countess murmurs to her companion as they pass. "Just returned from his estate. They say he conducts strange experiments there. Things the church would burn him for if they knew."

Near the garden's edge, a small commotion draws my attention. A child, perhaps eight years old, stands beside an ornate rose bush while two adults speak in low tones. Even from this distance, I can see the telltale golden flecks beginning to appear in the boy's eyes, early shadow corruption taking hold. One of the adults places a gentle hand on the child's shoulder, guiding him toward a side exit with the practiced ease of someone who has done this many times before.

They recruit children. The shadow cult's reach extends even to the innocent.

I adjust my position slightly, allowing discomfort to show in the careful way I hold my injured shoulder. Not obvious enough to draw concern, but visible to those seeking signs of weakness.

"Lady Ravencrest." His voice reaches me before I glimpse him approaching. Deep and cultured, with that undertone of genuine passion that makes him more dangerous than mere ambition would. "Your presence graces our gathering after your unfortunate illness."

Blackthorne stands before me like darkness given form, dressed in black formal attire that makes him appear carved from midnight itself. The silver at his temples catches moonlight, creating a crown of frost upon dark hair. Those storm-gray eyes with their rings of darkness study me with an intensity that makes my skin prickle.

"Lord Blackthorne." I offer my hand. "Your concern honors me."

He takes my hand, and this time the kiss he presses to my knuckles sears like a brand. His lips linger, breath heated against my skin as he murmurs, "I was... concerned when you didn't respond to my messages. Illness can be particularly dangerous when it strikes those we've grown fond of."

The admission hangs between us, weighted with meaning. His thumb traces the delicate bones of my hand before releasing me, the gesture possessive despite its brevity.

"You appear somewhat pale still." His gaze moves over my face with scrutiny too intense to be merely courteous. "The night air might restore some color to your cheeks. Walk with me?"

It's phrased as a question but delivered as a command. The other nobles have noticed our interaction, creating a bubble of space around us as if his mere presence generates a force field.

"I would enjoy that." I allow a slight tremor in my voice, vulnerability displayed like bait. "The gardens are said to be particularly beautiful by moonlight."

"Everything is more beautiful by moonlight." His eyes never leave mine as he offers his arm. "Shadows reveal what daylight conceals."

I place my hand upon his offered arm with apparent hesitation, ensuring my hand trembles slightly on the fine fabric of his jacket. Heat radiates through the material, his body unnaturally warm despite the evening's growing chill.

We walk along carefully tended paths that wind between flowering hedges. As we move deeper into the gardens, I notice more familiar faces among the guests. Guards from the warehouse raid, their civilian clothes failing to disguise their military bearing. They position themselves at key places throughout the gathering, watching specific nobles with predatory attention.

Blackthorne's network extends into the highest levels of society. Tonight serves as more than mere entertainment.

"The garden proves far more pleasant than my sickroom," I say, changing the subject gracefully. I let my steps falter slightly, creating an opportunity for his hand to cover mine where it rests upon his arm.

"You've made quite an impression in Luridian society." His thumb traces small circles on the back of my hand. Each movement sends heat spiraling through my blood. "For someone so recently arrived from Valmeria."

Already testing for inconsistencies in my story. He suspects what I've shown.

The irony doesn't escape me. Blackthorne believes my shadow affinity springs from ancient bloodlines, never suspecting it flows from years of Sisterhood training. Mordreth's blessing manifests in ways that mimic inherited power. Let him see what he expects to see.

We reach a secluded section of the garden where roses bloom with unnatural vibrancy under moonlight. Their petals unfurl in slow, sensuous movements, releasing fragrance that fills my lungs with sweetness that borders on intoxication. The scent reminds me of the corrupted incense at the temple, beauty masking darker desires.

"These specimens come from Nocthys borderlands." His voice drops to that teaching cadence that transforms him from noble to scholar. "They bloom only under moonlight, storing its energy in patterns visible only to certain eyes."

He moves behind me, not quite touching but close enough that I feel the heat radiating from his body. "Can you see it? The faint luminescence along the veins of each petal?"

I follow his gesture toward a particularly large bloom whose deep crimson petals appear almost black in the moonlight. For a moment, nothing seems unusual. Then my vision shifts somehow, clarity emerging from shadow. Lines of silver light trace delicate patterns through each petal, creating constellations in miniature.

"Yes." The admission feels dangerous. "They're beautiful."

A test. I've revealed what he suspected.

Satisfaction transforms his features. "Most can't perceive it without significant exposure to void essence. Your natural sensitivity must be quite exceptional."

The observation sends warning racing along the back of my neck. He sees too much, knows too much about what I should keep hidden. My hand itches for the knife secured at my thigh, but I force it to remain calm on his arm.

"You speak as though such sensitivity serves a calling." I let confusion color my words, prey appearing unaware of the trap closing around it.

"Everything has a calling, Lady Ravencrest." He guides me toward a stone bench positioned between rose bushes, creating an alcove separated from the main garden. "Particularly gifts as rare as natural affinity for shadow magic."

We sit closer than propriety dictates, his thigh nearly touching mine through layers of silk and formal attire. The garden sounds recede around us, conversations and music growing distant as if we occupy another reality within this small space.

"You seem troubled tonight." His voice gentles.

His concern seems authentic despite everything I know about him. The contradiction makes him more dangerous, not less. My cue arrives with perfect timing. I allow my eyes to lower, my shoulders to curve slightly inward. The posture signals distress without the obviousness of tears or trembling hands. A performance of vulnerability that requires no artifice given my genuine condition.

"Disturbing dreams plagued my fever." I speak just above a whisper, forcing him to lean closer to hear. His scent fills my lungs with each breath. "Shadows that moved with form. Golden eyes watching from darkness."

His body stiffens beside mine, surprise momentarily overcoming his careful control. "You dreamed of the shadow realm?"

I look up, allowing confusion to show clearly on my face. "Is that what it was? I thought I was merely delirious from the fever."

His hand finds mine, enveloping my fingers in unnatural warmth. "Your illness was no ordinary fever, was it?"

He believes he's uncovering my secrets while I feed him carefully selected truths.

The question cuts closer to truth than he knows. I allow hesitation to precede my answer. "I don't understand."

"Forces touched you." His thumb traces my pulse point at the wrist, the contact uncomfortably intimate.

I pull my hand away, the movement both defensive and inviting in its vulnerability. "You speak of things beyond my understanding, Lord Blackthorne."

"Do I?" His eyes hold mine with intensity that makes my breath catch despite myself. "Or do I simply name what you've experienced but can't explain?"

His perception proves more dangerous than anticipated. I feel control of our exchange slipping, the hunter becoming the hunted. This requires a different form of vulnerability than I originally planned.

"The dreams terrified me." I allow genuine emotions to show through, fear remembered from the temple confrontation. "Creatures twisted beyond recognition. Darkness that breathed with intent. Golden eyes watching from shadows that shouldn't move."

His expression transforms with triumph wrapped in careful concern. "You've been touched by void essence. Recently and directly."

A partial victory I grant him deliberately.

I let an apparent realization dawn slowly across my features.

"The night before my illness..." I hesitate, as though struggling with memory. "I explored the Lower City, seeking local color for artistic inspiration. An alley... shapes moved that shouldn't have... then darkness."

"Yet you survived." Wonder colors his voice. "Untrained and unprepared, you encountered a void manifestation and lived to speak of it."

"I remember little after that moment." The lie flows easily. "Only waking with fever and wounds I can't explain."

His hand returns to mine, enfolding my fingers in his larger grasp. "You've been blessed, though you don't yet understand how."

"Blessed?" I allow incredulity to sharpen my voice. "I nearly died."

"Death and transcendence often walk hand in hand." His gaze drops to my lips, hunger visible under barely masked restraint. "What kills the unprepared merely transforms the worthy."

Part of me responds to him, a recognition I can't fully explain or dismiss. The conversation veers into territory that reveals too much of his ultimate intent. I allow tears to gather in my eyes, vulnerability interrupting dangerous revelation. "I'm afraid. The dreams continue even after the fever broke."

His free hand rises to my face, fingers brushing away a tear I release with careful timing. The contact burns on my skin. "Fear is the natural response to encountering power past ordinary understanding."

"You speak as one familiar." I turn my face slightly into his touch, the movement designed to encourage further contact.

"I am." Pride warms his voice, a hint of what I've glimpsed under the aristocratic facade. "I've spent years studying what others fear or deny. The shadow realm contains wisdom lost to modern kingdoms through superstition and religious restriction."

His thumb traces my cheekbone, lingering at the corner of my lips. The touch sends desire I can't entirely attribute to the mission. My body responds to him with awareness that training should suppress.

This response to him disturbs me more than any wound. My flesh betrays what my mind knows.

"What wisdom justifies such fear?" My question carries a breathless quality that requires no pretense. The game between us shifts with each heartbeat, predator and prey exchanging roles with fluid unpredictability.

"The understanding that darkness and light represent false dichotomy." His face moves closer to mine, his breath warm on my lips. "That what we consider corruption merely represents transformation toward a more perfect existence."

Before I can respond, his mouth claims mine. This kiss is nothing like gentle seduction. This is possession, hunger, barely controlled need. His tongue traces the seam of my lips, demanding entry I grant with a soft gasp.

The kiss deepens, his hand tangling in my hair to angle my head for better access. I taste wine and shadow-smoke, danger and desire. My body responds unbidden, pressing closer, seeking more contact. His other arm wraps around my waist, pulling me close until I can feel the rapid beat of his heart through our clothes.

For a moment, I forget myself entirely, lost in sensation that eclipses training and devotion alike. My hands tangle in his hair, pulling him closer. The darkness I've trained to fight calls to instincts within me, and this time I answer its call.

When he finally pulls back, we're both breathing hard. His eyes have gone nearly black with desire, the rings of darkness seeming to pulse with life.

"Tell me you feel it too." His voice is rough, pleading. "Tell me I'm not alone in this madness."

"You're not alone." The admission tears from my throat, too much truth for safety.

"Then come to me again. Tomorrow night. Let me show you what we could be together."

Mordreth guide your servant through shadow's test.

The prayer rises belatedly, trying to restore clarity to thoughts scattered by unexpected passion. I pull back slightly, trying to regain control.

"Tomorrow." I manage, voice unsteady. "Yes."

A sound interrupts whatever response he might have offered, footsteps approaching along the garden path. Blackthorne shifts smoothly from intimate to courtly, creating distance between us with practiced ease.

Lord Hargrove appears around the hedge, his expression tightening at the sight of us seated together in the secluded alcove. "Lady Ravencrest. I've been looking for you. The Countess Mereswen was hoping for a conversation."

Blackthorne stands fluidly, offering his hand to assist me from the bench. The contact lasts longer than necessary, his fingers pressing meaning into my palm. "We shall continue our conversation soon, I hope."

"I would like that." The words carry warmth I ensure reaches my eyes.

"Tomorrow evening." His voice lowers for my ears alone. "My private collection contains knowledge I believe would resonate with your unique perspective. We can continue this... connection we've started."

The invitation falls exactly as planned despite the altered approach. My heart beats faster within my breast, the blood singing with calling fulfilled. The Raven's Kiss moves one step closer to his lips.

"Until tomorrow, then."

He bows elegantly before departing, leaving me with Hargrove whose displeasure shows in the tight line of his mouth. "I see Blackthorne wastes no time pressing his attentions."

"Lord Blackthorne has shown me great kindness during my recovery." I inject appropriate gratitude into my voice while moving toward the gathering with an apparent eagerness to meet the Countess.

These nobles play at intrigue while true darkness gathers beyond their perception.

The remainder of the evening passes in social performance despite my growing weakness as borrowed strength begins to fade. My wounds protest each movement with increasing intensity, blood warming bandages under my elegant attire. By the time my carriage arrives to return me to Crescent Court, pain threatens to overwhelm me completely.

Yet under the physical discomfort, satisfaction burns bright. The evening has revealed more than I dared hope. Confirmation of Blackthorne's final timeline, evidence of his recruitment network among the nobility, and proof that the shadow cult operates openly during public celebrations.

Three nights until the grand ascension. Three nights to gather final intelligence and prepare for judgment.

Tomorrow brings access to his private collection. Tomorrow the hunt reaches its conclusion.

I sink into the cushioned seats as the carriage departs, control slipping now that my performance no longer requires it. My breath comes in shallow gasps, sweat beading across my forehead despite the evening's chill. The wound at my shoulder burns, infection or corruption awakened and made worse by prolonged exertion.

Darkness threatens at the edges of my vision, yet my determination holds consciousness in place through sheer will. The mission proceeds despite my physical limitations. Vulnerability displayed as intended. Invitation secured for tomorrow's continued seduction.

Yet part of me troubles beyond physical pain. My response to him felt too genuine, too visceral. As if part of me recognizes part of him.

Crescent Court welcomes me with warm light burning in upper windows despite the late hour. The sight sends unexpected comfort through my chest. Another soul awaits my return, not for the mission's sake but for my own.

My body barely cooperates as I ascend the steps, each movement requiring separate focus. By the time I reach my chamber door, darkness threatens to claim me completely. I push through weakness with stubborn determination, refusing to surrender.

Liora rises from a chair near the fireplace as I enter, a book falling forgotten as she moves toward me. "You're back." Relief and concern war across her features. "How did it—"

The rest of her question vanishes as my legs finally surrender. The room tilts sideways, darkness rushing in from all sides. For the first time since my training began, my iron control fails me completely.

21

REVELATIONS

Strong arms catch me before I hit the floor. The world spins, then steadies as Liora guides my body to the bed. Her face swims in and out of focus, concern etched in every line.

"I told you this was too soon." Worry sharpens her voice as she helps me sit on the bed's edge. "The wounds have reopened."

I look down, seeing fresh crimson staining sage-blue silk. The sight should concern me, yet all I feel is bone-deep weariness that transcends physical pain. Not just my body but my spirit is exhausted by hours of careful deception while injured.

"The party served its purpose." My voice emerges rough with effort. "Blackthorne invited me to his private quarters tomorrow evening."

"That's what matters to you?" Anger flashes across her face. "While you bleed through your gown?"

The emotion catches me unprepared, her concern so different from the Sisterhood's cold evaluation or Blackthorne's careful attention. This care wants nothing beyond my wellbeing, expects no service or submission in return.

Her hands on my wounds feel entirely different from Black-thorne's touch. One seeking to heal, the other to possess. Yet both awaken something in me I never knew existed.

"The mission must proceed." The words emerge automatically, training asserting itself despite my exhaustion.

"The mission, again." She repeats the word as her fingers unfasten my gown. "Is that all that matters? Whatever sent you into the temple? Whatever had you fighting creatures that left these wounds?"

Her bluntness stuns me to silence. She knows more than she should, understands connections I've never confirmed. Yet her hands remain gentle as they help remove the blood-stained gown, her anger directed at circumstance rather than my deception.

My certainty wavers under her care. The Sisterhood taught that absolute devotion to mission provides clarity, but here, wounded and vulnerable, I find myself questioning not just my methods but the very foundation of my training. The papers from the temple revealed reversals might be possible for early corruption, how many souls had I condemned unnecessarily?

"Some things are worth the sacrifice." I find myself explaining without understanding why her opinion should matter. "Some causes serve greater purposes than individual comfort."

"And who decides what good is worth your life?" She kneels to remove my shoes, her head bowed over the task. "Who sends you into darkness alone?"

I have no answer that would satisfy her. No explanation that wouldn't sound like blind fanaticism to one outside the Sisterhood. The silence stretches between us as she helps me into a night shift, her hands careful around bandaged wounds.

"I've never had a choice." The admission slips out unbidden, vulnerability emerging after a night of exposure. "My path was predetermined when they found me."

Her eyes meet mine, understanding dawning like the sunrise. Another piece of the puzzle that is Seraphina rather than Lady Ravencrest clicking into place. Yet her expression holds no judgment, only a sadness that makes my chest ache with unfamiliar pressure.

"They saw something in you," she whispers, tracing the scar along my collarbone with careful fingers. "A rare quality they wanted to shape for their intent."

Her observation feels uncomfortably close to questions I've buried for years. Why Mother Superior selected me specifically for this mission. Why temple guardians hesitated before me. Why my eyes sometimes reflect gold when emotions overcome my control.

"We all have choices." Her voice softens. "Even when paths seem preordained."

She helps me lie back within pillows, her movements practiced yet personal in a way I've never experienced before. When she turns to leave, my hand catches hers, skin wrapping around her wrist with unexpected urgency.

"Stay." The request emerges without thought, just need. "Please."

Surprise flickers across her face before she nods, settling into the chair beside my bed. Her touch remains within mine, anchoring me somehow. We sit in silence as the fire burns lower in the grate, casting flickering patterns upon chamber walls.

"Did you learn anything that might help us understand what happened to my brother?" The question hangs between us just as I begin drifting toward sleep.

The temple guardians. My blade finding corrupted flesh. Black ichor washing over my hand as the creature died. The probability, the near certainty, that I killed what remained of Daven Tanner with blessed steel.

I can't tell her everything.

I can't destroy the fragile hope she still carries. Yet lying now, with her hand tender in mine and her concern wrapping around me feels like sacrilege.

"I saw a similar transformation last night." Truth serves where full honesty would only wound. "Golden eyes emerging after being exposed to whatever power Blackthorne channels."

Her touch tightens around mine. "So he is connected to the disappearances."

"Yes." I let my eyes close, exhaustion beginning to claim me. "Tomorrow I'll learn more. Tomorrow I'll find answers worth having."

Silence falls between us, comfortable rather than strained. My body grows heavier on the mattress, consciousness slipping toward darkness. The last sensation I feel is her free hand gently brushing hair from my forehead, the touch conveying more tenderness than I've known in years.

"I don't want your answers to cost your life," she whispers, perhaps believing me already asleep.

I drift into darkness with her words following me down, her hand still clasped in mine like an anchor to the shadow's pull. For the first time in years, my sleep contains no rituals, no prayers, no life obligations to divine mission. Just her touch tender in mine and her voice lingering in memory.

The sensation feels remarkably like peace.

Morning light finds us unchanged, her hand still within mine though she sleeps now, head resting awkwardly over the chair's arm. The sight sends heat spiraling through me.

I watch her in sleep, all artifice and guardedness stripped away by unconsciousness. Her face in repose shows both strength and softness, determination and vulnerability in balanced measure.

So different from Blackthorne.

She stirs, consciousness returning in visible stages. First confusion as she orients herself, then recognition as memory returns. An emotion almost like embarrassment follows as she realizes our hands remained joined through the night. She withdraws her touch carefully, straightening in the chair with wincing awareness of stiff muscles.

"You stayed." My voice emerges rough with sleep.

"You asked me to." The simplicity of her response catches me off guard. No explanation. No justification. Just truth without adornment.

"Thank you." The gratitude flows without hesitation, heat in the words I didn't recognize until I spoke them.

She rises, moving toward the window to draw curtains wider. Morning light illuminates her profile as she looks out toward the garden below. The sight burns into my memory with unexpected clarity—her slender form outlined in golden light, hair escaped from practical braids in soft waves around her face.

"I should prepare breakfast." She turns back toward me. "You need food to rebuild strength after so much loss."

"Liora." Her name feels different on my tongue this morning, weighted with meaning I can't fully articulate. "About last night..."

"You don't need to explain." Her voice carries no judgment, only quiet understanding. "We all have our burdens to carry."

"No." The refusal comes swift and certain. "You deserve more than silence after all you've done."

I push myself upright, ignoring how my wounds protest the movement. Life and pain mean nothing to this sudden need for honesty. Not the complete truth, that remains impossible, but greater connection than I've offered since arriving in Luridian.

"The garden party. Blackthorne." I search for words that won't compromise the mission yet still offer a real connection. "I played a role last night. Showed vulnerability where I should have shown strength. It left me... unbalanced."

Her eyes study my face, seeing more than I intend to reveal. "You're hunting him."

The observation lands like a blade between ribs, uncomfortably accurate. I keep my breathing steady despite my inner turmoil. "Why would you think that?"

"The way you speak his name. The papers from the temple. The wounds that match descriptions of those creatures from the Lower City." She moves closer, settling onto the bed's edge with a boldness that surprises me. "I'm not blind, my lady, whatever you might think of my station."

I've underestimated her perception. A dangerous mistake for an assassin.

An emotion breaks inside me at her words, at the quiet dignity in her bearing. At how she's tended my wounds without question, kept my secrets without demand.

"No. You see too clearly." I reach for her hand, surprising us both. Her skin feels tender over my cooler touch. "More than anyone should."

"Is that why you asked me to stay?" Her voice softens, eyes fixed on our joined hands. "Because I see you?"

The question pierces deeper than the temple guardians' claws ever could. I've been seen only as a weapon, as an instrument, as a blessed blade for so long that simple recognition as a woman, as a person, unravels a fundamental layer inside me.

"I asked you to stay because..." My voice falters, words failing within the tide of feeling rising in my chest. "Because with you I feel genuine connection."

Her breath catches audibly. Her touch tightens around mine, the pressure grounding me over confusion threatening to overwhelm.

"What do you feel?" The whisper barely disturbs the air between us.

I have no answer that my training would sanction. No explanation that doesn't threaten my mission focus. Yet—

"Alive." The word tastes strange on my tongue. "Not as a vessel or instrument, but as flesh and life. As a woman rather than an instrument of some god's will."

Her free hand rises slowly, giving me time to withdraw, to rebuild walls that crumble further with each shared breath. I remain still, pulse quickening in my chest as her touch brushes my cheek with reverent gentleness.

"You've always been more than you think." Her skin traces along my jaw, awakening sensations I've never permitted myself to acknowledge. "Even if they tried to burn the woman away."

No one has ever touched me like this. My skin responds to her touch, my life flowing tender through veins long trained to deadly stillness.

"They nearly succeeded." The admission costs more than crimson ever could.

Her hand cradles my face now, thumb tracing my lower lip with whisper-soft pressure. "Yet here you are. Still human despite everything."

An energy shifts between us, the air growing charged with memory of last night's garden confession. Her eyes drop to my mouth, and I see she's remembering too. That soft, careful kiss under moonlight, the trembling that followed, promises we're both too afraid to fully believe.

"We shouldn't," she whispers, but her hand still cradles my face. "You're injured, weak from whatever happened tonight."

"I'm never weak with you." The admission emerges raw, stripped of pretense. "You make me stronger in ways I can't explain."

Her breathing falters. Since our kiss in the garden, every moment between us carries new weight, every glance holds questions neither of us can answer. But now, with Blackthorne's touch still burning on my skin like a brand I need to wash away, I need her, need the truth of what we are together.

"Liora." Her name is both plea and prayer.

This time when our lips meet, it's nothing like the careful exploration of last night. This is desperate, hungry—as if we both sense time running short. Her mouth opens under mine, and I taste the salt of tears I didn't know she was crying. My hands tangle in her hair, pulling her closer, needing to erase every place Blackthorne touched with the honest heat of her.

She makes a sound against my lips—part sob, part surrender—and suddenly she's kissing me back with matching desperation. She frames my face like I might disappear, her thumbs stroking my cheekbones as if memorizing their shape. I taste mint and tears and that underlying sweetness that's uniquely hers, more intoxicating now that I know how rare such sweetness is in my world of darkness and crimson.

Where Blackthorne's passion felt like drowning, this feels like breathing. Where his touch claimed and conquered, hers heals and completes. The contrast is so sharp it makes me gasp, breaking the kiss to press my forehead to hers.

"I can taste the darkness on you," she whispers, voice breaking. "Whatever happened tonight, whoever touched you—I can feel it."

Shame floods through me. "I'm sorry. I shouldn't have—"

"No." She cuts me off, fierce despite her tears. "I'm not sorry. I just... I'm afraid I'm losing you to forces I'll never understand."

I pull back enough to meet her eyes, finding them bright with unshed tears and terrible understanding. She knows. Not the details, but the shape of it. That I walked into danger tonight. That someone else touched what she's beginning to think of as hers. That every kiss might be our last.

"You're not losing me," I promise, even knowing I can't keep it. "If anything, you're the only force keeping me tethered to who I really am."

When we part, both breathing faster than moments before, confusion and wonder war across her features. Her skin touches her lips as though confirming what just happened. Color blooms high on her cheeks, turning her ordinary features extraordinary.

"My lady, I shouldn't have—" she begins, lowering her eyes.

"No." I cut her off, refusing the lie propriety would demand. "If anyone should apologize, it's me." But the words feel wrong, hollow against the truth humming in my blood.

"Do you regret it?" The question carries a vulnerability that makes my heart ache. Her eyes find mine again, seeking truth she expects will wound her.

"No." The truth flows easily now that I've tasted this freedom. "Do you?"

Her smile transforms her face, eyes brightening with emotion I've never seen directed toward me. The simple joy there makes an emotion tighten in my chest.

"How could I regret a moment I've imagined since the first week in your service?" She looks away, nervously smoothing her skirt. "When you defended that street child from Lord Harlow's carriage. No fine lady notices such things."

The admission stuns me to silence. While I played roles and hid behind walls, she watched and wanted and waited without expectation or demand. The realization shifts a fundamental layer in my understanding of our relationship.

"I never knew." My voice emerges rougher than intended. *Trained to read death in a man's eyes, yet blind to this.*

"You weren't meant to." Her touch brushes hair from my face with gentle care. "What lady notices her handmaiden's heart?"

"One who learns to see beyond mission and position." I catch her hand, pressing my lips to her palm. The gesture carries nothing false or planned, just a genuine response to a connection I never anticipated. Her skin smells of lemon soap and carries tiny calluses from work she never complains about.

She draws a shaky breath, her composure cracking under the weight of intimacy neither of us expected. "This complicates everything."

"Yes." No point denying the obvious truth. "Your brother. My mission. Blackthorne's judgment."

"Your mission." She repeats the words, understanding darkening her eyes. "Tomorrow night with Blackthorne."

"I must go." Duty reasserts itself despite the heat of her skin over mine. "The invitation provides an opportunity I can't just ignore."

Pain flickers across her face, quickly mastered. "To learn more?"

I can't tell her about the Raven's Kiss or reveal that my lips will deliver death where they just offered connection. The contrast feels blasphemous somehow, each mission diminishing the other. *These lips are consecrated twice now. To death and to her.*

"Yes." The half-truth tastes bitter after such sweetness. "Information that might help me understand the disappearances. The transformations."

She nods, practicality overcoming emotion with visible effort. "Then you need to recover your strength today." Her voice softens to the practical tone I've come to rely on. "Your wounds need fresh dressing, and you need proper nourishment."

The shift to caretaking creates distance, allowing us both to recalibrate after the kiss. Yet her touch lingers within mine as she rises, the contact maintaining a connection despite her rational retreat.

"I'll prepare breakfast." She moves toward the door, composure almost restored save for her still-flushed cheeks. "Then we'll see to your wounds."

When she leaves, I touch my lips, still tender from her kiss. The sensation lingers like a benediction, holy in ways Sisterhood rituals never achieved. For the first time since childhood, I find myself wanting a future beyond mission's completion, beyond a divine calling.

Clarity of intent when doubt clouds judgment.

The prayer rises automatically, yet feels hollow over the memory of her lips on mine. For the first time, I wonder if my calling could ever include more than mission and judgment. A future chosen rather than assigned.

Tomorrow brings Blackthorne's seduction and judgment's delivery. Today brings an unexpected connection that threatens mission focus even as it awakens a force long dormant within my chest.

I close my eyes, centering breath and thought through sheer will. The woman must surrender to the weapon, at least until judgment flows from my lips to Blackthorne's. After tomorrow, perhaps, other possibilities might exist beyond my sacred purpose.

For now, the mission proceeds despite conflicting loyalties.

The Raven's Kiss waits in its wooden box, patient as judgment itself. My lips, which now know tenderness, must soon deliver death. The contradiction should trouble me more than it does.

May both blessed acts find favor in His sight.

22

TEMPTATION

I apply the Raven's Kiss carefully. My grip stays steady despite the pain pulsing through my shoulder. The crystal vial catches candlelight, liquid within gleaming like trapped blood. I layer it with religious devotion, the first binds to skin, the second activates the essence, and the third completes the binding.

"By Mordreth's shadow, bind this essence to sacred purpose," I whisper as I apply the first layer.

"By Mordreth's mercy, reserve judgment for the deserving soul," follows with the second.

"By Mordreth's will, release this judgment only when the vessel stands at pleasure's peak," I complete with the third.

The stain disappears completely into my lips, leaving death's promise for a full day as Mother Superior explained. The sacred venom waits like a serpent coiled to strike, requiring only the perfect moment to deliver its judgment. Until then, it rests dormant under my skin, a weight only I can feel.

Blood consecrates what shadow claims.

A soft knock interrupts my ritual. "My lady?" Liora's voice carries through the door. "May I enter to help with your hair?"

"Come." I close the ornate wooden box, securing it in my vanity drawer before she enters.

Liora moves behind me, weaving small braids into an elaborate pattern at my temples. Unlike her usual care, there's hesitation in her movements tonight, her touch occasionally brushing my skin as if testing boundaries established by yesterday's kiss. My body responds with warmth I can't afford tonight.

Her reflection catches my gaze in the mirror, questions lingering in eyes that saw too much of the woman within my careful disguise.

"I've never seen you use that shade before." She studies my lips in the mirror. "The color is extraordinary."

"A special lip stain," My voice stays casual despite my racing pulse. "Quite rare and absurdly expensive. Reserved for special occasions."

She continues braiding, her fingers gentle in my hair. "The color suits you perfectly. Like it was made for your lips alone."

"You won't find it anywhere in Luridian," I say, watching her work in the mirror. "The formula remains a closely guarded secret."

"You're meeting Lord Blackthorne tonight?" Her voice carries strain under practiced composure.

"Yes." I turn to face her, muscles protesting with fiery complaint. I search for words that will comfort her without revealing too much. "His private collection contains knowledge that could help us understand what happened to your brother."

The lie tastes bitter after yesterday's honesty between us, but the truth would frighten her more. Lady Ravencrest investigating mysterious disappearances makes sense. An assassin delivering sacred judgment does not.

"But after what happened yesterday..." Her words trail off, eyes lowering to study her fingers.

I think of the kiss and the unexpected connection neither of us planned. My chest tightens with memory I should suppress but don't want to either.

"What happened between us changes nothing about tonight." My voice emerges gentler than intended. "My purpose remains clear, even if my heart is less certain than before."

A flush spreads across her cheeks. "I shouldn't have mentioned it. Forgetting my place."

"There is no place between us when we're alone." The admission flows without permission. "Only truth neither of us expected."

She helps me into the midnight-blue gown, silk sliding cool over my skin while her touch works the fastenings efficiently. Her contact burns through the fabric, each point of connection searing into skin trained to register threat rather than tenderness.

"Lord Hargrove called again this afternoon," she mentions quietly. "His third inquiry this week."

"What did you tell him?"

"That you're recovering but not yet receiving visitors." Her fingers pause on the laces. "He seemed... agitated. Mentioned something about protecting you from dangerous influences."

Poor Hargrove. Still playing the gallant protector while I prepare to bed his enemy.

"His eyes follow you like you already belong to him." Jealousy colors her voice, the emotion naked and surprising. "I've seen how men like Blackthorne collect beautiful objects without caring if they break."

"I belong to no one," I say, my pulse heating through my veins. "Not to Blackthorne, not to those who shaped me for their purpose. My fate remains my own to decide."

Her touch is still at my back as she asks, "Will you return tonight?"

"Yes. Wait for me."

"Always." She says that single word again, with so much weight just like before.

Tonight I complete my sacred purpose, despite the wound in my shoulder and the unexpected tenderness blooming in my chest. The Raven God's judgment flows through willing hands, even when those hands have discovered gentler purposes to serve.

The carriage journey passes in weighted silence. Blackthorne's estate looms over the night sky, windows bleeding golden light that fails to penetrate the shadows clustering under stone eaves. The gardens smell of pine and damp earth, aristocratic control imposed on nature's wildness.

A servant guides me through corridors lined with artifacts that pull at power in my veins. Ancient masks with empty eyes track my passage. Ritual daggers displayed on velvet reflect firelight with hungry intent. My skin prickles with awareness, nerves registering their presence before my mind fully processes it.

The library door opens to reveal Blackthorne, firelight sculpting sharp planes across features too handsome for comfort. Formal attire emphasizes his frame, noble polish masking the darkness within. His smile ignites with immediate heat when he sees me.

"Lady Ravencrest." He crosses the space between us smoothly, taking my hand. His touch burns on mine, unnatural heat radiating from his skin. "Your recovery brings relief beyond mere courtesy."

My skin tingles where his thumb traces circles on my palm, nerves awakening with strange alertness. I curve my lips in a practiced response.

"Your invitation promised explanations..." I speak softly.

"And answers you shall have." His eyes darken, pupils expanding until gray barely remains. "But first, some refreshment."

A table near the fire holds crystal decanters filled with ruby-dark liquid. The scent reaches me before the glass. Rich berries undercut with a presence earthier, almost metallic.

"From my private reserve." He offers the glass, fingers brushing mine deliberately. "Saved for guests who might appreciate its unique properties."

The wine tastes of blackberries and night soil. Sweet touches my tongue first, then bitterness coats it like oil. Power within it recognizes my veins. A strange lightness fills my head, as though reality thins wherever his attention focuses. Not poison. An essence older. One that remembers when light and void flowed as one current.

Stop enjoying it. Stop responding to it.

"You notice the difference." Pride deepens his voice. "Most taste only sweetness, missing what lies below."

"There's an element underneath." I meet his gaze directly. "A presence familiar that has no name."

Satisfaction transforms his features, intensity replacing noble restraint. "Your natural sensitivity exceeds my expectations."

He guides me deeper into the library, past conventional texts toward shelves hidden behind ornate screens. The air thickens here, heavy with the scent of paper and preservative oils. Temperature drops with each step. My skin tightens into gooseflesh under silk.

Books line the shelves, their bindings fashioned from materials I recognize from Sisterhood archives. Human skin tanned to leather that retains body memory. Bones inlaid into decorative elements. Metals alloyed with life to create coverings that pulse at my touch.

"These collections contain wisdom the church would burn without reading." Passion overtakes his voice, the scholar emerging fully from the noble mask. "Knowledge from before kingdoms divided light from darkness, when power flowed freely between worlds."

His touch selects a volume bound in midnight leather with silver clasps that catch firelight like trapped stars. The book weighs heavy in my grasp, mass beyond physical dimensions pressing on my palms. Pages whisper over each other as I turn them, sound carrying intention beyond mere friction.

Diagrams show human figures in various stages of change. Notes in flowing script detail progression rates, individual variations, factors affecting resistance. The information mirrors Sisterhood knowledge yet contains elements Mother Superior either doesn't possess or deliberately withheld.

"What most fear represents evolution for those properly prepared." Blackthorne stands closer now, his body radiating heat at my side. "Those with natural sensitivity navigate the change, maintaining self while gaining gifts from beyond."

His hand settles over mine on the page. Together, we trace the diagram of golden-eyed figures standing between worlds. Contact sends shivers along my spine, consciousness briefly expanding beyond ordinary boundaries.

Don't respond to him. Don't let him see you want this knowledge.

"We're alike, you and I." His mouth hovers near my ear, breath burning on sensitive skin. "I sensed it from our first meeting. You walk the edge between worlds as I do."

His words resonate with unwelcome truth. The medallion responding to my touch. Temple creatures hesitating before me. Mother Superior selecting me specifically for this assignment, recognizing what she never named.

"How can you be certain?" I ask, breathless.

"Your survival after direct contact with the darkness. The way certain artifacts respond to your presence." His touch brushes hair from my face, contact lingering on my temple. "The golden flecks appearing in your eyes when emotion overcomes your control."

My breath stops completely. Golden flecks. The first sign of affinity, appearing in Brother Elias before his execution, in Daven Tanner before his transformation, in every victim before their claiming by the void.

Appearing in my own eyes, reflected in mirrors I avoid after intense combat or emotional breakthroughs.

"That's impossible." The denial sounds hollow even as I speak.

"Deny it if necessary." His smile carries understanding rather than mockery. "Your veins recognize truth even when your mind rejects it."

He takes the volume, replacing it with another bound in pale leather with black iron fastenings. This one falls open to pages detailing reversal rituals for early corruption, knowledge confirming temple discoveries while adding crucial components missing from those texts.

"Most believe the darkness corrupts." His voice fills with fervor. "But corruption occurs only when change happens without right guidance. Knowledge and acceptance determine whether one transcends or succumbs."

My touch traces diagrams showing ceremonial layouts matching the temple's hidden altar. The reversal components I memorized appear with greater detail and clarity. Quantities and timing critical for success laid out with clarity the temple texts lacked.

"You believe corruption can be reversed." I watch his face carefully.

"For those in early stages." His hand returns to mine, skin unnaturally warm over my cooler skin. "The first lunar cycle allows reversal through specific rituals. Beyond that threshold, change becomes permanent."

"Those who belong to darkness rarely recognize their nature until shown." His hand cups my face with disturbing tenderness. "Let me show you what you truly are."

"I never considered myself... different." The vulnerability in my voice isn't feigned.

He leads me from the library through corridors that feel increasingly dreamlike. The architecture shifts subtly. Walls curve where they should stand straight. Shadows pool in corners that receive more light than darkness. My skin prickles with awareness of watchers hidden in darkness, yet no servants appear.

We reach his private chambers, the space reflecting scholarly order rather than noble excess. Books line walls interrupted only by windows revealing night-darkened gardens. A massive bed dominates one wall, draped in fabrics that drink light rather than reflect it.

My heart hammers. The Raven's Kiss waits on my lips, prepared for the critical moment when pleasure peaks and death flows through sacred contact. I itch toward concealed weapons, instinct suppressed by practiced control.

"More wine?" He gestures toward a decanter different from the library's offering, liquid black as midnight within crystal.

"Perhaps a milder vintage." I smile, encouraging his confidence.

Approval warms his smile. "Sensitivity brings wisdom, it seems."

He selects water instead, crystal capturing candlelight in fractured patterns. The liquid tastes impossibly pure on my tongue. Cleaner than mountain springs. Clearer than Sisterhood ritual water. My body responds with immediate thirst, each swallow awakening deeper hunger.

"Sensitivity heightens all perception." His voice lowers as he approaches. "Taste. Touch. Scent. Everything becomes more intense as connection strengthens."

I feel his words manifest as truth across my skin. Silk suddenly registers with painful intensity on my skin. The chamber's scent separates into distinct elements. Leather-bound books. Beeswax candles. Blackthorne's unique signature of sandalwood and darkness. Sounds sharpen until I hear my own pulse rushing through veins, his heartbeat across the room matching mine in steadying rhythm.

His hand reaches for mine, drawing me closer with gentle insistence. "Join me in understanding what flows in your veins. Your natural affinity grants protection others lack."

His invitation offers an unexpected opportunity. Access to knowledge I've been denied. Understanding of my own nature beyond Sisterhood teachings. My mission adapts with each revelation, judgment temporarily delayed for personal truth.

"Tell me," I breathe close to his ear, playing my role while the Raven's Kiss pulses cold on my lips. "Tell me what you really want from me."

He pulls back to look at me, and tension fractures in his expression. The controlled nobleman shatters like a mask held too long. What remains is raw, hungry, almost feral.

"Everything." The word tears from his voice. "Fuck, Sera, I want everything."

His hands frame my face, thumbs pressing into my skin like he's trying to memorize me through touch alone. "Do you know how long I've searched? How many empty faces, empty souls, empty godsforsaken nights?"

The genuine pain in his voice catches me off guard. This isn't the seduction I prepared for.

"Is that what happened to you?" I ask, the question slipping out before wisdom can stop it. "Someone you loved?"

His touch stills on my skin. For a moment, power raw and ancient flickers in his eyes. "My sister. Celeste." The name falls like a stone between us. "She was thirteen when the shadows first sang to her. I was meant to protect her, guide her. Instead, I..." His voice cracks. "I tried to understand what took her. Spent years in forgotten libraries, chasing whispers in ancient texts. By the time I learned enough to matter, she was gone. Not dead. Worse. Hollow."

"So you seek others like her."

"I seek to become what she became, but without losing myself." His laugh is bitter. "The Void keeps showing me the path, but the price..." His touch traces my jaw. "Until you. You're already touching that edge without drowning. You're what I've been trying to become for fifteen years."

"Then take it," I whisper, my body already responding to his desperation with matching heat.

He crashes into me like a drowning man finding air. The kiss is nothing like our previous encounters. No finesse, no control, just raw need. His teeth catch my lower lip, drawing life that makes us both moan. His hands tangle in my hair, pulling hard enough to hurt, angling my head so he can devour me properly.

"Gods." He breaks away, breathing hard. "I can't—I need—"

"Stop talking." I grab his jacket, pulling him back. "Show me what you mean."

We collide again, harder this time. Clothes don't get removed. They get destroyed. His hands tear at the fastenings of my gown with impatience that borders on violence. The expensive fabric rips, but neither of us care. I work at his shirt, buttons scattering across the floor.

"I knew," he pants over my neck, teeth scraping sensitive skin. "The moment I saw you at that damned gallery. Those eyes. That control hiding wildness underneath."

The shadows in the room respond to our combined hunger. They rise from corners, reaching toward us with visible curiosity. Where they touch our skin, sensation amplifies. Every nerve ending suddenly hyperaware.

"The shadows," I gasp as darkness pools over us.

"They know." His laugh is dark, broken. "They've been screaming for you since that first dance. Can't you feel it? How they reach for you?"

He's right. The darkness moves differently about me now, less like observers and more like participants. They slide across my exposed skin, leaving trails of sensation that make me arch into him.

His mouth finds my breast, no gentle exploration, just ravenous need. He bites down on my nipple through the thin fabric still clinging to my body, and I cry out, not from pain but from the electric pleasure that shoots straight to my core.

"Mine," he growls over my skin. "Finally, completely mine."

His hands map my body like territory to be conquered, each touch a claim staked in flesh. Gripping, claiming, bruising. The careful control he's maintained for weeks is completely gone. This is the real Blackthorne, the one who's waited for someone who could match his darkness.

"Not yours," I manage, even as my body betrays me, arching into his touch. "Never yours."

"Liar." He spins me suddenly, pressing me face-first on the wall. His body cages mine, one hand tangling roughly in my hair while the other tears away what remains of my skirts. "Your body knows the truth even if your mind won't admit it."

23

PASSION

His touch finds me already wet, already ready, and we both gasp at the discovery.

"So perfectly wet for me." His voice is wrecked. "Is this what you've been hiding from me?"

He doesn't wait for an answer. His fingers plunge deep without warning, two then three. His hand works between my thighs like he's playing an instrument only he knows the music to, fingers curling and stroking until I'm nothing but sensation and need. Gods, the fullness overwhelms, his long fingers reaching places that make stars burst behind my eyelids, and my knees nearly buckle from the sudden claiming. Only his body pressing me to the wall keeps me upright.

"Look at you," he breathes close to my ear, movements brutally controlled. "The proper widow falling apart on my hand. Is this what you wanted? Is this why you came here tonight?"

The Raven's Kiss pulses on my lips, reminding me of my purpose, but coherent thought is fracturing under his assault.

His thumb finds my clit, circling with pressure that borders on too much, and I can't stop the sounds tearing from my voice.

"That's it." His teeth find the junction of neck and shoulder, biting down hard enough to mark. "Let me hear you. Let me hear what I do to you."

The shadows thicken over us, drawn by our combined need. They slide between our bodies, amplifying every sensation until I can't tell where I end and they begin. It's like being touched everywhere at once. Phantom hands and mouths working in concert with his.

"I need to be inside you." The words are more growl than speech. "Need to feel you come apart on my cock."

He spins me again, lifting me easily. My back hits the wall as my legs wrap over his waist on instinct. I can feel him hard at me, separated by too much fabric.

"Wait—" I start, some vestige of training trying to reassert control.

"No more waiting." He tears at his remaining clothes with one hand while the other keeps me pinned. "I've waited long enough. We've danced over this for weeks."

When he finally frees himself, pressing at my entrance, we both freeze for a moment. Eye to eye, breath mingling, shadows writhing about us like living entities.

"Last chance," he says roughly. "Tell me to stop."

Instead, I pull his hair hard, forcing his head back. "Take me like you mean it."

He slams into me with no further warning. The fullness is overwhelming, my body stretching to accommodate him. The shadows seem to help, reshaping me from within to take him deeper.

"Gods, you're tight." His forehead drops to my shoulder. "So godsdamned exquisite."

He starts to move, each thrust driving me harder on the wall. There's no rhythm, no finesse. Just primal urgency. The portrait frames over us rattle with the force of it.

"Is this what you wanted?" He pulls back to watch my face. "To make me lose control?"

"Yes." The admission tears from me without thought. Because it's true. I wanted to see him break as badly as he wanted to break me.

His hand grips my hair again, forcing me to maintain eye contact as he fucks me harder. The shadows respond to our violence, creating a cocoon of darkness over us. Through them, I can feel what he feels—the tight heat of my body gripping him, the burning need for more, always more.

"Your eyes," he chokes out. "Gods, Sera, look at your eyes."

"Extraordinary," he murmurs, his gaze traveling over my face with reverent hunger. "Those eyes... violet fire. And this—" His finger traces along my sharp cheekbone without quite touching. "Every line of you speaks of power." His attention drops to the star-shaped scar above my left hip, visible where my torn dress hangs open. "Every mark tells a story, doesn't it?"

I catch our reflection in a nearby mirror. My violet eyes are shot through with gold, the flecks more prominent than ever before. But it's the expression on my face that shocks me, wanton, wild, completely without control.

"Beautiful," he breathes. "So beautiful like this."

The position isn't enough. He pulls out suddenly, making me whimper at the loss. Before I can protest, he's carrying me to his desk, sweeping books and artifacts to the floor with one arm.

"Need more." He bends me over the desk, one hand pressing between my shoulder blades. "Need all of you."

He enters me again from behind, the angle letting him go even deeper. His hands grip my hips hard enough to bruise as he sets a punishing pace.

"Take it." His voice doesn't sound human anymore. "Take all of it. Show me what you really are."

The shadows love our violence. They pulse with each thrust, creating patterns on the walls that match our rhythm. Some of them slide inside me alongside him, the sensation impossible and overwhelming.

"Can't—it's too much—"

"You can." He pulls me up by my hair, my back on his chest, changing the angle again. One hand moves to work my clit while he continues his relentless pace. "You were made for this. Made for me."

The dual sensation of his thrusts and touch, amplified by the shadows' contact, sends me spiraling toward release faster than expected. My body tightens, pleasure coiling at the base of my spine.

"That's it." His teeth find my ear. "Come for me. Let me feel you break."

The orgasm crashes through me, leaving me whimpering. My body convulses about him, inner muscles clenching rhythmically as waves of pleasure crash through me. The shadows explode outward, reality bending at the edges as I scream my release.

But he doesn't stop. Doesn't slow. If anything, my orgasm drives him to greater urgency.

"Not enough." He pushes me forward again, still driving into me through the aftershocks. "Need more. Need everything."

His hand trails down my spine, thumb pressing at my other entrance. The touch sends a shock through my oversensitive body.

"Has anyone touched you here?" His voice is dark, possessive.

"No." The admission comes out as a whimper.

"Good." His thumb presses harder, not entering but promising. "Mine to claim. Mine to ruin."

The possessiveness in his voice should anger me. Instead, it sends fresh heat through my core. The shadows seem to agree, pooling where his thumb presses, adding their own pressure.

"Please." I don't even know what I'm begging for anymore.

"Please what?" He slows his thrusts, making me feel every inch. "Tell me what you need."

"I need—" The words fracture as he rolls his hips. "I need to see you."

He pulls out, turning me to face him. His eyes are completely black now, no white remaining. The shadows have claimed him as thoroughly as they're claiming me.

"On the desk." Not a request.

I sit on the edge, legs spreading automatically. He steps between them, cock pressing at my entrance but not entering.

"Watch." He grips my chin, forcing me to look down at where our bodies almost join. "Watch me claim you."

He pushes in slowly this time, making me watch every inch disappear inside me. The visual combined with sensation makes my head fall back.

"No." His hand tightens on my jaw. "Eyes on me. I want to see them when you come again."

He starts to move, slower than before but deeper. Each thrust is deliberate, designed to drive me insane. The shadows writhe over us, some sliding over my clit, others teasing my nipples.

"You're mine," he says, punctuating each word with a thrust. "Whether you admit it or not. The shadows know. Your body knows."

"Not—" I try to deny it, but he angles his hips, hitting a place inside that makes me see stars.

"Say it." His thumb finds my clit, circling with exquisite pressure. "Say you're mine."

"Never." But the word comes out as a moan.

He takes me harder, the desk creaking under our weight. His free hand wraps over my neck, not choking but possessing.

"Your eyes tell the truth." He leans down, lips brushing mine without kissing. "All that gold mixing with violet. You're changing, Sera. Becoming what you were meant to be."

The Raven's Kiss pulses on my lips, so close to his. This is the moment. I could end it now, deliver death with pleasure at its peak.

But he pulls back suddenly, denying me the opportunity. His hand leaves my neck to grasp my hair, yanking my head back.

"I want to watch you shatter." His voice is completely wrecked. "Want to see those golden eyes when you come on my cock."

His thumb presses harder on my clit, combining with the brutal pace of his thrusts. The shadows join in, sensation everywhere at once. It's too much, too intense.

"Can't—I can't—"

"You can." He forces me to meet his black gaze. "Come for me, Sera. Now."

The command breaks tension inside me. My second orgasm crashes through me even harder than the first. My body bows backward, only his grip keeping me from falling. The shadows explode over us, reality fracturing as pleasure whites out everything else.

I'm dimly aware of him following me over, his release triggering aftershocks that seem to go on forever. This is it—the crucial moment for the Kiss.

But I'm drowning in sensation, my body bent too far back, his face a distant star I can't reach through the haze of ecstasy. The Kiss pulses on my lips, ready, but I can't—can't think, can't move, can't remember why I need to—

By the time the pleasure fades enough for coherent thought to return, the moment has passed.

My first failed mission.

We collapse together on the desk, breathing hard. His weight presses me into the wood, but I can't find the energy to care. The shadows retreat slowly, leaving us in the aftermath.

"Hells." His voice is hoarse on my neck. "That was..."

"Not enough." The words surprise us both.

He pulls back to look at me, power still blazing in his slowly lightening eyes. "No. Not nearly enough."

Before I can respond, he's lifting me, carrying me to his private study. The room smells of old leather and forbidden knowledge. He sets me on the edge of a massive oak desk, scattering papers that I dimly recognize as ritual diagrams.

"The shadows respond to you," he says, wonder coloring his voice. "Do you see how they reach for you?"

He's right. The darkness moves differently here, curious tendrils exploring my skin with phantom touches. Each brush of shadow sends shivers through my already sensitized body.

"What are you?" he breathes, positioning himself between my spread thighs.

"Yours," I lie, pulling him closer. "Just yours."

He enters me again, and this time the shadows join us fully. They wrap over our bodies, amplifying every sensation until I can't tell where I end and they begin. His thrusts are deep, desperate, each one sending the shadows into frenzied motion.

"Look at me." His hand grips my chin. "I want to see those golden eyes when you shatter."

The second orgasm builds faster, harder. The shadows seem to pull it from me, demanding my surrender. When it crashes through me, I scream—a sound that doesn't seem entirely human. The shadows explode outward, shattering a nearby mirror.

His release follows immediately, but once again the angle is wrong. He pulls me on his chest, our mouths inches apart but not touching. The Kiss burns on my lips, unfulfilled.

"Gods." He holds me as we both shake. "What have you done to me?"

If only he knew. The Raven's Kiss throbs with unspent power, judgment delayed by passion and poor positioning. My first failed mission becomes another opportunity—a chance to learn what he knows before delivering death.

As we recover, he begins to speak of his research, his plans, the ceremony tomorrow night. Information flows as freely as our passion did moments before. He trusts me now, believes we share profound connection.

"Your sensitivity to shadow is remarkable." His touch trails along my collarbone. "Most people fear what they don't understand, but you respond to it naturally."

"Tell me about the reversal rituals," I prompt, playing the eager student. "The texts you showed me before—they suggested early corruption could be undone?"

His eyes light with scholarly passion. "Yes! The church suppresses this knowledge, but I've verified it myself. Within one lunar cycle, the transformation can be reversed with the right components and someone with natural resistance to provide the catalyst pulse."

"Someone like me?" I ask, though I already know the answer.

"Exactly like you." He kisses my forehead, still unaware that death waits on my lips. "Together, we could change everything. Save those the church would condemn."

The irony tastes bitter. Here I am, sent to kill him, learning that we might have been allies in another life. But the Kiss demands its due, and I am nothing if not dutiful.

"Show me," I whisper. "Show me everything."

His smile carries triumph wrapped in tenderness. "I knew you would recognize the truth when presented properly." He kisses my forehead with unexpected gentleness. "Rest now. The knowledge waits for you when you're ready to embrace it fully."

Soon his breathing steadies into sleep. My failure burns like acid in my veins. The Raven's Kiss remains viable for a full day, but the perfect moment has passed. Judgment delayed feels like judgment denied, a failure I've never experienced before.

Yet under the shame rises tension unexpected—possibility. Not completing the mission tonight means I can extract crucial knowledge before delivering final judgment. The reversal rituals might save lives beyond whatever satisfaction Blackthorne's death would bring.

Let wisdom guide mercy. Let truth illuminate darkness.

When certain he sleeps deeply, I slip from the bed. My wounds protest movement after such exertion, the fresh life warming bandages as I retrieve my scattered clothing. Each garment returns to its right place, all evidence of vulnerability erased except what serves my purpose.

I move silently to his private study adjoining the bedroom. Moonlight spills through tall windows, illuminating shelves lined with forbidden knowledge. My touch finds the leather-bound volume he'd shown me earlier, the one detailing reversal rituals for early-stage corruption.

I carefully remove several pages containing the crucial information—exact measurements, timing relative to lunar phases, necessary components. The theft creates risk of discovery, yet the knowledge matters more than perfect concealment now. This information might save innocent lives before they're lost completely to shadow's embrace.

The night embraces me as I slip through the gardens, my body still warm from his touch even as my mind figures out my next approach. I failed in my purpose tonight, but gained power perhaps more valuable—knowledge that might allow mercy beyond death's release.

Leaving Blackthorne's estate, I feel caught between worlds. His heat still burns on my skin, stolen knowledge heavy in my pocket. My shoulder throbs with renewed intensity, the exertion proving more taxing than I'd anticipated.

Yet my thoughts turn increasingly toward Crescent Court, toward soft touch and honest care. The contradiction in my desires should fracture my purpose. Instead, it creates a strange clarity—I can complete my mission while preserving knowledge that might save others from transformation's grasp.

The carriage returns me to Crescent Court in silence broken only by horses' hooves on cobblestone. The building rises over the night sky, a single window still illuminated despite the late hour. The sight sends warmth through my chest, an unexpected comfort.

She waits for me. Raven Lord watch over me.

The prayer feels hollow, words without conviction under the weight of tonight's revelation. My hand finds the stolen pages hidden under my cloak, knowledge worth the risk of discovery. Blackthorne's life is forfeit, but his research might serve a purpose greater than his ambition ever could.

Crescent Court welcomes me with familiar silence. My feet find the stairs as I climb to my bedroom. The chamber door awaits, salvation promised behind solid wood.

Liora rises from a chair near the fireplace as I enter, exhaustion evident across her face. Relief brightens her features, quickly replaced by concern as she studies my appearance.

"You're back." Her voice barely disturbs the air between us. "I worried when midnight passed."

Conflicting emotions flood me at the sight of her. Shame about my failed mission. Guilt at my response to Blackthorne. Warmth at her genuine concern. Being with her feels like truth after hours of performance, her expression holding nothing but honest worry without expectation of return.

"I found knowledge that might help others like your brother," I say, producing the stolen pages. "If we reach them early enough."

Her eyes widen, hands accepting the papers with reverent care. "What did you have to give for this knowledge?"

The question cuts deeper than any blade. Inside my mind, truths I can never speak aloud claw for release—how I failed in my mission, how pleasure claimed me so completely I forgot my duty in the critical moment. How the darker aspects of my purpose remain hidden from her gentle eyes.

"Nothing that matters measured on the lives this might save," I answer, the half-truth bitter on my tongue.

Her touch brushes mine as she accepts the pages, the contact sending warmth up my arm that carries its own gentle fire, so different from the shadow-touched heat still lingering on my skin. A foundation has shifted between us since yesterday's kiss, a connection neither of us fully acknowledges yet both feel with increasing clarity.

"Let me help tend your wounds," she says, her eyes moving to my shoulder where fresh life stains my gown. "Then you can tell me what you've learned."

As she works at my gown's fastenings, I realize my path has forever changed. I will complete my mission, deliver Mordreth's judgment as ordained—but not before using Blackthorne's knowledge to save those not yet fully claimed by shadow.

My failure tonight becomes an opportunity. A chance to prove mercy exists beyond blade's edge, beyond Mother Superior's teachings. The reversal rituals might save innocent lives caught in early corruption.

And after judgment flows from my lips to Blackthorne's? What then?

I look at Liora's face, focused on cleaning my reopened wound. Power grows between us that has nothing to do with Lady Ravencrest's mission or Seraphina's devotion, an energy neither of us expected yet both now cherish.

Whatever comes after Blackthorne's judgment, I can't return unchanged to the Sanctuary. Not after knowing her light and his darkness. Not after discovering that mercy takes forms beyond my blessed blade. The Sisterhood molded me as death's instrument, but in Liora, I've begun to imagine life's possibilities instead.

The thought should terrify me. Instead, it feels like waking from a dream I mistook for reality.

24

FORBIDDEN

The stolen papers burn my fingertips. Candlelight bathes Blackthorne's elegant script in blood-red glow. My shoulder throbs with each heartbeat, the temple corruption still fighting against my healing flesh.

I spread the documents across my desk and breathe in their musty sweetness. The scent reminds me of the Sanctuary archives where forbidden knowledge stays locked away from those deemed unworthy. My stomach knots as each page reveals truths Mother Superior never shared.

"These measurements seem impossibly exact," Liora says beside me. She narrows her eyes as she studies a diagram showing crystallized shadow essence. Her arm presses against mine as she leans closer, the simple cotton of her dress carrying the faint scent of lavender that has become oddly comforting.

"One drop too many and the mixture dies," I say, feeling her breath warm my skin. "Similar to noble marriages. Pretty on the surface while the husband poisons his wife's wine at dinner."

Liora's lips curl upward. During our evenings together, she's grown accustomed to my bitter observations. Her smile lingers longer than necessary, catching my attention like a shadow where none should exist.

The pages show what I never suspected. Early transformation can be reversed. The golden flecks in the eyes do not mean permanent corruption. They mark the threshold where salvation remains possible.

How many have I killed who might have been saved?

My stomach twists. Bile burns the back of my throat. Each execution felt righteous as my blade opened willing flesh. Now each memory tastes like ash.

"Some of these herbs look familiar," Liora says, pointing to a list of botanical components. Her touch brushes mine as she turns the page, neither of us acknowledging the contact nor pulling away. "My mother used similar combinations for fever purges."

I watch her face in the candlelight. The amber glow softens her features, making her ordinary beauty suddenly striking. Her eyes reflect golden pinpoints from the flame, reminding me of a memory I can't quite place. "Your mother worked with herbs?"

"She knew remedies passed through generations." Her fingers trace diagrams with sure movements. "Nothing this complex, but she understood how certain plants affect both body and mind together."

Her knowledge surprises me. Most commoners treat the symptoms they can see, missing the invisible currents flowing under the surface. Yet Liora sees connections others miss, much as she sees through my carefully constructed masks.

I find a section detailing recovery stages. The copper taste of blood fills my mouth as I realize what it means. "These remedies could help people recently affected by shadow influence."

I think of Amara at the temple ritual. Honey-blonde hair and eyes bright with misplaced trust. Golden flecks had just begun appearing in her gaze, her body still human beneath the shadow's early touch.

"Your wound." Liora's voice cuts through my spiraling thoughts, grounding me in the present. Her hand moves to my shoulder where fresh blood has begun bleeding through the bandages. "You've been pushing yourself too hard."

"It's nothing." The automatic deflection falls flat as pain lances through me, sharp enough to steal breath.

"It's not nothing." Her voice carries gentle reproach as she rises, moving to gather supplies. "Let me tend it properly this time."

I should refuse. Maintaining distance would be wiser, safer for us both. But the concern in her eyes undoes my resolve. "Very well."

She works with quiet purpose, helping me remove enough clothing to access the wound. Her intake of breath when she sees the full damage makes my heart pound.

"This is no simple fall injury." Her palms hover near the corrupted flesh, not quite touching. "These marks... what did this to you?"

"Does it matter?" I keep my voice steady despite the intimacy of the moment. Her touch on my skin, her breath warm against my shoulder as she leans close to examine the damage.

"Everything about you matters." The words slip out soft and raw before she catches herself, color rising in her cheeks. "That is, your health matters. For the work ahead."

I turn my head to look at her, finding her face closer than expected. "Just for the work?"

Her touch stills against my skin. For a moment, we simply breathe the same air, the space between us charged with everything we're not saying. Then she returns to her task, movements careful but no longer quite clinical.

"My mother taught me that healing requires more than herbs and bandages." Her voice has dropped to barely above a whisper. "It needs genuine care. Someone who sees the person, not just the wound."

"And what do you see?" The question emerges vulnerable, nothing like the controlled woman I pretend to be.

Her fingertips pause again. When I meet her eyes, they're bright with unshed tears. "I see someone carrying burdens they shouldn't bear alone. Someone who saves others while bleeding herself. Someone who..." She stops, biting her lip.

"Someone who what?" I prompt gently.

"Someone who makes me forget what's possible and what isn't." The admission hangs between us like a physical thing.

My good hand rises without permission, hand brushing a strand of hair that's escaped her braid. "I told you, not all impossible things stay that way."

"Don't." Her voice breaks slightly. "Don't give me hope if you don't mean it. I couldn't bear it."

"Liora." Her name feels like a prayer on my lips. "I've never meant anything more in my life."

She searches my face, looking for the lie she won't find. Whatever she sees makes her breath catch. Slowly, giving me time to pull away, she leans forward until her forehead rests against mine.

"You're going to break my heart," she whispers. "I can feel it coming like a storm on the horizon. But I can't seem to care."

"If anyone's heart breaks, it will be mine." The truth of it aches in my chest. "I'm not... I don't know how to do this. How to be what you deserve."

"I don't need you to be anything but yourself." Her hand cups my cheek, thumb tracing my cheekbone with devastating tenderness. "The truth beneath all the masks you wear."

The irony cuts deep. She wants the real me, but the real me is an assassin sent to kill. Yet in this moment, with her touch gentle on my skin and her breath mingling with mine, I feel more myself than I have in years.

"The wound," I remind her weakly. "You should finish bandaging it."

"Always so practical," she murmurs, but draws back enough to resume her work.

Her touch remains gentle but now carries weight, each brush of her fingertips an acknowledgment of what grows between us. As she secures the fresh bandage, she glances toward the window with sudden tension.

"We should be careful," Liora warns quietly. "I saw Lady Mereswen's carriage pass by twice today. She's watching the house."

The name sends a chill through me. Mereswen's knowing gaze at the gallery, her warnings about Blackthorne being impossible to escape. What does she suspect?

When she finishes with the bandage, her palms linger on my shoulders.

"There." Her voice has gone husky. "Try not to reopen it again. I'm running out of creative lies about your clumsiness."

"What would I do without you?" The question slips out more serious than teasing.

"Let's hope you never have to find out." But fear flickers in her eyes, a premonition perhaps, or just the natural fear of one who's already lost too much.

We return to studying the documents, but everything has changed. Now we sit closer, her thigh pressed against mine, fingers brushing with increasing frequency as we turn pages. The air between us hums with promise and peril in equal measure.

Whatever happens with Blackthorne, with the mission, with the sacred judgment I'm bound to deliver, this moment exists outside all of that. This connection neither of us sought but neither can deny.

"These notes mention people recovering if treated within the first month," I say, carefully hiding my true knowledge source. "Eight of Blackthorne's followers might still be saved if we act quickly."

Pain stabs through my wounded shoulder. I bite back a gasp as my muscles tense. The temple corruption spreads beneath my bandages, black tendrils fighting within my flesh.

Liora notices immediately. Her hand moves to my arm, the touch soft yet sure. "Your wound is troubling you again." Her eyes find my bandaged shoulder, concern warming her gaze. "That fall reopened it worse than I first thought."

The lie hangs between us, fragile as spun glass. We both know wounds like this don't come from simple falls, yet neither of us acknowledges what we're not saying. Her eyes hold questions she won't ask, and I'm grateful for her discretion even as guilt twists in my chest.

"It heals slowly," I admit. Her touch lingers on my arm, warmth spreading from the point of contact. "The wound fights with normal treatment."

She studies my face, her palm still resting on my arm. Her perception cuts through the masks I wear like gauze. "Your recovery exceeds what my remedies could accomplish alone. Your blood fights unusually hard."

Warmth rises up my neck, intensified by her continued touch. She comes too close to the truth without knowing it. The golden flecks appear in my eyes when my emotions run high. Blackthorne sensed something different about me. Mother Superior selected me for qualities she never fully explained.

"Perhaps." I turn another page, redirecting her attention but not moving away from her touch. "What matters now is how these formulas might help others."

Liora returns to the diagrams, her touch slowly sliding from my arm, fingertips trailing across my skin in a way that catches my breath. She arranges pages in proper order, her natural ability speaking of intelligence far beyond what her station suggests.

"The reversal needs seven days of preparation," she says, glancing up at me through her lashes. "We must gather ingredients immediately if we hope to help anyone before it's too late."

Seven days. The ritual requires preparation while the moon wanes. I recognize elements that mirror ceremonies I've witnessed in the Sanctuary, though these serve healing rather than judgment.

"The most important ingredient is blood freely given by someone with natural resistance," I say quietly, watching her reaction carefully.

Our eyes meet, understanding dawning. An electric current passes between us, intensity building in the small space separating our bodies. "Someone whose body naturally fights against shadow corruption."

My hand rises to my wounded shoulder where temple corruption still battles within my flesh. The truth sits heavy on my tongue but stays unspoken. How could I explain the golden flecks Blackthorne saw in my eyes? The connection I've denied since childhood?

"Someone with unusual healing abilities," I say instead. "Like myself."

Surprise flickers across her face, followed by an emotion deeper. Her gaze drops briefly to my lips before returning to my eyes. Her acceptance warms a place long cold inside my chest.

"Your blood could save them," she says, wonder filling her voice. "Where Blackthorne corrupts, you could heal."

The contrast hits me like a fist to the gut. I came to deliver death, yet I now find the possibility for life. Healing instead of destruction for souls not yet fully transformed.

"These people deserve mercy," I say, pressing my fists hard enough to make the wood creak. "If reversal remains possible, we can't stand by while innocents suffer."

Liora watches me, her fingers hovering near mine without touching, offering connection should I choose it. The air between our skin feels charged, alive with possibility.

"You believe this knowledge is true," she says, voice dropping to an intimate whisper. "Even though it contradicts everything commonly understood about shadow corruption."

"I believe mercy comes from complete understanding." My voice hardens with conviction, while my fingertips edge closer to hers. "Too often we condemn those who deserve second chances."

A shift occurs between us. This servant sees me more clearly than anyone has before, recognizing the truth beneath Lady

Ravencrest's careful mask. Her eyes hold mine with intensity that makes my heart quicken.

"We need a specific location for this ritual," she says, her practicality grounding my racing thoughts, even as her finger brushes against mine. "Somewhere private yet accessible, protected from interruption."

"The gardener's cottage behind the rose maze would work," I say, voice roughening as her fingertip hooks over mine. "Abandoned since before I arrived, but still structurally sound."

She nods, having already considered it. "I'll gather herbs from the garden tonight. Several grow there though you might not have noticed them among the decorative plantings."

"You planted them deliberately?" I look at her with new respect, admiring the quiet rebellion of this woman who appeared so obedient on the surface.

Her smile carries secret pride, eyes sparkling with mischief I hadn't noticed before. "Perhaps I saw their value beyond pretty flowers. Night blooms hold properties daylight flowers lack."

Her quiet rebellion goes beyond aristocratic expectations and reminds me of my own work. While nobles obsess over appearances, she cultivates practical medicines right under their unseeing eyes.

As darkness deepens outside, we study with renewed focus. I feel each component carefully, memorizing diagrams with intense concentration. The reversal ritual takes shape between us, possibility born from stolen knowledge and shared mission.

Our fingers brush together with increasing frequency, each contact lingering longer than the last.

"How do such secrets stay hidden?" Liora asks, tracing lunar phases on weathered parchment. "If salvation remains possible for those affected early, why does everyone believe otherwise?"

Her innocent question stabs between my ribs. My chest tightens as I consider possibilities I've avoided despite mounting evidence.

"Power," I say, tasting bitterness. "Knowledge creates options beyond absolute control. Questions undermine the certainty required for blind obedience."

I think of carefully measured truths, of knowledge doled out according to a servant's usefulness rather than their right to understand. How different is Mother Superior from Blackthorne, with his selective sharing of secrets among chosen followers?

The walls suddenly feel too close. My skin crawls with awareness of watching eyes and listening ears. I need space to breathe, to think. To feel whatever is growing between us without the weight of these walls pressing down.

"We should continue in the garden," I say, gathering the papers and hiding them inside my bodice. My fingers brush the skin along my breasts as I secure the documents. Liora's eyes follow the movement before quickly looking away, color rising in her cheeks. "These questions need open sky, not candlelight and confinement."

Moonlight spills through tall windows, painting silver patterns across the hallway floor. The house sleeps around us, servants long since retired. Our feet make no sound as we move toward the garden door, our bodies remembering how to travel unseen.

The stolen knowledge burns upon my skin, papers crackling softly with each breath. In this house, too many eyes watch, too many ears listen. Servants report to other masters, neighbors note unusual behavior, society punishes those who step outside their assigned place.

My shoulder throbs steadily, temple corruption fighting with my body's resistance. The pain keeps me present, anchoring me in reality while my mind races with possibilities.

"What happens after we try this ritual?" Liora asks softly. In the narrow hallway, she walks close enough that our arms brush with each step. "After we help those we can reach in time, what becomes of Lord Blackthorne himself?"

"Justice finds him regardless," I say, certainty steadying my voice despite new complications. The Raven's Kiss waits on my lips, though she knows nothing of its presence or intent. I have enough to try again, even as what I wear fades.

"And what happens to you?" she says, surprising me with her focus. She catches my hand in the darkness, stopping me before we reach the garden door. "After justice is served and those still savable find healing. What then becomes of Lady Ravencrest?"

The question hits me like a slap. I've never thought beyond completing my duty. Yet now, with stolen knowledge pressed close to my heart and this woman's warm hand in mine, new possibilities bloom like night flowers.

"I don't know," I admit, my voice rougher than intended. I step closer to her, close enough to feel her breath on my face. "My plans only reached as far as seeing Blackthorne face justice."

Her eyes search mine in the dim light, seeking an answer beyond what I've given. "You've changed since coming to Luridian," she says carefully. "The woman who interviewed me would never risk herself to save strangers caught in early corruption."

Her words slice deeper than any blade. An energy has shifted inside me since finding the reversal possibilities, since seeing golden flecks in my own eyes, since meeting this woman whose kindness awakens feelings I never allowed myself.

"I used to believe justice only required punishment," I say, acutely aware of her hand still holding mine, her body's warmth radiating in the cool hallway. "That mercy comes from simply ending suffering quickly."

"Now I see some souls deserve healing rather than judgment," I say, my voice dropping to a whisper as I step closer. Our faces are inches apart in the dim hallway. "Including those condemned without knowing salvation remained possible."

Her eyes widen slightly, pupils growing larger in the low light. The moment stretches between us, filled with possibility. The garden door remains forgotten as her free hand rises to touch my face, trembling slightly.

"You've come alive since I met you," she whispers. "The woman who first arrived was all perfect surfaces. Beautiful but cold as marble."

Her words should offend me. My training created that perfect exterior. But truth resonates in them. I was a honed blade, shaped for a single mission. Now edges blur, possibilities multiply. I've become a force unpredictable, even to myself.

"And what am I now?" I ask, turning my face slightly into her palm.

"Dangerous," she says with a small smile. "But alive. Breathing. Human."

Human. Not weapon, not instrument, not sacred blade. The word settles into my chest like a stone dropped in still water, ripples spreading outward. Human, with all its messy implications of choice and consequence.

My grip tightens around hers. "We should go to the garden," I say, though I make no move to open the door. "Anyone could find us here."

"And that would be scandalous," she says, her thumb tracing my lower lip with unexpected boldness. "The noble widow and her servant girl, standing too close in darkened hallways."

"Liora." Her name comes out rougher than intended. Warning or invitation, I'm not certain.

"My lady." Her response carries similar ambiguity, formal words belied by intimate tone.

The papers crackle upon my skin as I inhale sharply. We should move. This hallway offers too much exposure, too little protection. Yet neither of us steps away.

I'm the one who finally reaches for the door, though my other hand remains intertwined with hers. Cool night air rushes to my heated skin as we step into the garden. Stars pierce the black sky, watching with indifference. The rose maze stretches before us, flowers releasing a sweet scent that fills my lungs.

"This way," Liora says, tugging me toward a hidden path I hadn't noticed before. Her confidence in these gardens matches my comfort in the shadows. We each know the terrain that shaped us.

She leads me through narrow openings between hedge walls, moonlight catching in her hair. The pain in my shoulder remains sharp but distant, overwhelmed by more immediate sensations. Her hand in mine. The brush of her dress to my legs as we navigate tight passages. The sound of her breathing in the quiet night.

25

HEALING

The maze opens suddenly to its heart, a small circular clearing with a stone bench beneath a latticed arch heavy with night-blooming roses. Stars shine through gaps in the floral canopy, creating patterns like sacred symbols across the ground. The space feels protected, separate from the world beyond.

"I come here when the house feels too small," Liora says, pulling me toward the bench. "No one else bothers with the maze. Too many thorns, too little goal."

"Perfect cover for rebellion," I say, admiring her clever thinking.

"I've learned to hide important things in plain sight." Her smile holds secrets I've only begun to uncover. "People see what they expect to see."

We sit close together on the stone bench, her hip pressed close to mine. Night-blooming flowers fill my lungs with sweetness. The papers crackle between us as I withdraw them from my bodice, spreading them across our laps. Moonlight provides just enough light to make out the diagrams.

"These formulas," I say, forcing my attention back to our mission. "You were right about the herbs. You've grown everything we need right here."

She leans closer to examine the pages, her hair brushing my cheek. "The timing must be just right. The new moon in three days gives us perfect conditions for this reversal ritual."

I follow her finger tracing lunar phases on the weathered parchment. The closeness of shared mission feels different from planning with Sister-assassins. There's no rank here, just joined knowledge forming a force greater together.

"How did you know how to grow these specific plants?" I ask, truly curious about her foresight.

Her shoulder lifts in a small shrug that presses her more firmly close to me. "I didn't know their specific goal. But my mother taught me to prepare for possibilities I couldn't yet see. 'Some medicines aren't needed until the moment they become a truth essential,' she would say."

She turns slightly, our faces close in the darkness. "I've planted healing gardens wherever I've served. Mostly they go unused. But I sleep better knowing they exist."

"You've been preparing for this without knowing it," I say softly. "Just as I've been trained for purposes I'm only now beginning to understand."

Her eyes search mine. "What do you mean?"

The truth rises to my lips, dangerous yet necessary. "My blood naturally fights shadow corruption. It's why I heal so quickly, why corrupted creatures hesitate before attacking me. My blood resists what claims others."

Understanding dawns in her eyes. "That's why you're so drawn to him despite the danger. Your blood protects you where others would fall to corruption."

I nod slowly. "I was chosen for what I am as much as what I can do. Mother Superior has never shared the full truth of why I was selected as a child. Now I wonder how much she knows about my nature that I don't."

Liora's hand finds my wounded shoulder, gentle fingertips tracing the edges of bandages visible above my neckline. "Your blood can save those caught in early stages."

"Yes." I cover her hand with mine, holding it close to my skin. "The ritual requires fresh blood from someone with natural resistance. Mine will serve healing rather than destruction."

"Strange how paths appear," she murmurs. "You came to deliver death, yet now find ways to preserve life instead."

Her observation strikes deeper than she knows. Each execution I performed felt righteous, necessary. Now doubt creeps in like shadow at noon.

"I was taught that shadow corruption was absolute and irreversible," I say. "That death provided the only mercy possible. Now I question whether that teaching served truth or control."

Her fingertips brush my cheek, bringing my focus back to her face. "You question what once seemed certain. That's rare in people with power."

"Power," I laugh softly. "I've never thought of myself as having power."

"Yet you do," she says with sudden intensity. "Over life and death. Over your own choices now. Over me."

The last words hang between us, charged with meaning. Her eyes hold mine, refusing to look away despite the admission's vulnerability.

"I have no power over you," I whisper.

"Don't you?" Her fingertips trace my jaw. "You could destroy everything I care about with a single word to the right authorities."

"I would never."

"I know," she interrupts. "That's why I trust you. Why I..." She hesitates, words failing as her gaze drops to my lips.

Time suspends itself between one heartbeat and the next. The ritual papers slide forgotten to the ground as I lean forward, crossing the last distance between us. Our lips meet with gentle hesitation that quickly deepens into certainty.

Unlike our first impulsive kiss, this one builds slowly, deliberately. Her fingers slide into my hair, loosening pins until strands fall around my shoulders. I trace the curve of her waist, feeling warmth through simple cotton. She tastes of mint and smells of garden herbs, real in ways Blackthorne's practiced passion never approached.

When we finally part, breathless, she rests her forehead close to mine. "Remember this moment," she whispers. "Whatever happens after, remember we chose this freely."

The weight of her words sinks into me. Choice. Freedom. Concepts foreign to my training yet suddenly essential to my understanding. This kiss wasn't a mission or manipulation. It was a genuine desire, freely given and received.

"I'll remember," I promise, the words holding more significance than she can know.

She smiles, reaching down to collect the scattered papers. "We should continue our planning. Dawn comes too quickly, and we have lives to save tomorrow."

The shift back to work feels natural rather than abrupt. Our connection doesn't require constant acknowledgment to remain present between us. Instead, it gives our shared mission greater meaning.

We spread the papers across our laps again, heads bent together as we discuss reversal components. My finger traces the ritual circle diagram. "The timing must be just right. Sunset tomorrow begins preparation, with the reversal completed at midnight."

"I can gather all the herbs before noon," Liora says, her voice steady though her body remains pressed close to mine. "The gardener's cottage has everything else we need. Proper space, protection from interruption, access to water."

"We'll need to prepare the space first," I say. "Cleansing rituals, protective boundaries."

Her eyebrow lifts. "Boundaries for what?"

I hesitate, wondering how much to reveal about shadow energy's nature. "The process of drawing corruption from a body creates... disturbances. Better to contain them with proper precautions."

She studies me, accepting the partial explanation. "Then we should begin tonight with space preparation. The cottage has stood empty long enough to collect negative energies."

Her practical approach to mystical concepts surprises me again. Most servants would fear ritual work, dismissing it as superstition or fearing divine punishment. Yet Liora approaches it with the same steady mindset she applies to herb cultivation.

"You're not afraid of this work?" I ask.

"Should I be?" Our gazes meet directly. "If reversing corruption requires stepping beyond common boundaries, I'll gladly cross that line."

Her courage impresses me. She understands the risks yet commits completely. So different from my own training, where obedience substituted for choice, where commandments replaced conviction.

"We should gather materials now," I say, rising from the bench. "Basic cleansing can be done tonight, with specific ritual components prepared tomorrow."

Liora stands too, fingers brushing mine as she helps fold the papers. "The gardener's shed has salt, sage, and other basics. I've kept supplies there knowing they might be needed someday."

Again her foresight impresses me. This woman has built resources and knowledge without notice from aristocratic noses, preparing for possibilities she couldn't name but somehow sensed approaching.

We move through the garden together, collecting materials from hidden caches she's established throughout the grounds. Salt from hollow statuary bases. Dried herbs from pouches concealed in decorative urns. Candles stored in weatherproof containers beneath benches.

"You've created an entire apothecary under the aristocrats' noses," I say, admiring her cleverness.

"The upper classes see only what they expect to see," she repeats, pride evident in her voice. "A servant girl tending flowers holds no interest for those who believe themselves important."

Her methods mirror mine in surprising ways. We both use others' expectations as concealment, cultivate resources without notice, prepare for contingencies before they arise. Different training, similar results.

The cottage appears before us, small and weathered but sturdy. Climbing roses have nearly swallowed its stone exterior, thorny protection disguising its potential. Liora produces a key from her pocket, unlocking the simple door easily.

"You maintain this place," I observe as we enter. The interior, while dusty, shows signs of basic upkeep.

"I keep it usable," she says, lighting a lantern she retrieves from a cabinet. "Clean water in the barrel, roof intact, floor swept. Simple guards for decay."

The space consists of three small rooms. Main living area with stone hearth, tiny bedroom, and storage space lined with shelves. Practical, defensible, isolated enough for our needs. I approve even as other parts of me note the strange closeness of entering this space together.

"Perfect for our needs," I say, surveying the main room. "Large enough for ritual work but small enough to control any unwanted effects."

Liora nods, already arranging our collected supplies on a small table. "We should begin with salt boundaries tonight. Full cleansing at dawn, then preparation throughout the day."

I watch her work, admiring how she handles mystical elements with steady confidence. She treats ritual components with the same attention she gives to medical herbs. Respecting their power without fear or superstition.

"You've done this before," I observe.

She glances up, moonlight from the small window catching amber highlights in her eyes. "Not this specific ritual, but similar protective work. My mother taught techniques for keeping negative influences away from sickrooms."

"Folk traditions often contain real power without understanding its source," I say, thinking of Sisterhood rituals that mirror older practices. "Knowledge survives when its origins are forgotten."

Together we begin the cleansing process, working in comfortable harmony. I clear the space while she prepares salt mixtures with dried herbs. Our movements flow around each other naturally, anticipating needs without speaking. When our fingertips occasionally brush, neither of us pulls away.

As night deepens around the cottage, we establish basic protections. Salt at thresholds, simple sigils sketched on windowsills, cleansing smoke filling corners. Tomorrow will require more complex preparations, but tonight's work makes the space suitable for planning.

"It's a beginning," Liora says, satisfaction evident in her voice as she surveys our work. "Tomorrow we can truly prepare."

I nod, suddenly aware of tiredness pulling at my limbs. The day's revelations combined with my still-healing wound leave me drained. Liora notices immediately, her palm touching my arm with gentle concern.

"You need rest," she says. "The ritual will require your full strength tomorrow."

"Yes," I agree, though reluctance colors my voice. This bubble of shared mission feels too precious to abandon, even temporarily.

She steps closer, her touch sliding from my arm to my waist. "We should return to the house separately. It's getting very late"

Practical wisdom, yet I find myself unwilling to part so soon. My hand rises to her face, thumb tracing her lower lip much as she did mine earlier. "Not quite yet."

Her smile holds understanding beyond words. She turns her face into my palm, lips brushing sensitive skin. "Not quite yet," she agrees.

In the cottage's sheltered darkness, we find each other again. This kiss carries greater heat than before, bodies pressing closer without the garden bench between us. Her hand slides close to my cloak, finding the curve of my hip, the small of my back. I trace her neck, her collarbone, the place where her life beats steady and true.

We pull apart before passion overwhelms practicality, both aware of all we must accomplish tomorrow. Her eyes hold mine in the lantern's dim glow, saying things words can't express.

"Tomorrow," she says, smoothing my disheveled hair with gentle fingertips. "After the ritual preparations are complete."

Promise fills that single word. Tomorrow. Stretching beyond immediate tasks to an understanding neither of us names but both acknowledge. An emotion growing between us with each shared touch, each moment of understanding.

"Tomorrow," I agree, memorizing her face at this moment. Flushed cheeks, bright eyes, kiss-swollen lips. So different from the composed servant who first entered my service.

We part at the cottage door, separating to follow different paths back to the house. I watch her disappear into the rose maze before taking my own route, planning timing to ensure our returns don't coincide suspiciously.

My shoulder throbs as I walk alone through moonlit gardens. Temple corruption fights with my natural healing, black tendrils seeking purchase in flesh that rejects their influence. The pain serves as a useful reminder of all that hangs in balance tomorrow. Lives that might be saved, corruption that might be reversed, truths that might be uncovered.

Stars wheel overhead with indifference. The path stretches before me, silver beneath moonlight guiding my steps through darkness. My fingertips touch my lips, still warm from her kiss, as though preserving the sensation for future reference.

Tomorrow brings duty beyond anything my training prepared me for. The ritual we prepare serves life rather than death for the first time in many years. My blood will heal rather than spill. These changes should terrify me, yet instead they feel like awakening after long sleep.

Possibility grows inside my chest, hope beyond limitation or corruption. A force that belongs only to me.

Let mercy flow from understanding rather than ignorance. Let life rather than death fulfill my duty.

The prayer rises from lips trained to different words, yet feels more genuine than any ritual from my past. Tomorrow we save lives rather than end them, blood serving healing rather than destruction.

Whatever comes after justice finds Blackthorne, mercy matters more than any command.

26

CONVICTION

Before dawn, I practice the ritual forms in my bedchamber. My body flows through sacred positions honoring each aspect of Mordreth's divine nature. Silence. Shadow. Sacrifice. Secrecy. Suffering. Surrender. Salvation. The motions pull at my healing flesh, the corruption in my shoulder throbbing with each movement.

Sweat slides down my spine despite the morning chill. My muscles burn with satisfying heat. Pain keeps me anchored when doubt threatens to pull me under. My blood rushes beneath my skin, alive with purpose yet conflicted in direction.

Nearly three months in Luridian. Tonight Blackthorne dies. Months of deception end with a kiss.

Show me clarity where shadows cloud judgment.

The prayer rises unbidden. Words learned at Mother Superior's knee before I could even hold a blade. The familiar plea feels hollow now, like calling into a well that returns no echo.

Dawn light spills through parted curtains, painting my skin gold where it touches. Sleep has eluded me. My body aches with more than physical exertion. Blackthorne's stolen research lies scattered across my bed. Pages revealing reversal rituals for early corruption. Knowledge that shatters everything I believed true.

I complete the final form, my breath coming harder than the exertion warrants. I see Brother Elias bleeding out on the execution altar. I see temple guardians falling to my blade. Their corruption might have been reversed if I had known. If Mother Superior had told me.

My fist strikes the floor. Pain shoots up my arm with clarifying force. Mother Superior's voice echoes in memory. The necessity of execution. The absolute nature of shadow corruption. All certainties now floating untethered in my mind.

I rise and cross to the mirror. Violet eyes stare back, shadowed by sleepless nights. Midnight hair falls wild from ritual exertion. Black tendrils spread from the wounded shoulder, corruption fighting to claim territory my blood refuses to surrender.

What am I?

The question burns through my veins. Blackthorne saw golden flecks in my eyes during our passion. Temple guardians hesitated before attacking me. Mother Superior selected me specifically for this mission, recognizing qualities she deliberately kept unnamed.

A soft knock interrupts my thoughts. Three gentle taps against wood. Liora.

"Enter," I call, wrapping a silk robe around my sweat-dampened shift.

She appears in the doorway, morning light catching honey-brown strands escaping her practical braid. She carries a tray with tea and fresh bread, her eyes immediately finding my bandaged shoulder where black stains spread through clean linen.

"You've been training." Concern softens her features as she sets the tray down. Her tone carries no accusation, just worry.

"The forms help me think." I touch the bandage where fresh blood stains the linen.

She moves closer without hesitation, fingers already reaching toward my shoulder. This easy intimacy between us still surprises me. "May I?"

I nod, turning to give her better access. Her touch feels warm and gentle compared to the clinical handling I'm accustomed to from Sisterhood healers. She peels back the edge of the bandage, revealing the wound that has finally begun to heal, though faint dark lines still trace across the skin.

"It looks better today," she says, relief evident in her voice. "The herbal poultice is working."

I glance down at the healing skin. "Your mother's remedy proved effective."

"She learned from her mother, who learned from hers." Pride warms her voice as she prepares fresh bandages. "Some knowledge survives despite what nobility might prefer."

"I should redress this." Her voice turns practical as she gathers fresh bandages.

"After I've eaten." I take her hand before she can turn away. "Join me?"

Surprise flickers across her features, quickly replaced by pleasure. "Of course."

We share the simple meal, sitting closer than propriety allows. The bread tastes of honey and fresh grain. The tea carries mint and something earthier that warms my blood. Her knee occasionally brushes mine beneath the small table, each contact sending warmth through my body that has nothing to do with the tea.

"Tonight is Lord Blackthorne's celebration," she says after comfortable silence.

"Yes." I watch her face, memorizing details I've never fully appreciated. The small scar at her temple. The exact shade of amber that flecks her brown eyes. "I must attend."

"Even with your wound?" Worry clouds her expression. "You need rest, not another night of pretending to enjoy noble company."

I smile at her blunt assessment of my social obligations. "Some invitations can't be declined."

"Because of Lord Blackthorne's special interest in you?" Her voice carries an edge I've never heard before. Jealousy, perhaps.

"His interest serves my purpose." I cover her hand with mine, enjoying how her fingers automatically turn to intertwine with mine. "Nothing more."

"And when your purpose with him is complete?" She looks down at our joined hands. "What then?"

The question catches me unprepared. After. A concept foreign to my mission-focused existence. "I haven't thought beyond tonight."

She looks up, surprise clear in her expression. "Truly? You who plan everything so carefully?"

I laugh, the sound rusty with disuse. "I plan actions, not futures."

"Everyone deserves a future." Her thumb traces circles against my palm, the simple touch more intimate than Blackthorne's orchestrated seduction. "Even women who pretend they don't need one."

Her insight cuts to the heart of something I've never acknowledged. The Sisterhood trained me for purpose, not longevity. Mission completion, not personal satisfaction. Sacred duty, not human connection.

"What would you suggest for this hypothetical future?" I ask, surprising myself with the question.

"Somewhere quiet." Her eyes take on a distant look. "A small house near the sea, perhaps. Gardens without stone walls. A life where no one watches from shadows."

The image burns into my mind with unexpected clarity. Salt air instead of incense. Growing things instead of death delivered in darkness. Freedom from constant observation and judgment.

"It sounds peaceful." My voice emerges softer than intended.

"It could be." Her eyes return to mine, something unspoken passing between us.

The implication steals my breath. Not just a future, but a shared one. The possibility had never entered my mind until this moment.

"I should prepare for tonight." I stand, needing distance from possibilities I'm not ready to face.

She nods, gathering the breakfast tray. "I'll draw your bath."

While she's gone, I approach my wardrobe. Tonight's attire must balance beauty with functionality. The burgundy gown hangs like liquid blood, silk promising both attraction and concealment. Beside it, underpinnings that will secure the knife against my thigh.

The wooden box containing the Raven's Kiss rests on my vanity. I trace the carved surface, feeling cold power pulsing within. Death sleeps inside until awakened by sacred purpose and perfect timing.

Three sharp knocks announce Liora's return. She enters with steaming water for the copper bath, scenting the air with lavender and rosemary.

"You need proper rest before tonight," she says, pouring the final pitcher.

The water embraces me as I slip into the bath, heat seeping into sore muscles. Liora works cleansing oils through my hair, fingers strong as they work. Her touch carries only simple care, gentle and relaxing.

"Will you return tonight after the celebration?" she asks, her voice carefully casual.

"Yes." I close my eyes as she rinses my hair. "The carriage will bring me back."

Her hands stop. "I'll wait for you."

The simple promise warms something cold inside my chest. "No need to sacrifice your sleep."

"I want to." Her fingers resume their gentle work. "I worry when you attend these noble gatherings. You return different somehow."

Closer to truth than she knows. Each encounter with Blackthorne pulls me deeper into performance that threatens to become reality. "Different how?"

"Colder. More distant." She moves to my shoulders, working tension from knotted muscles. "As though you leave pieces of yourself behind."

Her perception unsettles me. I've spent years perfecting the art of seamless transition between roles. That she sees the fractures beneath my performance speaks to something beyond ordinary observation.

"Tonight will be different," I promise.

After my bath, she helps me dress in simple day clothes. The afternoon passes in quiet preparation. I rest at her insistence, though sleep eludes me. My mind circles endlessly around the evening ahead. The Raven's Kiss will find its target tonight. Blackthorne's judgment approaches with relentless certainty.

Yet beneath this divine purpose, something else grows. I find myself contemplating a future previously unimagined, a connection I never planned to form. Liora's quiet presence in my chambers has become more necessity than luxury, her touch more comfort than service.

As sunset approaches, she helps me prepare for the evening. Her fingers work through my hair, weaving small braids into an elaborate pattern. Unlike her usual practiced movements, there's tenderness today, fingertips lingering against my skin.

"Will you use your special lip stain tonight?" she asks, securing a final pin.

Our eyes meet in the mirror. I know which one she means, the Raven's Kiss she watched me apply before my last meeting with Blackthorne. The ornate wooden box sits on my vanity, waiting.

"Yes. This occasion calls for it." I reach for the box, opening it to reveal the crystal vial. The dark liquid shifts as if alive, responding to my presence with eager anticipation. She goes to fetch my gown as I begin.

I lift the small brush of raven feathers, its bone handle cool against my fingers. I dip it into the vial, feeling resistance as if the liquid possesses weight beyond its volume. I bring it to my lips with ceremonial care, applying the first thin layer across my lower lip. Cold burns where it touches, spreading through my flesh like frost across a window.

"By Mordreth's shadow, bind this essence to sacred purpose," I whisper, too low for her to hear.

The black liquid shimmers at my incantation, seeping slightly into my skin. I apply a second layer, feeling the cold intensify, spreading through my face and down my throat.

"By Mordreth's mercy, reserve judgment for the deserving soul."

My heart beats faster, pumping heat to combat the spreading chill. The sensation borders on pain yet carries a strange pleasure with it. I apply the third layer with steady hands.

"By Mordreth's will, release this judgment only when the vessel stands at pleasure's peak."

The black liquid glimmers once more, then seems to disappear entirely, leaving no trace on my lips. The cold sensation recedes, replaced by awareness of something new waiting beneath the surface. Power sleeps in my flesh, patient as winter. Death for Blackthorne waits in my kiss, ready to activate only at the height of his pleasure.

Liora returns with my burgundy gown draped carefully over her arms, her timing perfect as always. Her eyes find mine in the mirror, a knowing look passing between us.

"The color suits you perfectly," she says softly, echoing her words from before. Her eyes linger on my lips with unusual intensity, as if trying to memorize their shape. "There's something different about them tonight. They seem to shimmer, like they're holding secrets." Her fingers rise as if to touch them before catching herself, a flush spreading across her cheeks at the near-intimate gesture.

"You won't find it anywhere in Luridian," I reply, closing the box with a soft click. A secret shared between us, even if she doesn't know its true nature.

"It suits you," she says simply, though her expression suggests she knows I'm hiding something. She retrieves the gown, holding it open for me to step into. "Although you hardly need enhancements."

I slip into the burgundy silk, feeling it settle around my body like liquid shadow. Liora's fingers work the small buttons along my spine, each touch careful and deliberate. Her presence sends warmth through my body that contrasts with the lingering cold of the Raven's Kiss.

"What are you thinking about?" she asks softly, her breath warm against my neck as she secures the final button.

"Tonight." The half-truth comes easily. "And what comes after."

I turn to face her, adjusting the gown's drape. "I noticed Lord Hargrove's name appears nowhere on the invitation. His withdrawal from Blackthorne's circle seems complete."

"Perhaps that's for the best," Liora says carefully. "He never approved of your... association."

"Lady Mereswen, however, remains on the list." I frown slightly. "Her presence tonight could complicate matters."

"The Countess sees much but says little," Liora observes. "Be careful around her."

"You speak as though everything changes tonight." Her hands rest lightly on my shoulders.

"Perhaps it does." I turn to face her, careful to maintain enough distance that she won't touch my lips by accident. "Liora."

"My lady?" Her voice barely disturbs the air between us.

Words fail me. How to explain what grows between us without revealing truths that would endanger her? "Thank you for everything these past weeks."

Her expression shifts, disappointment quickly masked. "Of course. It's my duty."

"No." I take both her hands in mine, interlacing our fingers. "It goes far beyond duty. We both know that."

Color blooms in her cheeks. Her eyes drop to our joined hands. "My lady, I—"

"Wait for me tonight," I interrupt gently. "I'll return before dawn."

Her eyes are full of hope, something fragile awakening in their depths. "You promise?"

"Yes." I bring her fingers to my cheek rather than my lips, the touch warm against my skin. "Before dawn breaks, I will return to you."

Air stills between us, her body swaying slightly toward mine. "And then?"

"And then we'll talk about futures neither of us planned for." The words fall from my lips without premeditation, truth I hadn't known until speaking it.

Something transforms in her expression, hope blooming into certainty. Her hands slip from mine, rising to frame my face with unexpected boldness.

"No." Her voice carries steel I've rarely heard from her. "No more dancing around this. No more pretending we're just lady and servant."

"Liora—"

"I've watched you prepare for him." Her thumbs stroke my cheekbones, touch firm rather than tentative. "Watched you armor yourself in silk and lip stains. But when you're with me, you're different. Real."

The truth of her words cuts deeper than any blade. With Blackthorne, I perform, every touch measured, every response designed for maximum effect. His passion burns hot and consuming, all power and possession. But here, with her hands warm against my skin, I simply exist.

"You don't understand the danger," I whisper.

"I understand enough." Her eyes flash with quiet fire. "I understand that he takes from you. That each time you return from him, there's less of you left. But when we're together, when I tend your wounds, when we share meals, when you let me see past your masks, you come alive."

My hands rise to cover hers, feeling the calluses from years of honest work. Where Blackthorne's touch demands submission or challenge, hers offers sanctuary. Where his passion drowns, hers breathes life.

"What do you want from me?" The question emerges raw.

"Everything." No hesitation, no doubt. "Not the lady, not the hunter, not whatever role you play for him. Just you. The woman who trains before dawn because stillness terrifies her.

Who memorizes my brother's journal because she can't bear my grief. Who looks at me like I'm something precious instead of just useful."

The fierce possession in her voice undoes me.

"After tonight—" I begin.

"No." She pulls me closer, our bodies nearly touching. "Not after. Now. Before you go to him, I need you to know where your heart truly lies."

The quiet certainty steals my breath. In all my careful planning, I never imagined being seen so thoroughly by someone who should have no claim on me.

"Liora." Her name is both warning and plea.

"I know you'll go to him tonight." Her forehead touches mine, breath mingling in the space between us. "I know you have reasons I can't understand. But first, give me this. Give me something real to hold onto while you're gone."

She leans forward slowly, giving me time to pull away. Time to remember the Raven's Kiss sleeping beneath my lips, bound by divine will for another's judgment. I should retreat. Should protect her from the death I carry.

Instead, I close the distance between us.

Her lips find mine with desperate certainty, nothing like our careful first kiss in the garden or the reunion after my injury. This is need made manifest, desire breaking through every barrier of propriety and station. The intensity of it sends heat racing through my blood.

Where Blackthorne's kisses taste of power and darkness, hers carry sunlight and clean earth. Where his touch corrupts, hers purifies. Each difference burns itself into my memory even as I lose myself in the sensation. The way she angles her head to deepen the kiss, fingers tangling in my carefully arranged hair, the small sound of triumph she makes when I respond with matching hunger.

I find her hips, pulling her fully against me. The simple cotton of her dress is soft beneath my palms, honest fabric instead of silk designed to entice. She whimpers into my mouth when I nip at her lower lip, and the sound sends lightning through my veins.

This is what I never knew to want. Not the orchestrated passion of seduction, but the raw need of two people choosing each other despite every reason not to. Not the divine ecstasy promised by the Sisterhood, but the simple pleasure of being truly seen and wanted anyway.

When we finally part, we're both trembling. Her breath comes in quick, excited gasps, cheeks flushed with more than embarrassment. My carefully styled hair hangs loose around my shoulders, pins scattered on the floor.

"Remember this," she whispers, voice rough with desire. "When he touches you tonight, remember how it feels when someone touches you with love instead of hunger. Remember that you have a choice."

The gentle certainty in her voice makes my knees weak.

"You don't know what you're asking," I whisper.

"I'm not asking." She straightens my cloak with steady fingers, though her eyes still burn. "I'm hoping. Come back to me tonight. Whatever you have to do, whoever you have to be for him, come back to me after."

"And if I'm different?" The question slips out before I can stop it. "If what I do tonight changes me?"

Her smile holds something fierce and protective. "Then I'll help you remember who you really are. I'll bring you back to yourself, no matter how far you've gone."

Her eyes search mine, understanding dawning. "You're hunting something tonight."

The perceptiveness startles me. "What makes you say that?"

"The way you hold yourself. Like my father before tracking deer." Her hand traces the line of my jaw. "Whatever you seek, be careful. Lord Blackthorne sees too much."

"I'll handle him." I step away from her touch, retrieving my pearl earrings from the vanity. "Trust me."

"I do." The simple assertion warms my blood. "More than you know."

The carriage bell sounds from below. She helps with final preparations. A velvet cloak fastened with silver clasps, gloves of butter-soft leather that will allow dexterous movement while maintaining noble appearance.

At my chamber door she stops me, straightening my cloak with fingers that tremble slightly. "Come back to me," she whispers.

"I will." The promise feels more binding than any sacred oath I've sworn. "Wait for me."

Her eyes meet mine, filled with unspoken promise. "Until the stars fade," she whispers, the vow resonating between us like a prayer.

Returning to Crescent Court, I find myself wondering what story I'll tell her when I return. The truth feels both impossible and necessary. I carry the memory of Liora's touch against my cheek, warming me against the sacred venom that waits to deliver judgment.

As the carriage pulls away from Crescent Court, I touch my lips where the Raven's Kiss sleeps. Death waits for Blackthorne, but Liora offers me a promise I never thought to seek. Tonight brings mission completion, but dawn offers something entirely new.

The contradiction should trouble me. Instead, it feels like the first honest prayer I've offered in years.

Blood and shadow. Death and life. Let both find blessing in true sight.

27

— · —

JUDGEMENT

Blackthorne's estate rises in the night sky, windows blazing like fever-bright eyes in a dark face. The carriage wheels crunch over gravel, each stone grinding under weight with satisfying clarity, and my heart beats in perfect time with their rhythm. Tonight completes what began in Mother Superior's chamber, with the crystal vial cold in my palm and divine intent burning in my blood.

I trace the edges of my silk fan. The ribs feel smooth on my skin, familiar as a blade's hilt. The Raven's Kiss pulses on my lips, invisible but present, a cold fire waiting to consume its target. I taste it even now, metallic promise lingering at the edges of my awareness.

The burgundy gown slides over my skin as I step from the carriage, its whisper almost loud in the quiet night. The footman's hand feels warm on my gloved skin. His pulse jumps under my touch, his eyes lingering a moment too long. Lady Ravencrest's smile settles across my face, practiced and perfect.

My eyes take in the estate with hunger. I count three guards at the main door, never far from concealed weapons. Six more patrol the balconies, their movements betraying professional training under servants' attire. Others lurk in shadows designed to conceal them, their presence betrayed only by subtle shifts in the night air.

Soft music spills from the ballroom. The strings cry toward heaven, their sound carrying both beauty and sorrow. The scent of night-blooming jasmine mingles with beeswax candles and expensive perfume as I breathe in the heady mixture with each breath. Anticipation tastes sharp and sweet on my tongue, like copper pennies and overripe fruit.

"Lady Sera Ravencrest," the herald announces. Heads turn. I've crafted this moment through whispers and well-placed appearances as the mysterious widow who has caught Lord Blackthorne's interest. Eyes follow my progress across polished marble. Women measure the cut of my gown with their own while men imagine what lies underneath it.

Torchlight turns everything golden, casting shadows that dance like living things. I spot initiates mingling with aristocracy, their corruption betrayed by golden flecks in their eyes. Most remain early enough for potential reversal, their humanity still dominant despite the shadow's touch. The knowledge in my possession might save them, if judgment allows mercy alongside vengeance.

A server approaches with champagne. The glass feels cool in my palm, its surface slick with condensation. The liquid bubbles on my lips, but I only taste, never swallow. Nothing must dull my senses tonight. Nothing must delay Mordreth's judgment.

"Lady Ravencrest." Blackthorne's voice slides over my skin like oil. "You honor us with your presence."

I turn, allowing surprise to brighten my features though I sensed his approach from halfway across the room. He stands closer than expected, magnificent in black formal attire that emphasizes his height. The shadow pendant hangs at his throat, its surface drinking light rather than reflecting it.

"Lord Blackthorne." I offer my hand, wrist turned slightly to display the delicate bones under thin skin. He closes around mine with established intimacy. His thumb strokes across my knuckles, skin rough on mine. The contact sends familiar heat through my veins, memories of our previous encounter rising unbidden. "Your gathering exceeds even the rumors that reached me. A magnificent display."

"Beauty demands proper setting." His eyes never leave mine as he speaks, tracking my reaction with a predator's focus. "Some treasures require special attention to fully appreciate their worth."

My lips curve in response to his flattery, the expression balanced between invitation and amusement. The Raven's Kiss warms slightly, recognizing its target's presence. "Your collection certainly justifies such attention. Few in Luridian possess your eye for rare beauty."

His gaze heats with genuine pleasure. He believes I reference his artifacts, the relics forming the foundation of his cult's power. The trap closes tighter as his grip presses into mine.

"Perhaps you'll allow me to show you my newest acquisitions later this evening." His voice drops, meant for my ears alone. "Items that might interest a woman of your... unusual perceptions."

I press into his grip, promises in the subtle pressure. "I would be honored. Your previous offerings proved most illuminating."

Our words carry layers that neither of us speak aloud. His lips part slightly as pupils dilate with interest. The scent of him reaches me through the crowd's collective perfume. Expensive cologne masks the shadow-oil clinging to his skin, but my trained senses detect it nonetheless.

"Until then, enjoy the festivities." His hand releases mine with obvious reluctance. "My attention is unfortunately required elsewhere for a time."

His body moves through the gathering, stopping to speak with various nobles and officials. Every person he meets bends toward him like flowers seeking sunlight. Conversations pause when he approaches, then burst into laughter at his smallest joke. The shadow-touched among the crowd turn toward him unconsciously, their bodies aligned with his presence.

The string quartet plays a complex melody in the corner, their bows moving in perfect unison. I drift through the ballroom, becoming Lady Ravencrest with every gesture. My fan opens and closes, speaking silently to those versed in its language. I sample delicacies that taste like ash under the anticipation coating my tongue.

Lady Mereswen catches my eye across the room, her expression unreadable. She raises her glass in a subtle toast. To what, I cannot say. Warning? Acknowledgment? Farewell?

Near the doors, I glimpse a familiar figure. Lord Hargrove, uninvited but unable to stay away, watches from the shadows. His face twists with emotions I have no time to decipher.

Through it all, my awareness never leaves Blackthorne. I track him through mirrors and reflective surfaces. Three women approach him, each beautiful in different ways. His smile offers distinct appeal to each, one receives charm, another spiritual promise, the third pure carnal invitation.

Yet his eyes find me repeatedly across the crowded rooms. The seventh time our gazes meet, he excuses himself from a trade minister and moves toward me with unhurried intent. My heart beats faster, blood warming as he approaches.

"You've been watching me, Lady Ravencrest." His voice wraps around my name like a caress.

"Have I?" My fan closes with a soft snap. "Perhaps I simply recognize beauty when I see it."

His expression changes, hunger replacing practiced charm. "I promised to show you rare treasures. Items that exist between worlds, much like yourself."

The invitation I've waited for arrives exactly when I want it. I offer my arm, fingers resting lightly on his sleeve. "Lead on, my lord."

We ascend the grand staircase side by side. Each step moves us further from witnesses. I feel gazes following our departure but refuse to acknowledge them. The weight of their stares presses into my back like physical touch. I imagine whispers beginning the moment we're out of sight, speculation about where Lord Blackthorne leads the mysterious widow.

The upper hallway stretches before us, carpeted in midnight blue that swallows our footsteps. Paintings line the walls, their subjects' eyes seeming to follow our progress. Blackthorne's hand rests at my lower back, his palm radiating heat through silk directly to my skin.

"Your interest in shadow knowledge continues to intrigue me." His voice has lost some of its public performance, revealing more genuine depth inside. "Few women of your station look beyond the visible world."

"I find the visible world rarely contains the whole truth." I brush his arm with crafted familiarity. "Under every surface lies deeper meaning."

"Indeed." His smile shows genuine pleasure at my response. "You speak my thoughts before I voice them."

The corridor ends at carved double doors, their surfaces etched with symbols I recognize from forbidden manuscripts. Blackthorne produces a key unlike any common locksmith would craft. The metal seems to absorb rather than reflect the hallway's soft light. The lock turns with sound like distant bells rather than mechanical clicking.

"After you, Lady Ravencrest." His hand guides me forward into darkness that breathes like a living creature.

I step into his private chambers. The room serves as half temple, half bedchamber. The walls shimmer midnight blue with silver constellations painted in patterns unlike any visible from Luridian's night sky. Sacred objects rest on pedestals of polished obsidian, each singing with power my trained senses perceive. A massive bed dominates one wall, its frame carved from wood darker than ebony, sheets black as shadow itself.

The air feels thick with incense and earthier elements. Shadow-oil's scent clings to everything, subtle but unmistakable to one raised in the Sisterhood's traditions. I breathe it in, allowing appropriate awe to shape my features.

"Beautiful," I whisper, the word serving both my cover and my genuine impression of the space's impact.

"I knew you would appreciate it." He closes the doors, the lock engaging with finality. "So few do."

I move toward a pedestal holding a silver chalice, its surface etched with symbols similar to those used in Sisterhood rituals, though corrupted in ways that change their meaning entirely. My hands hover above it without touching, feeling the power sleeping within its metal.

"Your collection has grown since I last visited." My voice carries genuine interest. Everything here holds knowledge I crave, even as I prepare to end his life.

"I collect what sings to me." He moves closer, standing just behind me, close enough that his breath warms my neck. "As I found you."

I turn to face him, allowing one eyebrow to rise in challenge. "Found me? I am not one of your artifacts."

"Aren't you?" His hand rises, tracing the air beside my cheek without quite touching skin. "I discovered you among the dullness of Luridian society. A rare treasure that vibrates with ancient power."

His words strike truth I've tried to ignore, that the shadow's response to my presence, the golden flecks appearing in my eyes during moments of intense emotion, Mother Superior choosing me for this specific mission.

I lean into his touch, playing my role while keeping my aims clear. "Show me," I whisper, voice catching. "Show me what others can't see."

There's a difference in his eyes tonight. A sharpness under the cultured charm, as if he senses danger but can't quite place its source.

"You're different tonight." He studies me with an intensity that makes my skin prickle. "More... focused. Like a blade finally drawn from its sheath."

The observation cuts too close. I force a laugh, light and dismissive. "Perhaps I'm simply tired of pretending to be less than I am."

"Yes." His grip closes around mine, firmer than usual. "I think that's exactly it. The question is, what are you really, Sera?"

The way he says my name carries warning. This is still the game we've played, but the stakes feel suddenly higher. Good. Let him suspect. It will make his surprise all the sweeter.

"Why don't you tell me?" I challenge, stepping closer. "You claim to see so much."

His other hand comes up, gripping my waist with possessive force. "I see hunger that matches mine. Power that could reshape the world if properly channeled. A woman who walks between shadows as easily as breathing."

"Pretty words." I press into him, feeling his body's immediate response. "But what do you want from me? Really want?"

His control fractures slightly, grip tightening. "Everything. Your body, your power, your submission to what we could become together."

There it is. The truth under his careful seduction. Not love, not partnership, but possession. Domination. Control.

"And if I'm not interested in submission?" I let my own mask slip slightly, showing him the predator inside the widow's facade.

His pupils dilate with genuine excitement. "Then we have an interesting evening ahead of us."

He backs me to the wall with sudden force, his body caging mine. This is established territory, the physical chess match we've played before. His mouth finds my throat, teeth grazing skin with barely restrained violence.

"I've thought about this," he growls at my pulse. "How you surrendered so completely last time. How you screamed for me."

"Did I?" I arch into him, nails finding his shoulders through expensive fabric. "I remember it differently."

"Liar." His hand fists in my hair, pulling my head back to expose my throat further. "Your body remembers the truth even if your pride won't admit it."

He's right, partially. My body does remember the intensity, the pleasure that caught me off guard. But not surrender. Never that.

His mouth claims mine with bruising force, all pretense of gentility abandoned. This is what he truly is under the civilized veneer, a predator who takes what he wants. I respond with equal violence, biting his lip hard enough to draw blood.

He pulls back with a harsh laugh. "There she is. The real Sera."

"You have no idea who I really am."

"Then show me." He works at my gown swiftly, tearing when fabric resists. "Stop hiding behind these masks."

The irony almost makes me laugh. If only he knew which mask I'm truly wearing.

We move toward the bed in a tangle of partially removed clothing while competing for dominance. He is everywhere, gripping, claiming, trying to arrange me where he wants. I allow it to a point, matching his aggression while keeping my own control.

When he pushes me onto the bed, I let him think he's won. His weight settles over me, pinning without crushing. The shadows in the room respond to our combined energy, pooling around us with palpable hunger.

"The shadows sing for you," he says, voice rough with desire. "Can you feel how they want to claim you?"

"Is that what you think this is?" I arch under him, drawing a groan. "The shadows claiming me?"

"Among other things." His mouth travels down my body, each kiss a brand of possession. "By dawn, you'll understand what you truly are. What we are together."

Always the teacher, even now. Always positioning himself as the one with answers, the one in control. The Raven's Kiss pulses on my lips, ready.

His mouth finds the center of my need, and I allow myself to respond. No point in pretending the pleasure isn't real. My body's reaction to him has never been feigned, just carefully managed. He works me with skill born of years of practice, building each sensation with care.

But there's a difference tonight. A possessive edge that borders on desperate. As if he senses this might be his last chance to claim what he sees as his.

When the first orgasm builds, I let it come. My back arches, a cry tearing from my throat that echoes off stone walls. He rises above me with predatory satisfaction, wiping his mouth with the back of his hand.

"Beautiful," he says. "But we're far from finished."

He settles between my thighs, the hard length of him pressing to my entrance. Our eyes lock, storm-gray to violet, predator to predator.

"Tell me you want this," he demands.

"I want what you can give me," I say truthfully. The knowledge, the power, the completion of my mission. All things he'll provide tonight.

He enters me with one brutal thrust, forcing a gasp from my lips. There's no gentleness, no tender build-up. Just raw possession as he sets a punishing pace.

"Mine," he growls with each thrust. "You've been mine since that first dance."

"Never yours," I manage between gasps. "No one owns me."

"We'll see." His hand wraps around my throat, not quite choking but asserting dominance. "By the time I'm done with you, you'll beg to belong to me."

The shadows writhe around us, feeding on our violence. I can feel them trying to penetrate deeper, to claim me as they've claimed him. But resistance in my blood holds, has always held.

He must feel it too because his rhythm falters slightly. "Why do they hesitate with you?" Wonder mingles with frustration in his voice. "What are you?"

Your death

I think but don't say. Instead, I pull him down for a kiss that's all teeth and desperation.

We roll across the bed, each fighting for control. When I end up on top, I set my own pace, using him as he tried to use me. He grips my hips hard enough to leave bruises, but his eyes show the truth. He loves that I fight him, that I refuse to simply submit.

"Gods," he groans as I ride him. "You're going to destroy me."

If only he knew how right he is.

The second climax surges toward me, my body tense, ready. This is the moment—the Kiss ignites with dark fury. Pleasure crests through me as I lean forward, capturing his mouth. I feel him pulse, throbbing deep inside as my body clenches around him, pulling him into release alongside me.

For three perfect heartbeats, he kisses me back, lost in what he thinks is shared ecstasy. Then the Raven's Kiss activates, cold fire passing from my lips to his.

His body stiffens immediately. Not from pleasure now, but recognition. His eyes fly open, rage replacing passion.

"You—" The word comes out strangled as the poison begins its work. "No. Not you. Not like this." His voice rises to a snarl. "Sisterhood."

"Mordreth sends his regards," I whisper at his lips.

He reaches for my throat, trying to crush even as his strength fails. "I offered you everything. Power beyond imagining."

"You offered me chains." I catch his weakening wrists, holding them almost gently. "Golden ones, perhaps. But chains nonetheless."

"My followers will destroy you." His voice grows weaker, body beginning to convulse. "They'll hunt you to the ends of the earth."

"They'll try."

The rage in his eyes shifts to a different emotion, not acceptance, but a kind of bitter admiration. "I should have known. You were too perfect. Too ready for what I offered."

"You saw what you wanted to see," I tell him. "A woman you could mold into your dark queen. You never saw the blade."

"No," he gasps, body failing faster now. "I saw it. I just thought... thought I could turn it to my aims."

His arrogance even now is almost admirable. Thirty more seconds and it will be over. Twenty. Ten.

"The world I would have built," he manages with his last breath. "You would have been... magnificent."

Then nothing. His eyes remain open, staring at nothing. I close them with professional detachment before rising from his still form.

The shadows in the room wail, reaching for their master. Some brush over me, leaving that strange tingling sensation, but they don't linger. Whatever darkness passes from him to me is minimal, a whisper, not a shout.

I clean myself methodically, erasing evidence of our encounter. The stolen knowledge from his collection goes into my cloak. His body I arrange to suggest heart failure during solo pleasure, not uncommon for a man of his appetites.

As I prepare to leave, my thoughts turn to Crescent Court. To gentle touch that heals rather than possesses. To quiet conversations that feed my soul rather than challenge my dominance. To Liora.

The contrast is stark. Where Blackthorne was fire and possession, she is warmth and acceptance. Where he tried to claim me, she simply sees me.

The job is done. My twentieth kill, though certainly one of the more complex ones. Tomorrow the city will mourn or celebrate, depending on their allegiances. The shadow cult will fragment without his leadership.

And I? I'll return to arms that ask nothing but honesty. To a love that doesn't demand submission or transformation.

To home.

I leave through the balcony, descending into gardens wet with midnight dew. The carriage waits where arranged, the driver asking no questions.

As we roll through empty streets, I touch my lips where the Kiss delivered death. They've served their end tonight. Tomorrow, perhaps, they'll remember gentler uses.

Rain begins to fall as we reach Crescent Court, gentle droplets washing away all evidence of the night's sacred work. I pay the driver and watch the carriage disappear into shadow before climbing the stairs to the front door.

What will I tell Liora? What story explains my actions without endangering her with knowledge too dangerous to possess? The questions fade as I see light in her window, a beacon guiding me home.

Home. The concept feels foreign yet compelling. I have never had a home beyond the Sanctuary's cold stone walls.

I touch the door handle, pausing before entering. Whatever waits beyond this threshold, I am no longer quite the same woman who left hours earlier. The shadow's touch has marked me. Blackthorne's blood has consecrated me. And Liora's love has transformed me.

Gods, does she love me? I pray she feels what I feel.

The thoughts rise unbidden, words never taught by Mother Superior. They taste of truth nonetheless as I open the door to whatever waits beyond.

To her.

28

LIORA

lood still sings in my veins as the carriage stops before Crescent Court. The night opens its arms to me, stars glittering like scattered diamonds across black velvet. My feet touch cobblestone with lightness unknown since childhood. The burden has been lifted. The mission is complete. For the first time since I can remember, possibility stretches before me instead of obligation.

Blackthorne's death stains my lips no longer. The Raven's Kiss completed its sacred purpose, delivered judgment as ordained by Mordreth's will. Yet tonight, that divine purpose feels distant compared to what waits within these walls. With who waits.

Liora.

Her name flows through my blood like honey and sunlight. The memory of her lips on mine this morning burns brighter than any execution fire. Her promises echo with each heartbeat. A future neither of us planned but both now yearn toward with unexpected hunger.

A small house near the sea. Gardens without stone walls. Life where no one watches from the shadows.

I trace the manuscripts hidden within my cloak. Knowledge stolen from a dead man, capable of saving lives that Blackthorne would have sacrificed to his ambition. Mercy beyond death's release. Another gift I bring to her tonight, another promise of the life that might await us.

The night gardens welcome me with heady perfume. Climbing roses reach toward me with thorny branches as I pass. The key turns in the lock with the sound like distant bells. The entrance hall greets me with familiar shadows that no longer feel like lurking threats but instead like old acquaintances.

A letter waits on the entry table, red wax seal broken. I recognize the stationary. It's mine, taken from my writing desk. My heart leaps at the sight, a reaction so foreign to my training that I almost laugh aloud. I lift the folded paper, wondering what words she chose, what courage it took to commit such feelings to permanent form.

My dearest Sera,

As I write these words, my hands tremble, not with uncertainty about your heart, for I know it beats with mine, but with the magnitude of what I'm about to ask.

Tonight you face whatever night calls to you. I see it in your eyes, the weight of obligations I'll never fully understand. You speak of duties that bind tighter than rope, of chains I cannot see. Yet in our stolen moments, when your guard falls and you let me glimpse the woman beneath the warrior, I've dared to dream of impossible things.

You told me once that not all impossible things stay that way. Tonight, I'm choosing to believe you.

I know what I'm asking goes beyond everything. Your secrets, your purpose, the life you've built in shadows I cannot follow. But when you hold me, when you whisper my name like a prayer, when you look at me as if I'm worth choosing over everything else... in those moments, I see a different future.

The life I dream of for us. A small house by the sea, gardens without walls, mornings where we wake beside each other without having to pretend. A life where you tend to healing instead of... whatever weighs so heavily on your conscience.

I've saved enough coin for passage to the coastal towns. I know how to disappear, servants always do. We could be gone before dawn, before whatever holds you here can reclaim you. Before duty steals you away from me forever.

If you come to our garden tonight, come ready to leave with me. Bring nothing but yourself. I have everything else we'll need. If you don't come... I'll understand. I'll treasure what we had and ask for nothing more.

I'll wait until dawn among our roses. After that, I'll know your answer.

Forever yours, if you'll have me, Liora

The words blur as unexpected moisture fills my eyes. So much courage in each carefully chosen phrase. So much hope in each stroke of her pen. My chest aches with unfamiliar fullness as I fold the letter and tuck it close to my heart.

My feet carry me faster now, urgency building with each step. The corridors feel endless, time stretching like pulled taffy as I move through the sleeping house.

The garden door opens under my hand, night air rushing cool across my heated skin. Moonlight bathes the grounds in silver, transforming ordinary shrubs and pathways into territories magical and sacred. The rose maze beckons, its thorny walls guarding the secret heart where she waits.

I move through narrow passages with growing anticipation. I brush against leaves and flowers, gathering their perfume on my skin. Each turn brings me closer to her, to promises neither of us expected to make. To a future without bloodshed and sacred blades. Without Mother Superior's gaze or Mordreth's endless demand for sacrifice.

The thought should terrify me. Instead, it fills my lungs with air sweeter than any I've breathed before.

I round the final corner, the maze's heart opening before me. The stone bench waits beneath the rose trellis where we shared secrets and kisses. Moonlight spills across the small clearing, painting everything in silver and shadow.

My steps falter.

Everything is wrong.

The scent reaches me first, metallic and sharp under floral sweetness. A smell I know too well from execution chambers and sacred offerings. My pulse stutters as my eyes find a small figure curled on the stone bench.

"Liora?"

She doesn't move. Doesn't answer. Moonlight reveals her face, still and pale as carved marble. Her arm extends toward the ground, fingers curled loosely around an object that gleams in scattered light. My wooden box. The ornate container lies open on stone, crystal vial uncapped beside it.

Dark liquid smears her lips.

The raw Raven's Kiss essence.

My world shatters. My body moves before thought forms, lungs forgetting how to pull air as I fall hard beside the bench. Stone tears through silk and skin, blood warming my knees as I reach for her face with trembling hands.

"No no no no no." The word repeats without permission, raw and broken, tearing from a place inside me I never knew existed.

My touch shakes on her throat, searching frantically for life under cooling skin. I find it, a pulse fluttering weakly, unsteady and fading like the last ember in dying coals. Her breath whispers between parted lips stained black, each inhale shallower than the last.

The venom. Mother Superior's warning burns through my mind. Death in hours. Mordreth's mercy twisted into cruel judgment.

"Liora." Her name shatters on my tongue as I gather her into my arms. Her body weighs nothing, impossibly light, already half-surrendered to darkness. I press my face into her hair, breathing in lavender and rosemary as tears spill hot and unfamiliar down my cheeks. "Please. Not now. Not like this."

Sobs wrack my body, sounds I've never made tearing free from my chest. My hands clutch her nightdress, bunching fabric as though I could anchor her to life through sheer will. I rock her like a child, broken prayers falling between gasps for air.

"Please." The word means nothing and everything, repeated until my throat burns raw. My tears fall on her face, mingling with the venom staining her lips. "Don't go where I can't follow."

My mind scrambles for answers, for rituals, for anything to halt death's advance. Nothing. Nothing in all my training prepared me for this hollow terror. This loss without purpose or meaning.

I've never begged before. Never pleaded. Sisters take what Mordreth sends with cold acceptance. But tonight, prayers rip from my throat without grace or dignity.

"Please." I rock her body with mine, soaking her nightdress with tears I didn't know I could shed. "Not her. Take me instead. My blood for hers. My breath for hers. My future for hers."

My voice breaks into animal sounds of grief, words dissolving into raw noise that tears my throat raw. I press my forehead to hers, lips moving on her skin, begging anyone, anything, that might listen.

"Mordreth, shadow lord, take what you want from me. Everything. Anything. Just let her live."

Night thickens around us. Stars dim overhead as though turning away from human suffering. The silence grows absolute, pressing on my ears until even my broken sobs make no sound. The shadows under the rose trellis writhe and gather, darkness itself coalescing into presence with weight and form. Air freezes in my lungs. Tears crystallize on my cheeks. Time stutters and stops between heartbeats.

A raven descends from the night sky.

Not a bird but power wearing its shape. Its wings span wider than possible, each feather a slice of absolute darkness that drinks starlight. It settles on the garden wall, massive, eyes burning molten gold in the night.

The air hums with power. The ground under me vibrates with unseen energy. The roses close their petals as though in fear.

When it speaks, the voice bypasses my ears and resonates directly within my skull, sounding like mountains grinding together, like oceans crushing ships, like stars dying in distant reaches of night.

"Your heart has strayed from sacred purpose."

Reality bends around the creature. Its form shifts and flows, shadows peeling from its body to dance independently across the garden. Those golden eyes burn through my flesh to the hidden chambers of my soul, judging every secret I've kept even from myself.

"The Sisterhood faces peril greater than you know."

Visions flood my mind. Void corruption spreading across kingdoms, golden-eyed cultists gathering by thousands, forces vast and hungry stirring under ancient ground, breaking chains forged when the world was young. My skull nearly splits with the force of these images, blood trickling from my nose.

"Mordreth's faithful servants grow few while the void grows stronger."

I clutch Liora tighter to my chest, feeling her heartbeat fading to nothing. "Save her," I beg through blood and tears. "Please."

"What would you sacrifice for this insignificant mortal?" The raven's head tilts, movement too fluid for bone and flesh. Its voice scrapes on the inside of my skull. "What offering could possibly balance her worthless life?"

"Anything." The word tears from my soul without hesitation.

Laughter fills my mind, sounds like glaciers calving, like mountains splitting apart. The garden trembles with it. "Anything means nothing, Blade of Mordreth. Name your sacrifice or watch her die."

Terror and understanding bloom together in my chest. A divine bargain. A test of love over duty. Liora's pulse flutters like dying moth wings under my touch.

"My love for her." Truth rips my throat raw as I offer what means most. "My memories of everything we shared."

"Meaningless trinkets." The raven's voice cuts through my mind like frozen steel. "She diverted my blade from its sacred purpose. The price must match the crime."

Its wings unfurl wider, blotting out moon and stars until the garden exists in a bubble of consuming void. Only its golden eyes remain, twin suns burning in midnight emptiness.

Understanding comes with brutal clarity. My hands tighten on her shoulders, fingernails leaving crescents in her skin through the thin nightdress.

"My service then." The words taste of ash and surrender. "My complete devotion returned to the Sisterhood and your will. My life for hers."

The raven's form grows impossibly larger, night spreading outward until it swallows the garden whole. The night sky vanishes behind wings that span beyond physical bounds. "And your void affinity sealed away, dormant until I require it for greater purpose."

My soul shatters as I understand the full price. Not just my love but my awakening self-knowledge. Not just memories but identity. Not just my future with her but my understanding of what I truly am.

I memorize her face one final time, burning details into whatever part of me might survive. The tiny freckle under her left eye. The slight crookedness of her nose. The calluses on her hands from years of work. The scar at her temple from childhood fever.

"I accept." No hesitation. No bargaining. Only absolute certainty as I sacrifice everything I've become.

The raven launches from the wall in a rush of power. Its wings engulf the entire garden in consuming void as it settles beside us. Its massive head lowers until golden eyes burn level with mine, judging the truth of my offer.

Its beak touches Liora's lips. Black poison mist rises from her mouth, pulled into the creature's form where it dissipates like smoke. With each breath drawn from her body, color returns to her cheeks. Warmth flows back into her limbs. Her heartbeat strengthens under my touch. Life reclaims what death had marked as its own.

As Liora's life returns, I feel memories beginning to blur at the edges. Our first kiss in my chambers. Her hands in my hair. The way she looked at me. Each moment fractures like ice under spring sun, breaking into pieces too small to hold.

Her eyelids flutter open. Confusion clouds her gaze momentarily before recognition dawns. "Sera?"

My name on her lips sends pain through my chest. Already her face seems less familiar, details slipping away like water through cupped hands. Each heartbeat pulls me further from her and back toward the cold certainty of the Sanctuary's stone walls.

"What happened?" Her voice sounds stronger, though confusion lingers.

"Listen to me." Words tumble out between sobs as I feel memories already beginning to blur. "I'm an assassin. My real name is Seraphina. They sent me to kill Blackthorne. Lady Ravencrest isn't real. Nothing but my feelings for you were real."

My voice breaks as I clutch her hands. I force the truth out through tears, desperate to share everything before it vanishes forever. "The Raven's Kiss, the lip stain on my lips killed him tonight. You found the vial. It wasn't meant for mortal touch."

"What's happening to you?" Her grip tightens on mine, eyes wide with terror.

"I made a bargain." The words come faster now as faces and names slip like water through my grasp. "Your life for my memories. For us. For everything we might have been."

"No!" Her voice breaks as understanding dawns. Her hands grip my face, forcing me to look at her. "You can't do this. Not for me."

I struggle to hold her features in my mind, already forgetting the exact shade of her eyes. "The manuscripts will save others like your brother. You need blood from someone with shadow resistance. Someone like me."

"Please." Her tears fall on my cheeks, hot on cooling skin. "Don't leave me."

"I don't know how to stay." The truth tears from my chest as fog thickens in my mind.

She pulls me to her with desperate strength, crushing her lips to mine. The kiss tastes of salt and venom and heartbreak. I cling to her, hands tangling in her hair as my heart memorizes what my mind soon won't remember.

Her body presses warm and alive with mine. Our tears mingle on joined cheeks. I breathe her in, trying to burn this moment into whatever part of me might survive the bargain. Her heart beats with mine, strong where moments ago it faltered.

"I'll find you again," I whisper fiercely to her mouth. "I don't care how long it takes."

Words in my voice steady her in my soul even as her name begins to fade from thought. "The garden cottage. The ritual ingredients. Remember for both of us."

"Your devotion is noted, Blade of Mordreth." The raven's voice fills my mind one final time. "Return to the Sanctuary. Mother Superior awaits."

My mission. Blackthorne. The judgment was delivered. These memories remain crystal clear while others blur and vanish. The girl before me watches with strange intensity, tears streaming down her face. The emotion in her gaze makes me uncomfortable, intimate in ways I can't understand.

"You're safe now," I tell her, my voice strangely hollow. "These texts seem important. I leave them in your care."

She grabs my wrists, her touch sending unfamiliar warmth through my skin. "Sera, please." The name she calls me sounds right and wrong simultaneously.

Her words mean nothing yet stir emotions buried under layers of forgetting. I pull away, unsettled by sensations I shouldn't name.

"I completed my purpose here." The words taste true yet incomplete on my tongue.

She reaches for my face, touch trembling on my cheek. "Part of you will always remember us," she whispers, voice breaking. "I'll wait for you to find your way back. I love you."

I step away from her touch. My duty here is done. The Sanctuary calls me home. Mother Superior requires my report. Sacred purpose fills the empty spaces inside my chest.

I turn away, following paths through thorny walls that my feet know without guidance. Behind me, soft weeping punctuates the night air. The sound pierces depths within me, bringing unexpected tears to my eyes though I can't understand why.

The night wraps around me as I leave Crescent Court for the final time. Stars watch with indifference as I walk away from... someone important. Someone precious. Someone I forgot.

With each step, divine purpose grows stronger. The Sisterhood awaits. Mother Superior calls me home.

Yet within my breast, an unfamiliar ache spreads like spilled wine. My lips tingle with phantom warmth. Echoes of memories I can no longer remember.

As I reach the road leading from Crescent Court, I pause once to look back. A figure stands framed in moonlight at the garden's edge, watching me leave. For a heartbeat, memories struggle through chains of forgetting, desperate and wild.

Then nothing.

Blood consecrates what shadow claims.

The prayer whispers across my lips, bringing familiar comfort as I walk beneath cold stars. The road stretches before me, leading home to stone walls and sacred purpose.

Who was that woman?

— · —

EPILOGUE: MERCY

The Sanctuary rises over the horizon like a memory, seven towers piercing the morning sky. I trace the familiar spires with my gaze. Satisfaction fills me yet feels strangely hollow, as though an essential piece remains in Luridian, abandoned without name.

My flesh remembers Blackthorne's death with perfect clarity. His eyes widened in recognition as the Raven's Kiss activated. His limbs stiffened as venom flowed from my lips to his. *Crimson consecrates what darkness claims.* Yet what happened afterward blurs at the edges, details dissolving whenever I try to grasp them. I recall fragments only. A garden. Moonlight. A bargain. My body carries memory my mind cannot access, muscles tensing at thoughts that disappear before forming.

The Mother Superior waits in her chambers, white robes catching sunlight until she glows with internal radiance. Her silver hair, pulled severely back, emphasizes angular features that have watched over me since childhood.

"Daughter Seraphina." Her voice fills the space with quiet authority. "Is the blessed task complete?"

I bow gracefully. "Blackthorne's life became Mordreth's offering as ordained."

"And the darkness responded strangely, you mentioned." She studies me with penetrating focus, her eyes cataloging changes I can't name.

"When life left his body, gloom in the room seemed to... touch me." My voice sounds strange to my own ears. "Briefly. Then disperse."

Mother Superior approaches with unhurried steps, stopping closer than protocol allows. Her hands rise to my face, turning it toward light spilling through tall windows. She examines me with unusual intensity, searching for details only she can see.

"Just as I anticipated." Her thumb traces my cheekbone before she steps away, nodding at whatever she finds in my eyes.

What does she see that I can't?

"What happens next?" I ask, questions crowding my throat that years of training lock behind my teeth.

"Your next blessing." She removes a sealed document from within her robes. "You and three carefully selected Sisters will travel to Nocthys and deliver mercy to Prince Valtheris, whose corruption threatens to spread darkness beyond its borders."

"Nocthys?" The name sends cold shivers along my spine.

"The shadow kingdom grows restless. Blackthorne's cult was merely one manifestation of a larger threat." Her voice lowers. "Your... unique qualities make you ideal for this offering. The renewed commitment I see in you serves greater purpose than you can comprehend."

The phrase strikes a dissonant chord within me. When did my devotion waver? What necessitated renewal? I swallow these questions behind practiced composure.

Renewed from what? My blood knows answers my mind refuses.

"I exist to serve Mordreth's will," I respond automatically.

"Yes, Daughter. You do." She dismisses me with a cold smile that never touches her eyes. "Rest today. Your team awaits introduction at evening meditation."

As I turn to leave, a strange urgency fills my chest. "Mother Superior?"

She looks up, surprise flickering across her features. "Yes?"

"Are there records of... reversing corruption? In early stages?"

The question emerges without thought. Mother Superior's expression freezes momentarily before resuming perfect composure.

"Heresy," she dismisses. "Mordreth's mercy comes through blessed steel, not false hope of restoration."

The answer should be satisfying. Instead, it leaves a strange hollowness in my gut, as though an important truth has been denied.

The weeks of preparation pass in disciplined focus as my team forms around me. Each Sister brings distinct skills that complement our holy work.

Sister Bryn plans our approach to Nocthys with maps spread before her, her analytical mind capturing details others would miss. "The western route provides better cover but extends our journey by two days," she notes, hands tracing mountain passes with scholarly care.

Sister Leigh sharpens our weapons with methodical focus, testing each blade over her thumb. Her northern pragmatism grounds our combat training in brutal efficiency. "Nocthys guards will see through typical concealment," she warns, voice rough from years in harsh climates. "We must adapt accordingly."

Young Sister Eliza, still soft-faced where others have hardened, prepares compounds with surprising skill. Her hands move with delicate intent among vials of shadow-oil and dried herbs. "The lunar phase affects potency," she explains. "What works in ordinary kingdoms fails in perpetual twilight."

I observe them from a central position, feeling strangely disconnected despite our closeness.

Faithful servants of Mordreth, devoted without question.

These Sisters, selected specifically for this divine offering, remain somehow unfamiliar compared to someone whose absence I feel without understanding why. Someone whose methods complemented mine differently than ritual training could achieve.

The thought dissolves before fully forming, leaving a hollow absence in my chest where certainty once resided.

Our training establishes perfect coordination, each Sister knowing her role without excessive explanation. Yet sometimes during combat forms performed in flawless unison, I feel absent from movements my body executes without thought. As if ritual and muscle exist separately from whatever constitutes my true self.

My mind repeatedly drifts toward fragments of memory from Luridian. A lavender scent clinging to simple cotton. Amber flecks in brown eyes watching me with understanding beyond station. Fingers brushing mine with tenderness rather than ritual purpose. These sensations feel more real than the stone walls surrounding me, though I can't explain why.

"You seem troubled," Sister Leigh observes during combat practice. Her directness carries the unfiltered honesty of northern territories, a trait the Sisterhood normally trains away.

"Readjusting after an extended mission," I explain, the lie bitter on my tongue, familiar as ritual oil. The answer feels both true and incomplete. I wonder when lying to my Sisters became so effortless, when truth became a resource I could parcel out in careful measures like shadow-oil.

The Mother Superior visits our preparations occasionally, her cold eyes tracking my movements with satisfaction that borders on hunger. "Your potential grows stronger," she observes while inspecting our weapons. "Your renewed dedication strengthens our blessed calling."

Another reference to dedication renewed rather than maintained. What happened in Luridian beyond Blackthorne's blessing? What transformation required restoration rather than continuation?

During one such visit, Mother Superior mentions the aftermath in Luridian. "Lord Hargrove has withdrawn from society entirely. Lady Mereswen, however, has risen in influence. She seems to have anticipated the power vacuum Blackthorne's death would create."

Lord Hargrove's face surfaces clearly in my memory. The silver-haired neighbor who first introduced me to society, his jealousy when I grew close to Blackthorne. Lady Mereswen too, with her knowing smiles and veiled warnings. I remember them perfectly, yet they feel distant, like characters from someone else's story.

The departure day arrives with crisp mountain air and cloud-streaked skies. Four horses wait in the Sanctuary's central courtyard, laden with supplies necessary for our journey. Mother Superior emerges from the central tower as the sun clears the eastern mountains, her white robes transforming ordinary fabric into divine radiance.

"Daughters of Mordreth," she addresses us, voice carrying perfect distance for privacy within public ceremony. "You embark on a purpose greater than individual understanding."

Mother locks her gaze on me. "Darkness stirs within the shadow kingdom. Prince Valtheris experiments with forces better left untouched. His blood will consecrate Mordreth's altar through your willing hands."

She places her thumb on each Sister's forehead in ceremonial blessing. When she reaches me, her hand lingers, pressing into leather with unusual urgency. "Remember your oath, Daughter Seraphina. Your renewed dedication serves purpose beyond ordinary offering."

"I live to serve Mordreth's will," I respond automatically, though the words feel somehow distant on my tongue.

We turn our horses toward the eastern gate. As we pass beneath the Sanctuary's massive gates, an impulse makes me look back once. Mother Superior stands motionless in the courtyard's center, her white robes billowing in the mountain breeze. Seven towers rise behind her, dark spires reaching toward heaven yet anchored in stone and darkness. For a brief moment, unexpected grief closes my throat, a physical weight pressing into my lungs though I cannot name its source.

The path descends from mountain heights through forests growing increasingly dense. By midday, we reach a lower elevation where pines give way to ancient oaks whose massive trunks speak of centuries watching human concerns with indifference.

We stop beside a small stream for a brief rest. I find myself standing slightly apart, studying the eastern horizon where the perpetual twilight marking Nocthys becomes visible.

A flicker of black wings catches my attention. A raven perches on a branch above the stream, larger than ordinary birds. It watches with an intensity that seems to assess more than mere physical presence.

My heart stutters in my chest. Memory fragments surface with sudden clarity. A garden at night. A bargain struck under moonlight.

Your heart has strayed from sacred purpose.

The words echo inside my skull, though whether memory or present communication remains unclear. The raven tilts its head, movement too fluid for ordinary bone and muscle.

Pain lances behind my eyes, sharp enough to make me gasp audibly. Sister Eliza looks up from her work, concern furrowing her brow.

"Sister Seraphina? Are you unwell?"

The bird launches into flight before I can respond, wings spreading wide as it soars toward the distant shadow kingdom.

"Just... adjusting to lower elevation," I manage, the lie slipping easily from trained lips.

We continue our journey as afternoon twilight lengthens across the landscape. Each mile brings us closer to the perpetual gloom visible on the eastern horizon. The border between ordinary kingdom and Nocthys manifests not as a physical barrier but as a gradual transformation of light quality. Colors dim. Darkness deepens.

At the Nocthys border, we pause for final preparation. Trees grow increasingly twisted, their branches reaching with almost deliberate intent. Flowers close their petals despite morning light. Animals fall silent, their ordinary calls replaced by watching stillness.

We form a circle, hands joining in a ritual pattern that creates divine protection. Ancient words pass between us, each Sister speaking her part of the traditional blessing.

"Mordreth guide our blades," Sister Bryn intones. "Mordreth strengthen our calling," Sister Leigh continues. "Mordreth preserve our sight," Sister Eliza concludes. "And may his mercy be swift," I finish.

As the words leave my lips, an emotion stirs within me. Deep within layers of forgetting, memory struggles toward the surface. I sense something important sacrificed willingly, a connection severed but not completely broken.

I mount my horse smoothly, positioning myself at our formation's head as we prepare to cross into perpetual twilight. My sisters fall into position behind me, trusting my leadership without question.

"Forward," I command, voice steady despite the turmoil beneath my surface thoughts.

We ride into Nocthys twilight, each step carrying us deeper into Mordreth's shadow realm. Colors fade around us, the world transforming into a muted palette where the darkness gains substance while light retreats. Trees whisper as we pass, their voices carrying meanings beyond wind through leaves.

Yet occasionally throughout the journey, strange sensations return without explanation. Fleeting impressions of something important forgotten. Brief scent of lavender triggering warmth in my chest. The phantom sensation of gentle touch brushing my cheek in a gesture holding nothing of ritual or duty.

These moments pass quickly, leaving only nameless yearning that I dismiss as irrelevant to sacred purpose. Yet as I lead my Sisters toward Nocthys gloom, shadow-oil coated blades ready for divine service, the inexplicable longing lingers like an unfinished prayer.

Remember this moment. Whatever happens after, remember we chose this freely.

The words appear in my mind with painful clarity, though I can't place their origin or their meaning. Beneath us, the horses move steadily forward. Above, a distant raven circles on wings that span wider than possible, watching our progress with ancient patience.

Guide your servant through darkness.

The path stretches before us into twilight.

A Raven's Mercy awaits.

A Note from E.S. Brandon

Thank you for diving into this adventure, for investing your heart in these characters, and for staying with us until the very last page. Stories come to life when readers like you take the journey, feel the emotions, and share in the joys and heartbreaks.

We truly hope you enjoyed the experience, and if the story touched you, We'd be incredibly grateful if you'd leave a brief, honest review on Amazon or Goodreads. Reviews are the lifeline for independent authors and help more readers discover these worlds we've built together.

If you'd like to stay connected, head over to https://esbrandon.com and join the newsletter. Subscribers receive:

- Exclusive bonus content and short stories

- Updates on upcoming releases, cover reveals, and special events

- Early access to new adventures and characters you'll love (and maybe love to hate)

Thank you again for reading, for feeling, and for supporting indie authors. Your passion means everything.

Warmest regards,

Elizabeth and Stephen

BOOK 2 COMING SPRING 2026

The first time Seraphina killed Prince Valtheris, she felt nothing but satisfaction. The second time, she felt terror.

Sent by the Sisterhood of Mercy, a blood cult cloaked in holy vows, Seraphina arrives in Nocthys to assassinate the cursed prince Valtheris and free his kingdom from its eternal night. But her heart is strangely hollow—as if something precious was torn away.

Trapped within the haunted palace, Seraphina is hunted at every turn, their game of predator and prey twisting into something darker. As she unravels his curse, she discovers his torment is no accident, and neither is her role in it. Yet phantom memories haunt her. Brown eyes, gentle touches, and love so profound she traded it all away to save... someone. If only she could escape to find the truth.

But Valtheris has no intention of letting her go. Not when the darkness calls her by name. Not when her blade belongs as much to him as to the gods.

In the end, only one of them will kneel.